Lord Kane's Keepsake

A DELICIOUS DENIAL

Gerald's answer to the charge that he was having an affair with the Countess of Purbeck came easily from his lips.

First in words, as he declared, 'I would never be unfaithful to you.'

Then, before Emma knew it, his lips came down on hers. His arm slid around her waist, drawing her to him, and she could feel his heart beating close to hers. Her lips trembled beneath his as she returned the kiss.

He drew back then, his eyes even darker. 'Do you trust me now?' he asked softly.

Had a spell been cast over her, she could not have been more under his influence. 'Yes,' she whispered, 'I trust you.'

But the question now was: Could she trust herself?

By the same author

A Scandalous Publication
A Perfect Likeness
An Impossible Confession
A Matter of Duty
The Second Lady Southvale

Lord Kane's Keepsake

SANDRA HEATH

ROBERT HALE · LONDON

© Sandra Heath 1992, 2008
First published in Great Britain 2008

ISBN 978-0-7090-8092-3

Robert Hale Limited
Clerkenwell House
Clerkenwell Green
London EC1R 0HT

www.halebooks.com

4 6 8 10 9 7 5 3

Typeset in 11/13½pt Classical Garamond Roman
by Derek Doyle & Associates, Shaw Heath
Printed by the MPG Books Group in the UK

1

LONG EVENING SHADOWS were cast by the fading mid-September sun as the carriage drove along the southern boundary of Hyde Park, on the last part of its one-hundred-and-twenty-mile journey from Dorset to Mayfair's fashionable Grosvenor Square. The team was tired, and the vehicle's dark-blue panels were spattered with mud from the open road because there had been rain earlier in the day. The horses' breath stood out in clouds, for the summer of 1809 had ended suddenly, and the chill of a surprisingly early autumn was already in the air.

There were two passengers in the carriage, twice-widowed Mr George Rutherford, of Foxley Hall, Dorchester, and his daughter by his first marriage, twenty-two-year-old Emma. It was on Emma's account that the journey to London was being undertaken, for in the spring she had become an heiress, having unexpectedly inherited a comfortable fortune through some distant connections of her late mother's family, and this change of circumstance had secured her a very advantageous match indeed. Instead of simply being the daughter of a minor Dorset landowner, with the prospect of sharing her father's wealth with her half-brother, Stephen, and with the consequent prospect of achieving a marriage within neighboring Dorset circles, she had attracted the attention of no less a gentleman than Gerald Fitzroy, Lord Kane, who would one day succeed his grandfather as the Earl of Cranforth. Gerald was handsome, sought after, and immensely wealthy, and his interest in someone as insignificant as Emma was regarded as nothing short of amazing, but on the strength of a single meeting in July, he had offered to marry her, and on her behalf her delighted father had readily agreed.

It was a calculated, businesslike arrangement, but one of considerable social importance, and when it became formalized on Halloween at a betrothal ball at the Earl of Cranforth's residence in Park Lane, most of London's *beau monde* would attend. Society regarded Emma as a very odd choice for someone of Gerald's rank and position, for he could have had his pick of aristocratic brides, and she not only lacked noble blood and social standing, she was not even considered to be a beauty. His friends believed him to be embarking upon an astonishingly unnecessary misalliance, and London was waiting with immense curiosity to see the future Lady Kane when she made her first appearance. Very few believed in their heart of hearts that the planned wedding would actually take place in the New Year.

She would not be Gerald's first wife, for he had been married before, and his adored wife, Margot, had died tragically in a carriage overturn. The first Lady Kane had been beautiful, fascinating, witty, and of noble birth, and few believed that someone like Emma Rutherford would ever be able to hold a candle to her. Losing her had plunged Gerald into despair, and he had vowed never to marry again, but his anxious grandfather had plagued him to do his duty, because Margot had not provided the necessary heir to ensure the continuation of the earls of Cranforth. At last Gerald had given in, and had begun to search for a suitable bride. He did not look in society circles, where everyone had known Margot, but instead looked beyond London to the provinces, and families whose daughters had no connection with the capital.

It was only by chance that he discovered Emma, for a friend of a friend had mentioned her name, and when he had troubled to find out more, for reasons he kept strictly to himself he had swiftly concluded that she would be ideal. He approached her father, and after the two gentlemen had met a number of times, Gerald was introduced to Emma herself. A further meeting was not considered necessary, for she was deemed to be all that was required to become the new Lady Kane.

Mr Rutherford had been astonished and delighted with the suddenness of this immense stroke of good fortune, for never in his wildest dreams had he thought that Emma would one day become a countess. It had not occurred to him to ask her whether or not she wished for the match, because in his view it was unquestionably advantageous, and since she had always been a dutiful daughter, he naturally believed that she would be as delighted and eager as he. His joy blinded him to the troubled look in her eyes, and made him oblivious of the slight hesitation in her voice whenever she spoke of her dashing husband-to-be. Even now, with the journey to London almost at an end, Mr Rutherford remained blissfully unaware of his daughter's reservations.

He had fallen asleep in the seat opposite her, and his head lolled against the shining dark-brown leather upholstery. He was a frail man whose poor health made him appear rather older than his fifty-five years, and he was very well wrapped up against the evening chill. There was a thick woolen rug over his knees, and his feet rested on a warm brick wrapped in a square of cloth. A shawl Emma had knit for him had been placed around the shoulders of his fur-collared greatcoat, and his mittened hands were thrust deep into a large muff. He looked for all the world as if he had embarked upon a journey in a Russian winter, and yet when he was awake he had still complained of feeling the cold.

His high-crowned hat had slipped forward, hiding a face that still retained an echo of the good looks that had made him so winning as a young man. He had china-blue eyes, fine features, and a kind mouth, and his figure had not yet succumbed to the thickening waistline that so often came with advancing years. His hair was white now, but had once been the rich dark-chestnut color that was now enjoyed by his son, by his second marriage, twenty-year-old Stephen, who also shared his handsome face and bright blue eyes.

Even in his sleep Mr Rutherford was mindful of his health, for he raised a hand to twitch the knit shawl more closely around his neck, to fend off the draft that was seeping through the carriage glass. He loathed traveling when the weather was cold, for such expeditions invariably led to several days in bed in order to recover his strength, and he had a horror of contracting a chill, no matter how slight, for on the last occasion he had been confined to his bed for several months. He would much have preferred to delay the betrothal until the following summer, but Gerald had been impatient to proceed without any unnecessary wait. Stephen had consequently been dispatched to London to find a suitable house to rent, and in due course the journey from Dorchester to Grosvenor Square had commenced.

Toying nervously with the strings of her gray corded-silk reticule, Emma sat in silence opposite her slumbering father. The future Lady Kane and Countess of Cranforth was of medium height, with a softly rounded figure and a face that was charming and attractive rather than lovely. Her eyes were large and green, with long dark lashes, and she had rich dark-brown hair. The Rutherfords were a curly-headed family, but her curls were thicker, more luxuriant, and more shining than Stephen's were, or her father's ever had been. When brushed loose, her hair tumbled in a shining mane about her shoulders, and the enviable curls did not need the assistance of papers or tongs. A great deal of patience and toil were necessary with comb and pins, however, for such hair did not submit easily to the neat, precise styles that were *de rigueur* for ladies of fashion. Never had Emma been more aware of this wearying fact than over the past three days, when she had been without the services of her maid, Dolly Makepeace, who had preceded her to London to see that her wardrobe was in readiness. It was as well that the not entirely satisfactory results of her labors could be safely concealed beneath a Gypsy hat.

But if her coiffure was slightly less than perfect, the same could not be said of the rest of her appearance, which was everything that was commendably modish for someone who had never set foot in London before. Emma was nothing if not practical, and had always assiduously subscribed to London fashion journals. She had a dressmaker in Dorchester who was particularly clever at copying the illustrations in such publications, and as a consequence, Emma's wardrobe was as stylish as any highborn London lady's. It was a fact that although she was inwardly far from assured and at ease about the prospect that now lay ahead, outwardly she gave every appearance of being poised, stylish, and prepared.

For the journey she was wearing a primrose velvet pelisse over a white jaconet gown, and her Gypsy hat was made of shining gray straw, tied on with primrose satin ribbons. Her dainty shoes were made of black japanned leather, and her kid gloves were dyed the same gray as her hat and reticule. The only jewelry she wore was the pair of drop-pearl earrings bequeathed to her by her mother, and they trembled slightly at the motion of the carriage.

She gazed out at the London scene. The roads had been busy for some time now, even though it was a Sunday evening, and it was all a far cry from rural Dorchester, where the daily arrival and departure of the Exeter mail was a noteworthy event. There were no empty streets now, but a constant flow of stagecoaches, hackney coaches, mails, carriers' wagons, carts, drays, and a generous sprinkling of private carriages, cabriolets, curricles, gigs, and phaetons. The sound of wheels and hooves filled the evening air, and Emma found it all a little overwhelming, as indeed she had found everything since she had so unexpectedly come to Lord Kane's attention.

The corner of Park Lane and Piccadilly lay ahead now, and she could see the first Mayfair mansions looking out over Hyde Park. She lowered her eyes, for her courage was weakening with each yard the carriage traveled. This match was a mistake, and if she had any wisdom at all, she would withdraw from it while there was still time. If she had any wisdom? Oh, it was easy enough to think such things, but when it came to carrying them out, then it was a very different matter, especially when one's heart had been set at sixes and sevens by a man whose heart was not even remotely engaged.

She twisted and untwisted the strings of the reticule, recalling her one and only meeting with Gerald. It had been in the library at Foxley Hall, and she had been wearing a cherry muslin gown that was embroidered with little white daisies. The July sunlight had been very bright, streaming in through the windows, and in the garden the flowerbeds had been a riot of summer colors. She had been waiting for some time, and in some trepidation, for it hardly seemed credible that a man like Lord Kane would go through with such an unlikely match. The library doors had opened suddenly, and her father had ushered their aristocratic guest in to meet her. She had found herself looking at the most devastatingly handsome man she had ever seen, and her foolish heart had almost stopped within her.

Gerald was thirty years old, with clear gray eyes and wavy hair that was so dark it was almost black. He was tall, with broad shoulders and slender hips, and there was an assuredness about him that came from centuries of privilege and position. He was impeccably dressed in a pine-green coat with a high velvet collar and shining brass buttons, and his white corduroy breeches clung to his form like a second skin. His waistcoat was made of costly white *piqué*, and it was only partly buttoned in order to reveal the starched white frills of his shirt. A pearl pin nestled in the folds of his silk neckcloth, and there was a gleam on his tasseled Hessian boots that must have taken his valet an age to achieve.

She had hardly heard her father introducing them, and a startling frisson of pleasure had passed through her as Gerald took her hand to raise it to his lips. His glance had taken in every inch of her appearance, but there had been no way of knowing whether or not she met with his approval. Her heartbeats had quickened almost unbearably, and she had been hard put to hide her confusion. Then she had noticed the pale mark on the fourth finger of his left hand, where his wedding ring had reposed so recently that he had probably removed it only as he approached Foxley Hall in his carriage. That pale mark was a sobering reminder that he was seeking a second wife only because he required an heir, and that any marriage he entered into would be one of convenience, not love. He had adored his cherished Margot, and Emma Rutherford, if she became the second Lady Kane, would never replace her in his heart, even though she might replace her in his bed. This was what had troubled Emma ever since, for her reaction to him had been so bewildering and responsive that she knew she was already perilously close to falling completely in love, and if that should happen, then immeasurable heartbreak lay ahead for her. Could she risk that? Or would it be infinitely more sensible to cry off now, before things proceeded any further?

The carriage turned north by Apsley House, entering Park Lane, which formed the western boundary of Mayfair. Fine houses and superior streets stretched away into the heart of the capital's most sought after area, and Emma glanced out at the late-evening sunlight as it flashed on the elegant windows. She knew that in a moment or so she would see Cranforth House, where the betrothal ball was set to take place the following month. Gerald did not reside there, for it was his grandfather's London residence, and Gerald had his own house a mile away in St James's Square. Cranforth House had been closed for a number of years, because the earl preferred to live at his country seat, Cranforth Castle in Derbyshire. The Park Lane house was being prepared for him, however, and there were lights in the windows as the carriage drove past.

Emma stared at the beautiful mansion, which was very splendid indeed, with a white portico and a carriage porch. A semicircular entry swept in and out through two wrought-iron gateways ornamented with the distinctive Fitzroy family crest, a double-headed phoenix. Behind the mansion, only briefly glimpsed through a postern gate, lay some of the most beautiful gardens in London, covering several acres of the finest part of Mayfair.

The carriage drove on by, and Emma turned to look back. Her misgivings had increased perceptibly, for there was something rather austere and forbidding about Cranforth House. She was used to the homeliness of Foxley Hall, which was a rambling red-brick Tudor house of comfortable proportions, and which bore no resemblance at all to this grand building overlooking Hyde Park.

Leaving Park Lane behind, the carriage turned east again, driving along Upper Grosvenor Street toward Grosvenor Square and the house that Stephen had secured for their stay. He had had some difficulty in finding a suitable property, but then had heard that Lady Bagworth, an elderly, infirm widow, had been instructed by her physician to take a lengthy cure in Bath. Ever thrifty, her ladyship had decided not to leave her London residence empty while she was away, and so Stephen had been able to take a six-month lease of the house, fully furnished, and complete with servants. In Stephen's opinion, the property was the perfect place for the future Lady Kane, and would be entirely appropriate when she received calls from the many new friends and acquaintances he was certain she would meet in London.

Emma's thoughts moved away from her impending betrothal and settled instead upon her rather wayward younger brother. She wondered what he had been up to during his month of freedom in London, for even though she loved him very much, she was well aware of his shortcomings, chief among which was his penchant for gambling. The two years that separated them in age were sometimes very evident indeed, for there were times when she felt infinitely more sensible and mature than he. He was so impressionable and headstrong that he was constantly getting into scrapes, and his liking for the green baize tables had brought him into several brushes with the duns. Their father had had more than enough of Stephen's misconduct, and before his departure for the capital had issued a stern ultimatum. Stephen was strictly forbidden to gamble at all during his stay in London, and if he did, then he would find himself without an allowance. Emma hoped that her brother had seen the error of his ways, but she doubted it very much, for Stephen was one of those people who only learned the hard way.

At last the carriage entered the southwestern corner of Grosvenor Square, which covered six acres and was the largest quadrangle in Mayfair. It had a leafy, railed central garden with a gilded equestrian statue of George I as a Roman emperor, and was surrounded by about fifty houses, most of them built of red brick, with stone facings, decorative fanlights, and pedimented doors. The houses had basements that were separated from the pavement by graceful wrought-iron railings that met in elegant arches before the entrances. As the September sun sank further and further in the west, more and more lights appeared in windows, and a lamplighter was going about his business, assisted by his boy. A flower girl was endeavoring to sell the last of her posies before going home, and as the carriage drew to a halt, Emma heard her calls: 'Roses. Buy my red roses.'

Lady Bagworth's house was on the southern side of the square, and Emma looked up at it. Like most of the others, it was built of red brick, and its door was approached by steps that bridged the basement area. It had four stories above ground level, with tall rectangular windows that diminished in size with each ascending floor. It possessed a quiet air of opulence and good taste, and was almost welcoming, a fact for which Emma was most relieved. But would she be married from here in the new year? Or would she soon be fleeing home to the safety and seclusion of Foxley Hall?

She wished she wasn't so full of doubt where Gerald was

concerned, but she couldn't help herself. If she had been able to approach the match as detachedly as he, then there would not have been any problem, but she could not, and so the problem was there. But was it an insurmountable problem? Once she knew the answer to that question, then she would know whether or not she could become Gerald's wife.

2

THE CEASING OF the carriage's motion awoke Mr Rutherford with a start. He pushed his hat back from his face and looked around.

Emma smiled at him. 'We've reached the end of the journey, Father.'

'We have?' He breathed a sigh of relief, glancing out at the house. 'Upon my soul, it's a handsome establishment.'

'And so it should be, considering the sum her ladyship saw fit to demand,' Emma replied.

The carriage's arrival had not passed unnoticed in the house, for the door opened suddenly and a butler emerged, ushering before him two liveried footmen who were instructed to attend to the unloading of the carriage boot. Emma knew from Stephen's one and only letter from London that the butler's name was Saunders, and that he had once served on the royal naval frigate commanded by the late Lord Bagworth. On that gentleman's retirement, Saunders had accompanied him, and had served the Bagworth family ever since. He was a sturdily built man of about forty-five, with eyes that were permanently narrowed from years of scanning the horizon for enemy vessels. He wore a plain brown coat, fawn breeches, white stockings, and black buckled shoes. His nose was sharp and pointed, and he had beetle brows that gave him a rather severe expression. It was impossible to tell if he still had hair, for he wore a powdered bagwig, but somehow Emma felt that he was completely bald. According to Stephen, he was a Bristol man who abided diligently by the old saying 'shipshape and Bristol fashion,' and so efficiently did he run the Bagworth residence that in Stephen's opinion the house could probably sail into battle and deliver the enemy a deadly broadside.

It was an amusing thought, and Emma had to hide a smile as the butler approached the carriage, lowering the rungs and then opening the door. He gave them a surprisingly graceful bow. 'Welcome to London, sir. Madam.'

Mr Rutherford tossed his traveling rug aside and picked up the walking stick which lay on the seat beside him. Then he edged himself stiffly forward, reaching out to accept the steadying hand the butler immediately offered.

Emma followed once her father had alighted, and as he paused for a moment to stretch his aching limbs, she glanced briefly toward the garden in the center of the square. The air was noticeably cooler, and she shivered. Goodness, how early autumn was this year. One day it had been summer, the next summer was gone.

The flower girl had given up her efforts and was hurrying away with her basket of flowers, and the lamplighter and his boy had almost completed their work, but the square was far from deserted. A number of pedestrians strolled the pavements, and several carriages rattled past on the cobbles. Two fine ladies crossed the square, accompanied by their maids. The ladies were very elegant, one wearing rose-pink, with ostrich plumes curling down from her jaunty little hat, the other in lime green with a high-crowned bonnet adorned with artificial flowers. The maids hurried in their mistresses' wake, bringing with them a number of little white dogs on scarlet leads. The dogs yapped and jumped around, looking longingly toward the central garden, but there was to be no such pleasure for them on this occasion. Emma studied the two ladies' clothes, concluding with some satisfaction that they did not appear to any more advantage than she, except, perhaps, in the matter of their coiffure. Oh, how good it would be to enjoy Dolly's services again, for hair was a very definite problem.

A rowdy party of gentlemen emerged from a nearby house, some of them appearing to be very much in their cups as they all made their way to two carriages waiting at the curb outside. Somehow they all managed to squeeze into the vehicles; which then drove smartly away, the sounds of their passengers' merriment still audible. As the two carriages left the square, a small pea-green cabriolet entered at speed, driven by a dandy who was dressed from head to toe in the idential pea green as his transport. The single high-stepping black horse had pea-green ribbons in its mane and tail, and Emma was quite certain that if it were possible to dye a black horse green, then such a fate would have befallen the unfortunate creature.

She watched as the astonishing cabriolet darted around the square toward the northwestern corner, where it vanished from sight into Upper Brook Street, which led west toward Park Lane and Hyde Park, parallel with Upper Grosvenor Street, along which the Rutherford carriage had driven a moment or so before.

Mr Rutherford's walking stick tapped on the pavement as Saunders assisted him into the house, and Emma left her perusal of the square to follow them. Behind her the two footmen had begun to unload the trunks and valises from the carriage.

From the doorway Emma stepped into a small outer hall, square in shape, with white walls that were elegantly adorned with swags of gilded plasterwork. There were two marble statues of Greek goddesses, their delicate robes so skillfully sculptured that they seemed real. Between the statues was the only piece of furniture in this outer hall, an exquisite inlaid table upon which rested a silver salver for calling cards. Emma noticed that a number had already been left. The outer hall gave onto a chandelier-lit inner hall of breaktakingly palatial proportions. A grand staircase rose up between soaring Ionic columns to the three floors above, where galleries edged with marble balustrades were all that could be seen. To one side there was a mural depicting figures leaning over a marble balcony to gaze down into the hall.

The floor was tiled in red, black, and white, and there were a number of doors, each one with impressive pilasters and pediments. A fire crackled in the hearth of an immense fire-place to the right, and there were beautiful crimson velvet sofas placed on either side of it. To the left, a console table stood against the wall, and above it there was a gilt-framed mirror that reflected the whole area.

Two familiar figures were waiting at the foot of the staircase, Emma's maid, Dolly Makepeace, and Mr Rutherford's man, Jacob Brown. Of Stephen there was no sign.

Saunders bowed low to Mr Rutherford. 'Would you and Miss Rutherford care to take some tea in the drawing room after your journey, sir?'

'We would indeed. Is my son at home?'

'No, sir, but he left word that he would return in time to dine.'

'Where is he?'

'I do not know, sir,' replied the butler after a fraction of a second's hesitation which Mr Rutherford did not notice, but Emma did.

'Then it seems we must wait to see him,' grumbled her father, nodding toward Jacob, who hastened forward to assist him.

As her father walked stiffly toward the staircase to go up to his room to change before adjourning to the drawing room for the promised tea, Emma turned her gaze upon Saunders, for she was suspicious about his replies. 'Saunders, have you no idea at all where my brother is at the moment?' she asked, watching him closely.

'None at all, madam,' he replied.

She didn't believe him, but knew that it would do no good to press the point.

'Will that be all, madam?'

'Yes.'

'I will see that tea is served directly, madam.'

'Thank you.'

As he walked away toward the door that led to the kitchens, Dolly approached her mistress, bobbing a curtsy and smiling. 'It's good to see you again, Miss Emma,' she said. She was Dorset born and bred, the daughter of a Dorchester tailor, and she was rosy-cheeked, with hazel eyes and fair hair that was cut short. Her plump little figure was neat and tidy in a pale-blue woolen dress, high-necked and long-sleeved, and her white apron was so crisply starched that it crackled when she moved.

Emma did not beat about the bush. 'What is my brother up to, Dolly?'

The maid lowered her eyes quickly. 'Up to, Miss Emma?'

'You know exactly what I mean. Is it the gaming tables?'

Dolly nodded reluctantly. 'I only know the talk in the kitchens, Miss Emma, and I've only been here a day or so, but it seems he

17

uses Lady Bagworth's town carriage most nights and sometimes during the day, to take him to Avenley House in Pall Mall.'

'Avenley House?'

'It's the town residence of Lord Avenley, Miss Emma, and it contains a private gaming club where they are said to play for the very highest stakes.'

Emma stared at her in dismay. The very highest stakes? Oh, no! 'Dolly, are you quite sure about this?'

'As sure as I can be, Miss Emma, for it's all the talk belowstairs. I wish it weren't true, for I know how upsetting it is to hear such things, especially when a gentleman like Lord Avenley is involved.'

'Why do you say that? What about Lord Avenley?' asked Emma quickly.

'He is said to be the most wicked and unscrupulous lord in all London, Miss Emma, at least that's what Mr Saunders says of him, and all the other servants agreed with him. Lord Avenley is not a man to tangle with.'

Emma's heart sank still further. 'How did my brother meet him?' she asked.

'It seems that Master Stephen went to a prizefight at the Fives Court, and that a mutual friend introduced them. At least . . .'

'Yes?'

'Well, I think Lord Avenley asked to be introduced to Master Stephen.'

Emma was taken aback. 'That cannot possibly be so, for why on earth would a man like Lord Avenley ask to meet someone like Stephen?'

'I don't know, Miss Emma, but that's how I think it happened. One thing is for certain, and that is that Lord Avenley has gone out of his way to befriend Master Stephen, calling upon him here and inviting him to the club in Pall Mall. Mr Saunders wasn't being entirely truthful a moment ago, for Master Stephen is with Lord Avenley now, but left instructions that his dealings with his lordship were not to be conveyed to Mr Rutherford.'

Emma sighed heavily. This was getting worse and worse. Oh, Stephen Rutherford, I could wring your foolish neck! She looked at the maid again. 'How does my brother seem? Is he in buoyant spirits?'

'Oh, yes, Miss Emma.'

'He doesn't seem like a man who has been losing?'

'Not at all, Miss Emma.'

'Well, that's something, at least, I suppose.' Emma turned, for the footmen were beginning to carry the luggage inside.

Dolly glanced at her. 'Let me show you to your room, Miss Emma, for tea will be served shortly.'

'Very well.'

Gathering her skirts, Emma followed the maid up the staircase, and on the next floor Dolly paused, pointing to a tall gold-and-white double door. 'That is the drawing room, Miss Emma,' she said, but before she could proceed to the bedrooms on the next floor, there was a sudden rapping of a cane on the front door.

The two footmen had been about to carry a large trunk up the staircase, but now they swiftly put it down and one of them hastened to see who was calling.

His voice carried clearly to the two women on the first gallery. 'Good evening, my lord.'

'I believe from the carriage outside that Mr and Miss Rutherford have arrived,' replied the gentleman at the door.

Emma's breath caught, for the voice was Gerald's.

The footman ushered him into the first little hall. 'Yes, my lord, they arrived about ten minutes ago.'

Emma looked swiftly at Dolly. 'Quickly, my hat and pelisse!' Her fingers shook as she fumbled with the pelisse's tiny buttons and then the ribbons of her Gypsy hat.

Dolly assisted her as best she could, and then relieved her of her gloves and reticule as well. Emma cautiously patted her hair, fearing that at any moment the pins she had labored with would give up the fight, but thankfully the dark, heavy tresses stayed in place.

As Dolly hastened on up to the bedrooms above with her clothes, Emma went cautiously to the balustrade, peeping over to look down just as Gerald followed the footman into the main entrance hall.

There were golden spurs on his Hessian boots, and they jingled softly on the tiled floor. A charcoal-colored Garrick greatcoat rested casually around the shoulders of his indigo coat, and his face was in shadow from his hat brim. Saunders materialized from the kitchens to assist him, taking his greatcoat, and placing hat, gloves, and cane carefully on the console table.

Emma could see Gerald's reflection clearly in the mirror above the table. He was the personification of Bond Street excellence, wearing beneath the indigo coat a waistcoat made of old-gold armazine silk, a frilled white shirt, and cream kerseymere breeches. There was a sapphire pin on the knot of his starched cravat, and it flashed in the light from the chandeliers as he turned to address the butler.

'Have someone attend to my curricle, for I fear the horses are a little fresh.'

'Certainly, my lord.' Saunders snapped his fingers at one of the footmen, who immediately hurried outside. Then the butler bowed to Gerald. 'I will inform Mr and Miss Rutherford that you have called, my lord.'

Emma composed herself, and then went to the staircase. 'You need only inform Mr Rutherford, Saunders,' she said, trusting that her voice sounded more confident than she felt inside. She looked at Gerald. 'My father and I were about to take tea in the drawing room, Lord Kane. Would you care to join us?'

'That would be most agreeable, Miss Rutherford,' he replied politely. There was no particular intonation in his voice, so that it was impossible to tell if he truly found the prospect agreeable or not.

As Saunders hastened away to issue fresh instructions concerning the number for tea, and then to use the back staircase to go to Mr Rutherford's room, Gerald began to ascend toward Emma.

She strove to give the impression of collectedness, but it was very difficult indeed. She had planned to look her very best for their first meeting in London, but instead the moment was being thrust upon her when she was very ill-prepared indeed. She felt anything but elegant, with her hair looking less than perfect and her jaconet gown crumpled from the journey. The gown wasn't one of her favorites, and she only ever wore it with the primrose velvet pelisse, because the gown's high, ruffed neckline emerged very prettily from the pelisse's collar. On its own, however, the gown was less than successful, and had been one of the few failures when copied from a journal illustration. What must she look

20

like to him? Surely he must think her provincial in the extreme, and a very poor substitute for his matchless Margot.

Her nervousness and lack of confidence intensified with each step he took, and her glance was drawn inexorably to his left hand. She could no longer see the mark left by his wedding ring, but she still felt as if it were there, reminding her that theirs was to be nothing more or less than a marriage of convenience.

She wished that her emotions had remained untouched, and that the feelings he had aroused that July day at Foxley Hall were now a thing of the past, but from the moment she had looked at him again, she knew that nothing had changed for her. She was trapped by her own treacherous heart, and although cold common sense bade her turn away from this match, every other sense conspired to shackle her. She was a moth to his flame, and there was nothing she could do to save herself from burning.

3

THERE WAS STILL no way of reading his thoughts as he reached her. 'I trust you will forgive this unannounced and perhaps inopportune call, Miss Rutherford, but I was driving past on my way from Upper Brook Street, and I could not help but see your carriage.' He bowed and took her fingers, drawing them to his lips.

His touch electrified her, and she felt warm color rush into her cheeks. 'There is nothing to forgive, Lord Kane, for it is most pleasing to see you again.'

He smiled a little. 'I do have a reason for calling, for there is something I wish to suggest concerning our first engagement together in society.'

'Shall we go to the drawing room?'

He offered her his arm, and they walked toward the double doors Dolly had pointed out earlier.

Lady Bagworth's drawing room was very sumptuous indeed, stretching from the front of the house to the rear, with windows that overlooked both the square and the gardens. The walls were hung with white silk patterned in gold, and the coffered ceiling was crimson and blue. On the floor there was a Wilton carpet that echoed the ceiling, and the chairs and sofas were upholstered in golden velvet. Dull blue velvet curtains were drawn across the windows, and the room was lit by three shimmering crystal chandeliers that moved gently in the rising warmth from the fire in the huge white marble fireplace. Gilt-framed portraits gazed down from the walls, and there were a number of Greek statues in the corners. Glass-fronted cabinets displayed the late Lord Bagworth's collection of Oriental jade, and Lady Bagworth's spinet, inlaid with lapis lazuli and mother-of-pearl, occupied a prominent position near the center of the room.

Gerald conducted Emma to a sofa near the fire. 'I trust that you had an agreeable journey from Dorchester,' he said politely, waiting until she was properly seated before taking a nearby chair himself.

'It wasn't as arduous as we had expected, although I fear my father still found it somewhat taxing. He will require a few days to recover, but if he is careful to rest and avoid too much exercise . . .' Her voice died away awkwardly as she realized she was talking a little inanely. Her cheeks became hot, and she lowered her eyes quickly.

He did not seem to notice her awkwardness. 'I hope that he will soon be able to put the rigors of the journey behind him, Miss Rutherford.'

'I'm sure he will,' she replied, forcing herself to meet his eyes again.

His gaze was upon her, very clear and gray in the light from the chandeliers. 'No doubt you are pleased to see your brother again,' he murmured.

'We have yet to speak to him, for he isn't at home.' She looked away, remembering what Dolly had told her of Stephen's activities.

'Is something wrong, Miss Rutherford?'

'Wrong?'

'You seem a little, er, distracted.'

'Perhaps I am, just a little.'

'If I can be of any assistance. . . ?'

'Are you acquainted with Lord Avenley, Lord Kane?' she asked suddenly.

His face became very still, and for a moment he didn't reply, but then he gave a brief nod. 'Yes, I am acquainted with him. Why do you ask?'

'Because I have been given to understand that my brother has been spending a great deal of time with him, and that it isn't at all a suitable friendship.'

'It most certainly is not, Miss Rutherford, and I suggest that you do all you can to discourage it. Avenley is a dangerous man, and your brother would be wise to keep away from him.'

She drew a heavy sigh. 'I was hoping that I had been misinformed, but it seems I was not. Lord Kane, you will not mention this in front of my father, will you? He has expressly forbidden Stephen to gamble, and I believe that Lord Avenley has a private gaming club in Pall Mall—'

'Your father will learn nothing from me, Miss Rutherford.'

'I . . . I don't want you to think that my brother and I are much given to deceiving my father, Lord Kane, for truly we are not.'

He smiled a little. 'I'm sure you are not, Miss Rutherford.'

At that moment they heard the tap-tap of a walking stick approaching the doors, and Gerald rose swiftly to his feet as Mr Rutherford entered. He had changed out of his traveling clothes and now wore his favorite gray coat, with no less than two warm woolen shawls around his shoulders. There was a tasseled cap on his gray hair, and his feet made no sound because he had forsaken his boots for silk slippers.

Gerald bowed to him. 'I am sorry to have called without warning, sir.'

Emma's father waved him to sit down again. 'Think nothing of it, my lord, for it is an honor to see you,' he said, his walking stick tapping as he went to sit down next to Emma on the sofa.

He had hardly taken his place when Saunders entered, accompanied by a footman carrying a silver tray. For a few minutes the silence was broken only by the polite chink of fine porcelain cups and saucers, and then the servants withdrew again.

Mr Rutherford sipped his cup and then smiled approvingly. 'I have to confess that although it is considered by some to be a poor beverage, very little refreshes me as well as a cup of good China tea.'

Gerald's cup and saucer remained untouched on the little table by his chair. 'Miss Rutherford was telling me that the journey tired you, sir,' he said politely.

'Tired me? My dear sir, it exhausted me. I abhor traveling at the best of times, but when autumn takes it into its head to arrive early in September, I have to admit that every mile on the open road is torture. However, I shall remain cozily inside for the next week, and then I will be able to sally forth safely again.'

'I was hoping that you would be able to accept an invitation for tomorrow evening.'

'Tomorrow evening? Oh, my dear sir, I would much rather not,' said Mr Rutherford, putting his cup and saucer down quickly. 'The last thing I wish to do is run the risk of my health keeping me from the betrothal ball next month, and that is indeed what might happen if I do not take every possible precaution now.'

'I quite understand, sir.'

'What was the invitation?'

'It is for you, your son, Miss Rutherford, and myself to join Lord and Lady Castlereagh in their box for the opening performance at the new Covent Garden theater. It promises to be an enjoyable occasion, with Madame Catalini singing, and Mrs. Siddons and her brother Mr Kemble playing in *Macbeth*.'

Mr Rutherford gave a wistful sigh. 'Catalini? Oh, if only you knew how much I'd enjoy to hear that paragon sing, but I fear I must be firm and stand by my resolve. However, I see no reason at all why my son and daughter should not attend.'

'I am delighted that you should take that view, sir, for it is an occasion which I feel will be perfect for Miss Rutherford's first London engagement. We are all also invited to an assembly at Manchester House on Friday, again in Lord and Lady Castlereagh's party, but it will be much more of an ordeal because it promises to be a considerable crush, and I gather that Prinny himself might be present.'

'The Prince of Wales? Upon my soul,' murmured Mr Rutherford, quickly sipping his tea.

'Perhaps Miss Rutherford and her brother will be able to attend then as well?' suggested Gerald tentatively.

'Oh, yes, yes, of course,' replied Mr Rutherford without hesitation. 'My dear Lord Kane, if my son and daughter had to remain at home on account of my indifferent health, I fear they would never set foot outside at all.' He smiled warmly. 'They will be delighted to accept both invitations.'

Emma sat forward a little awkwardly. 'Father, it may be that Stephen has prior engagements,' she pointed out.

'Eh? Oh, yes, I suppose that may indeed prove the case,' he conceded. 'I hadn't thought of that.'

'If I may make a suggestion?' said Gerald. 'If it should be that

Miss Rutherford is the only one who can come, then I will approach Lady Castlereagh to act as her chaperone. I am sure that that would satisfy propriety, and that Miss Rutherford will find Lady Castlereagh's company very congenial indeed.'

Mr Rutherford nodded approvingly. 'Yes, that is perfectly in order, Lord Kane. Tell me, are you very well acquainted with Lord Castlereagh?'

'I have the honor to name him among my close friends, sir.'

'I think him a very stout fellow, and his politics are much to my liking,' said Mr Rutherford.

'Then we are in agreement, sir,' Gerald replied, smiling.

Emma kept her eyes lowered to her cup. Lord Castlereagh was the war secretary in the government, and a very prominent man indeed. To be in his party at the theater was a daunting prospect in itself, but the further prospect of attending an assembly at which the Prince of Wales himself might be present filled her with alarm. Oh, how far away now the peace and tranquillity of Foxley Hall and the Dorset countryside.

Mr Rutherford studied Gerald. 'Lord Kane, I may just have arrived from the country, but rumor does occasionally reach Dorchester, and I have heard an unfortunate whisper or two that all is not well concerning Lord Castlereagh's position in the government. Is there any foundation in this?'

Gerald seemed totally nonplussed, staring at him in silence for a moment. 'What have you heard, sir?' he asked at last.

'Oh, it was just a snippet at a dinner with my fellow magistrates, concerning the machinations of the foreign secretary, Mr Canning. There appears to be a suggestion that Mr Canning, who is a mountebank of the first order, wishes to have Lord Castlereagh removed from office for incompetence, and that endeavors to this end have been secretly in progress for the past six months or so, unknown to Lord Castlereagh himself.'

Gerald remained nonplussed for a moment, but then gave a wry smile. 'You heard this in Dorchester, Mr Rutherford?'

'Indeed so.'

'So much for close-guarded secrets in high places,' murmured Gerald dryly.

'It is true, then?'

'I fear so, although I myself only heard it today. It seems that the foreign secretary has indeed been trying to have Lord Castlereagh sacked from office for mishandling the war effort, and that he has been threatening to resign unless this is done. The prime minister and the rest of the government are in turmoil over it all, and no one wishes to be the one to inform Lord Castlereagh of the situation. In my opinion he is being treated very shabbily indeed, if not dishonorably, and it is up to the prime minister himself to do the right thing and inform him of Canning's mischief. I find myself in an intolerable quandary now that it has come to my notice, for I have no wish to see a good friend treated this way, being allowed to continue in office when all the time plans are afoot to remove him, but at the same time I do not wish to precipitate a crisis in the government by telling him something which should come from the prime minister and the rest of the cabinet. I have therefore requested a meeting with the prime minister in the next day or so, at which I will ask him to rectify the situation or I will have no option but to inform Lord Castlereagh myself. It's a distasteful situation, and one for which I will never forgive Canning.'

Mr Rutherford exhaled slowly. 'I do not envy you, my lord, but I have to say that I am amazed that news of this should circulate in Dorchester before even you had heard it.'

'As I said, so much for close-guarded secrets in high places. I feel very badly for Lord Castlereagh, who in no way deserves what is happening. He is far from incompetent and cannot be blamed for the recent setbacks against Bonaparte and the French. The war swings like a pendulum, one moment going our way, the next the enemy's. I fear that I see Canning's overweening ambition shining through in all this. The prime minister's ill health and coming resignation on account of it has given the foreign secretary an opportunity to further himself, and this is the despicable way he's chosen to rid himself of his most formidable rival.' Gerald smiled apologetically and then rose to his feet. 'I think it is time that I took my leave, for you must wish to relax a little after your journey. Again I must beg your forgiveness for calling at such an inopportune moment, but I thought it best to approach you without delay on the matter of the invitations. I am pleased that Miss Rutherford will be able to accept both, for I am sure that the evening at the theater will be the very thing to introduce her to what lies ahead, and that after that she will find the Manchester House assembly by no means the ordeal it might otherwise have been. No, sir, please do not get up, for I am quite capable of finding my own way out,' he added quickly as Mr Rutherford made to rise from the sofa.

Emma put her cup and saucer aside and got up. 'I will show Lord Kane to the door, Father,' she said, resting a gentle hand briefly on her father's shoulder.

He sat back thankfully. 'Would you, my dear? Thank you so much.'

Gerald offered her his arm once more, and they left the drawing room. At the top of the staircase he paused, turning to face her. 'Miss Rutherford, I have been thinking about what you said earlier, concerning your brother's unsuitable friendship with Lord Avenley. If it would be of any assistance, I am quite willing to speak to Stephen about it.'

'Would you? I mean to reason with him myself, of course, but if I am not successful, then I would be very grateful for your help.'

'You have only to say the word.' He hesitated, looking seriously into her eyes. 'Miss Rutherford, I cannot overemphasize that Avenley is everything that is undesirable, for he is without a doubt the most disreputable man in London. He is entirely governed by self-interest, and is both ruthless and without conscience. You may be sure that he has an ulterior motive in cultivating your brother, and that that motive has nothing to do with friendship or kindness.'

Emma stared at him. 'But what ulterior motive could there possibly be?'

The ghost of a smile played on his lips. 'Who can say, Miss Rutherford, who can say?' he murmured, again offering her his arm.

After a moment she accepted, and they proceeded down the hall, where Saunders was waiting with Gerald's greatcoat. With the coat around his shoulders, Gerald took his hat, gloves, and cane and then turned to Emma for a last time.

'Until tomorrow evening, Miss Rutherford.'

'Until tomorrow evening, Lord Kane.'

'If by any chance your brother cannot accompany you, please send word to me, and I will enlist Lady Castlereagh's assistance as chaperon.'

'I will.'

He drew her hand to his lips. 'Good night, Miss Rutherford.'

'Good night, Lord Kane.'

She watched him go out to his waiting curricle and drive away, and as the door closed she thought how very formal and correct they had been. They were complete strangers, and yet they were to be man and wife.

She closed her eyes for a moment, and then turned to retrace her steps up the staircase. She paused at the top, where he had paused a few minutes before to speak to her about Lord Avenley. What had he meant about an ulterior motive? He had had something specific in mind, of that she was quite certain. But what could it be? Of what possible interest could Stephen Rutherford be to a man like Lord Avenley? She wished she knew, for she found the whole business very troubling indeed. Oh, plague take her feckless brother for becoming involved with such a dangerous and unpleasant man! She intended to give Stephen a sharp piece of her mind when she saw him, there was no mistake about that.

4

DINNER WAS SOON to be served, but Stephen had yet to return. Both Emma and her father were ready and waiting, and in the kitchen the cook grumbled as the fine piece of roast beef had to be kept, becoming less and less deliciously pink in the middle with each passing minute.

Mr Rutherford decided to wait another half-hour, and no more, and in the meantime amused himself by adjourning to the library on the ground floor, where he browsed quite happily through the late Lord Bagworth's considerable collection of books on the Orient, and swiftly became so engrossed that thoughts of dinner actually began to recede.

Emma joined him for a while, but the library was at the rear of the house, affording no view of the comings and goings in the square, and after a short time she crossed the hall to the morning room, which looked out to the front. It was a pretty blue-and-white-striped room containing a large sideboard and the circular table where it was the custom to take breakfast. The chandelier had not been lit, and so the only light came from the fire that flickered in the pink marble hearth. A second door gave onto the narrow passage to the kitchens, and in two alcoves there were shelves of shining silver-gilt plate that danced with the fire-light.

The royal-blue brocade curtains had been drawn across the single tall window, and Emma drew them aside to look out. For a moment her eyes were unaccustomed to the darkness, and she could see only her own reflection in the panes of glass. She wore a lime-green silk gown, low-necked with long, diaphanous sleeves, and there was a knotted white silk shawl resting over her arms. Her hair was immaculately combed and pinned into a knot on top of her head, and she still wore her mother's pearl drop earrings.

Gradually her eyes became used to the dim light, and she found that she could look past the reflection to the lamplit square beyond. There were stars in the velvety sky, and lights burning in most of the houses. Several carriages drove past, their lamps casting pale arcs over the cobbles, but of Stephen there was still no sign. Where was he? If he was still with Lord Avenley, she could only pray that he wasn't seated at a green baize table with a hand of cards. This really was too bad of him, for he knew full well the punctual hour their father liked to keep for dinner.

Behind her the clock on the mantelpiece began to whir, and then chimed. The roast beef would soon be done to a crisp, and no doubt fit only to sole boots. She scanned the darkened square again, and as she did so, another carriage approached. It was a gleaming town vehicle drawn by four dapple grays, and as it drew up at the curb she saw to her immense relief that her brother was preparing to alight. She turned from the window and drew the curtains across once more, watching through the open door as Saunders hastened across the hall to the front door.

His greeting carried clearly. 'Good evening, Mr Rutherford.'

'Good evening, Saunders,' Stephen replied, entering the inner hall and turning to give the butler his hat, gloves, and cane.

Emma watched him closely, anxious for any sign that all was not well, but he seemed in excellent fettle, if a little pale from too many late nights. His looks were very youthful and boyish, but it was clear that soon he would become a handsome man. He wore a damson coat and gray breeches, and there was the sort of shine on his top boots with which he would never have been concerned at home in Foxley Hall. His neckcloth was tied in a very complicated and exaggerated style, and was adorned with such a large pin that it gave him an almost dandified appearance that was again very far indeed from the Stephen Rutherford she had known

31

before. He had undergone a great change since coming to London, that much was quite clear, but she was doubtful it was for the better.

Saunders placed his hat, gloves, and cane on the console table, ready for Jacob to retrieve in a few minutes, and then he bowed to Stephen. 'Mr and Miss Rutherford arrived some time ago, sir, and they have been awaiting your return in order to commence dinner.'

'Oh, Lord, I completely forgot dinner! I say, you didn't tell them where I was, did you?'

Emma interrupted before the butler could reply. 'No, he didn't, Stephen, but I've found out anyway.'

Stephen whirled guiltily around, staring at her shadowy figure in the morning room doorway. 'Emma!'

Saunders beat a very prudent and hasty retreat, leaving brother and sister to face each other. Stephen glanced uneasily around, fearing that his father might also have heard, but Emma shook her head, nodding toward the closed door of the library, where their father's poor hearing and absorption in Lord Bagworth's excellent collection of books would have kept him in ignorance of his son's return.

Stephen crossed the hall swiftly, drawing her back into the morning room and then closing the door so that they were completely alone. 'I don't know what you think you know, Sis, but I promise you—'

'I've learned that you've fallen in with a very bad lot, namely Lord Avenley,' she replied, the firelight flickering in her green eyes as she held his gaze.

'You mustn't pay any attention to what's said of Avenley, Emma, for he's a splendid fellow and could not have been more friendly and agreeable toward me since my arrival.'

'A splendid fellow? Friendly and agreeable? That isn't what I've heard about him.'

'As I said, you mustn't pay attention to rumor, for in Avenley's case it's all false.'

'Forgive me if I choose to reserve judgment,' she said, Gerald's warnings echoing in her ears.

'I suppose Dolly Makepeace has been whispering to you, has she?'

'Does it matter how I know?'

He hesitated. 'It matters what Father knows.'

'If you are afraid that he's been regaled with your flagrant disregard for his wishes, then you may rest assured that he hasn't, at least, not as yet.'

'You mean to tell him?'

She drew back angrily. 'It would be no more than you deserve, sirrah! You know full well that you are not supposed to go anywhere near gaming tables, and yet you've been visiting Lord Avenley's private club almost every night, and apparently sometimes during the day as well.'

'Keep your voice down,' he pleaded, glancing uneasily toward the door.

'I had hoped that you'd behave a little more responsibly, Stephen, but it seems that you've paid no heed at all to Father's wishes and warnings.'

'How? Simply by going to Avenley's club? Sis, I may have been going there, but only because the company is so excellent. I swear that I haven't been sitting at the tables.'

'And you honestly expect me to believe that? I'd rather believe a cat would knit scarves for mice!'

'I'm not fibbing to you, Emma.'

'Not one card has soiled your lily-white fingers?'

'Not one.'

She searched his face, wanting to believe him.

He saw that she was no longer quite sure, and he pressed home his advantage. 'Emma, I swear that I've been observing Father's wishes about gambling, but I know how my friendship with Avenley must appear, and that's why I've been at pains to keep it secret. I like Avenley, and I enjoy visiting his club, and I see no harm in that, provided I adhere to Father's wishes concerning the tables. Besides, the stakes are so astronomically high there that I couldn't possibly indulge, even if I wished to.'

He was very believable, and against her better judgment she found herself being persuaded, but she still wasn't convinced that Lord Avenley was the angel he claimed. 'Stephen, why has Lord Avenley singled you out so?'

'We get on, it's as simple as that.'

'I'm told he asked to be introduced to you.'

'My word, chitter-chatter does get around, doesn't it?' he replied coolly. 'Very well, yes, he did ask a mutual friend, but only because someone told him I was an expert on gun dogs.'

'Gun dogs?'

'Yes. Avenley likes grouse shooting on his Scottish estate, and is always interested in gun dogs. It was a case of mistaken identity, but once we'd been introduced, we found that we hit it off. That's all there is to it, Sis, it's nothing untoward. I tell you, Avenley is an excellent chap.'

'I've been told that he's unscrupulous and dangerous.'

'Servants' tittle-tattle. I'm surprised at you, Sis, for since when have you listened to kitchen gossip?'

'I haven't heard it only from Dolly, Stephen.'

'Who else?'

'Lord Kane.'

He stared at her. 'Kane?'

'Yes, and he warned me most earnestly against your Lord Avenley. What reason could he have for telling untruths?'

'What reason? Only the extreme bad feeling that exists between him and Avenley. They despise each other, it's a well-known fact. Look, Emma, can't we talk about something else? You have my word that I haven't been plunging in at Avenley's tables, so can't we leave it at that?'

'Stephen—'

'Please, Emma,' he pleaded wearily. 'I haven't been straying, I promise.'

'I want to believe you, Stephen.'

'Then do so, and don't worry Father with wild stories about the bad lot I'm mixed up with, for it isn't true about Avenley. Just trust me.'

'I will, provided you give me your solemn word that you will stay away from the gaming tables.'

'You have my word.'

She smiled then. 'Then I won't say anything to Father.'

'Thank you, Sis.' He bent to kiss her on the cheek. 'So, you've already seen Kane, have you?'

'Yes, he called a few minutes after we'd arrived. Oh, Stephen,

I'm afraid that he caught me at a complete disadvantage. I was wearing that white jaconet gown, and it was all crumpled, and you know how poorly I manage my hair without Dolly. It looked like an untidy haystack.'

He grinned at her doleful expression. 'Come, now, I'm sure that even the Countess of Purbeck is sometimes caught at a disadvantage.'

'That I doubt very much,' Emma replied with feeling. Raine, Countess of Purbeck, was the acknowledged belle of London society. As the widowed Mrs. Backford she had taken the capital by storm, and had soon acquired a convenient second husband in the form of the elderly, infirm Earl of Purbeck, who doted on her, indulged her every whim, and who remained conveniently out of town at Purbeck Park in Sussex. Raine was golden-haired, with lilac eyes, a voluptuous figure, and the sort of fascinating ways that men apparently found irresistible. Emma's fashion journals were constantly extolling her virtues, describing her perfect taste, immaculate manners, and flawless beauty, and never failed to give full details of her clothes, jewelry, and hair at whatever function she attended. The Countess of Purbeck was *the* paragon of fashion, and the thought of her ever being caught as ill-prepared as Emma Rutherford had been that day was too ridiculous for words.

Stephen pulled a face. 'Sis, you shouldn't believe all you read about the countess, for she isn't all she's cracked up to be, you have my word on that.'

'You've met her?'

'Our paths have crossed,' he replied shortly.

Emma looked curiously at him. 'I take it that you don't like her?'

'She's a *chienne* of the highest order.'

Emma was a little surprised by the deep dislike the countess appeared to have aroused in her usually placid and easygoing brother. Stephen very rarely displayed antagonism, or aroused antagonism in others.

He smiled. 'Enough of her, let's talk about you and Kane instead. How did your first London meeting go?'

'Well enough, I suppose. He came to invite us all to join Lord and Lady Castlereagh's party at the theater tomorrow night, and again at a Manchester House assembly on Friday.'

'And happy chance brought him the very moment you'd arrived?'

'He said he was driving from Upper Brook Street and saw our carriage.'

Stephen's smile faded. 'Upper Brook Street? Are you sure?'

'Quite sure. Why?'

'Nothing. Go on.'

'Stephen, you can't just leave it at that. What is so significant about Upper Brook Street?'

'Nothing whatsoever.'

'Then why did you say it like that?' she demanded.

'I didn't say it like anything, Sis, you're imagining it. So, he came to invite you to the theater and to Manchester House, did he?'

'Not just me, I said it was all of us. Father can't come, of course, because of his health and the journey, but you and I are to go.'

'Ah, that presents a slight problem.'

'Problem?' She looked quickly at him.

'The Manchester House invitation I can accept, and do so gladly, but I'm afraid that tomorrow night is out of the question.'

She was dismayed. 'Oh, Stephen!'

'I have a prior engagement, Sis, and it's simply not done to accept something and then cast it aside in favor of another.'

'But it's my first time in London, Stephen. Can't you possibly wriggle out of this other invitation, just this once?'

'It's Donkey Shingleton's coming-of-age birthday tomorrow, and I'm dining with him and a party of other friends at White's. It's a special dinner, Sis, very grand, and my absence would be very glaring. Look, I'll gladly escort you on Friday, but I simply cannot do it tomorrow night. Surely you can conjure a chaperone from somewhere, if that's what's worrying you?'

'It's not just the matter of a chaperone, Stephen, because I am assured that Lady Castlereagh will gladly perform the duty, it's more that I'm dreadfully nervous and would feel much happier if you were with me.'

He smiled, pulling her into his arms and hugging her tightly.

'My poor big sister,' he murmured fondly.

She held him close. 'I don't know whether I can carry this match off, Stephen,' she whispered. 'I felt so painfully countrified when he called today, and I dread to think what he must have thought when he saw me. He must have compared me with his first wife and found me lacking in every single way.'

'If he found you so lacking, he'd never have embarked upon the match in the first place,' he pointed out gently. 'Look at me, Sis. Kane made all the approaches, and he decided upon you after a single meeting. Doesn't that tell you something?'

'Yes, that he didn't much care about anything, provided he found the necessary wife.'

'That isn't what it tells you at all,' he said reprovingly, tilting her face toward his. 'It tells you that he liked what he saw at Foxley Hall, and decided that you would more than do. He didn't have to proceed after that first meeting, did he?'

'No, but—'

'No buts, for that is the end of it. He saw you, liked you, and offered for you. What more is there to say? Besides, I doubt very much if you will be the main attraction tomorrow night, not if you are in Castlereagh's party. Rumors are flying all over town today concerning things that have been going on behind his back in the government, and odds are being laid as to when and how he finds out.'

'I know all about the rumors. It seems that Father heard them before we left Dorchester.'

'Did he, be damned?' Stephen gave a low whistle. 'Fancy old Dorset getting the sniff before London. Well, if you know about it, you'll understand why odds are even being laid that when Castlereagh finds out, he'll feel obliged to call Canning out over it.'

'A duel?' she gasped. 'Oh, surely not.'

'Castlereagh's honor has been gravely impugned, Sis. So, as I said, you will most definitely not be the only attraction tomorrow night, for his lordship will steal your thunder. You won't need me, Emma, and you'll carry it all off splendidly, I know you will. Now, then, shouldn't we show our faces for dinner?'

'Dinner! I'd forgotten all about it! Oh, that wretched roast beef will be a positive cinder!' She hurried to the door, but as she opened it, she turned to look back at him. 'Stephen, you haven't humbugged me tonight, have you?'

He met her gaze. 'No, Sis, I haven't. Everything I've told you has been the truth.'

She smiled, holding out her hand to him. 'Come on, let's go to Father.'

5

THERE WAS A thin mist the following morning, but it dispersed as soon as the sun rose, and soon the sky over London was clear and blue, although still with that crispness that accompanied even the most mild of autumn days.

Emma and Stephen breakfasted alone in the sunlit morning room, for the ordeal of the journey had now caught up with their father, who had elected to remain in his bed all day. Propped up on a mound of pillows, his room heated almost unbearably by a roaring fire, he breakfasted on several glasses of hot milk, consumed while he read a volume on Chinese plants that he had discovered the night before in the library.

A hearty breakfast was out of the question for Emma, who had awoken in a state of immense trepidation over the coming visit to the theater. Her anxiety made her pale, a fact which was not concealed by the judicious application of a little rouge to her cheeks, and although she wore a cheerful peach-and-white-striped muslin gown that was gathered beneath her breasts with a wide peach satin ribbon, she knew that she looked less than carefree. Her dark hair was piled up beneath a lace-edged day cap from which fluttered peach ribbons to match her gown, and she wore no jewelery at all.

She had hoped to wake up feeling a little more buoyant, but her courage seemed only to grow more feeble. She was nervous about facing society for the first time, especially without Stephen at her side, and even though he would be with her on Friday at the assembly at Manchester House, the prospect of royalty possibly being present was almost too much to countenance.

Her father had written to Gerald the evening before, as soon as he heard that Stephen would not be able to join the theater party, and a running footman had delivered the communication promptly to Gerald's residence in St James's Square. The footman had soon returned with Gerald's reply, an extremely courteous note written on cream vellum that bore the phoenix crest of the Fitzroy family. In it he reassured Mr Rutherford that Lady Castlereagh had agreed to act as Emma's chaperone, and that as a consequence there would be no danger at all to her reputation. To be certain of this, Lord and Lady Castlereagh would accompany him to Grosvenor Square at eight o'clock, and they would all four leave together for the theater. He added that should circumstances change as far as the Friday engagement was concerned, Lady Castlereagh willingly offered her services for that occasion as well.

Emma sighed, gazing at the slice of buttered toast on her plate. Her cup of coffee was now almost cold, and she had declined any thought of sampling the delicious bacon and scrambled eggs that her brother was enjoying with such gusto.

Stephen looked up, his glance encompassing her untouched meal and withdrawn expression. He poured himself another cup of the coffee, and then sat back in his chair, surveying her. 'No appetite, Sis?'

'Not really.'

'You're worrying about nothing, you know. The morning paper is full of speculation about the Castlereagh-Canning affair, which means that Castlereagh himself must be aware of it by now. It's bound to be the sole topic of interest at the theater, especially if Castlereagh is present, so you are going to come a rather poor second, I fear.'

'I hope you're right.' She paused. 'I think that poor Lord Castlereagh has been treated very badly.'

'And so he has. If he does decide that his honor must be satisfied, then very few will blame him.'

'Do you really think it would come to that?'

Stephen shrugged. 'There is a precedent. The late Mr Pitt fought a duel while he was still prime minister.'

She fell silent, returning her gaze to the toast.

Stephen tossed his napkin aside and got up. 'Enough of this

moping. What you need is a good brisk walk, and that is what Dr
Stephen Rutherford prescribes. What do you say to a look at the
Oxford Street shops?'

She smiled. 'It sounds a sovereign remedy, sir.'

'Then off you toddle to put on your walking togs,' he said, holding out her chair as she rose to her feet. 'I will await you in the hall
in a quarter of an hour.'

Shortly afterward, dressed in an orange wool pelisse trimmed
with brown braiding, and a brown beaver hat with golden tassels,
Emma emerged from the house on her brother's arm. Her brown-
gloved hand rested on Stephen's sage-green sleeve, and a brown
silk parasol twirled slowly over her shoulder.

Beside her, Stephen looked very much the young man-about-
town. The stand-fall collar of his coat was very high, as was the
stock around his throat, and his voluminous cravat was of a rather
startling green silk spotted with gray. His breeches were very tight,
his top boots sported rather large and ornate spurs that did not
simply jingle as he walked, but rang out clearly like bells, and an
ivory-handled cane swung elegantly in his hand. He wore his high-
crowned hat at a rakish angle over his forehead, so that he had to
tilt his head back a little in order to see where he was going, and
there was a definite hint of cologne about his person. His friends
in Dorchester would scarcely have recognized him, and his sister
found it difficult to believe the change that had come over her
hitherto rather untidy sibling. The Stephen Rutherford of Foxley
Hall had not been all that interested in matters of fashion; the
Stephen Rutherford of Grosvenor Square was a positive fashion
fiend.

They strolled west along the pavement, toward the junction of
South Audley Street and Upper Grosvenor Street, the latter along
which the carriage had traveled from Dorchester the evening
before. A light breeze rustled the trees in the square's central
garden, and the sun shone brightly on the gilded statue. The
flower girl was seated by the garden railings, her replenished
baskets beside her, and her plaintive calls rang out around the
house. 'Roses. Buy my red roses.'

Several carriages drove past, and a party of horsemen returned
from a brisk ride in Hyde Park. A chimney sweep had been called

to a house on the corner, and his cart had been left in a very awkward place, requiring Emma and Stephen to step out into the road in order to pass by. As they left the safety of the pavement, an expensive open landau swept past, its team of four creams stepping high.

Stephen pulled Emma swiftly back out of danger, for the carriage was really dangerously close. The coachman didn't even glance at them, even though he'd almost run them down, and the landau drove on down South Audley Street.

Stephen looked anxiously at Emma. 'Are you all right, Sis?'

She nodded a little breathlessly, gazing after the landau and its single lady occupant. 'Yes, just a bit shaken, that's all.'

As Emma looked, the lady turned to glance back. She was very beautiful indeed, with bright golden curls and a heart-shaped face of incredible sweetness. She was dressed from head to toe in turquoise corded silk, with soft silver plumes curling down from her elegant little hat, and would have presented an almost perfect vision of loveliness had it not been for the cold set of her mouth as her lilac eyes met Emma's.

For the space of several heartbeats the two women looked at each other, and then the lady turned to the front again, and the landau drove on. Emma glanced at Stephen. 'Who was she?' she asked, seeing that he too was now gazing after the landau.

'That, my dear sister, was Raine, Countess of Purbeck, the paragon whose example you think so unrivaled, and whose name fills the foolish pages of your fashion journals.'

Emma's lips parted in surprise, and she looked after the retreating vehicle. Stephen spoke again. 'I meant it last night when I called her a *chienne*, Sis, for she is no friend of mine, and she will most certainly be no friend of yours.'

'Why are you and she so hostile toward each other, Stephen?'

'It doesn't matter why. Suffice it that you should always be on your guard where she is concerned, for she will do her utmost to belittle you.'

Emma stared at him. 'Belittle me?'

'Yes.'

'Stephen—'

'That's all I mean to say concerning the dear countess, Sis. Just be very wary of her. Now, then, let's get on with this excursion to Oxford Street.' He took her hand firmly and drew it over his sleeve, leading her across the corner of the square to walk north-ward toward the other corner and the road that gave onto Oxford Street.

She said nothing more about the Countess of Purbeck, but she thought about her a great deal. What on earth could have caused such deep ill feeling? It was evident that Stephen wasn't going to explain anything, but whatever it was had to be very serious indeed for him to adopt such a position of implacable dislike. And what would cause the countess to wish to belittle his sister?

Emma puzzled about it as she and Stephen strolled toward the northwest corner of the square, where North Audley Street led to Oxford Street, and Upper Brook Street led west toward Park Lane and Hyde Park. Upper Brook Street. Emma's steps faltered a little as they reached the corner, and she looked along the street that seemed to have some mysterious connection with Gerald.

It was a handsome road, a place of fine mansions and high garden walls over which hung the branches of exotic ornamental trees. Beyond the walls she could hear the gentle splashing of foun-tains, the cooing of doves, and the occasional calls of peacocks. The sun shone brightly on gleaming windows and brass door knockers, and upon the panels and accoutrements of the hand-some private carriages that passed to and fro along the exclusive cobbled way. This was Mayfair at its most elegant, a place where only the most superior of persons would have their addresses, and it beckoned almost irresistibly to Emma, whose inquisitiveness had been aroused by Stephen's strange reaction the evening before.

At the far end of the street, across Park Lane, she could see the trees of Hyde Park, their leaves already showing the early tints of autumn, and she came to a sudden decision. 'Stephen, don't let's go to Oxford Street, let's walk to Park Lane instead. If I remember accurately from the street map that I studied so much before leav-ing Foxley Hall, we can walk down Park Lane and then back along Upper Grosvenor Square, and complete a comfortable circle home.'

Stephen shrugged. 'As you wish, although I would have thought the lure of shops would prove too great for you.'

'Not this morning. I'll be content with just a good walk in the fresh air.'

They turned west, continuing their leisurely stroll along the pavement of Upper Brook Street. The soft breeze stirred gently through the foliage hanging over the garden walls, and something startled a flock of doves so that they rose in a flutter from an unseen dovecote, their wings very clean and white against the blue of the sky.

Emma glanced all around as they walked. She studied fine mansion after fine mansion, but there was nothing unusual about any of them. She didn't really know what she expected to see, she only knew that there was something significant about this street, and that it concerned the man she was to marry. She glanced surreptitiously at her brother, but he seemed totally unconcerned, and certainly gave no hint of anything untoward; he even whistled softly to himself, his cane swinging to and fro.

They reached the end of the street, and the bustle and noise of Park Lane. In Hyde Park, the 'lungs' of London, carriages bowled along Rotten Row, and horsemen and women rode their mounts in the daily display performed by the *beau monde*.

Stephen paused, pointing with his cane. 'You and I will have to ride there soon, Sis. There's an excellent livery stable in South Audley Street where we can hire suitable mounts. Would you like that?'

She smiled. 'You know full well that I adore riding, Stephen Rutherford.'

'It's settled, then. We'll go one morning, before breakfast, and then you'll come back ravenous and eat properly.'

'I hope you're right,' she replied.

Before they turned south along Park Lane, she glanced back along Upper Brook Street, but it all seemed so innocent and quiet, and Stephen's attitude was now one of such unconcern that she began to think she had imagined it the evening before after all.

They had almost reached the corner of Upper Grosvenor Street, and the final part of their circular tour, when something made her suddenly turn to look at the traffic approaching from behind along Park Lane. Her gaze was drawn immediately to a travel-stained carriage drawn by a team of four exquisitely matched bays, for the coachman chose that moment to crack his whip to encourage the horses to come up to a smarter pace at the end of what had evidently been a rather long stage for them.

The carriage held Emma's attention, and she watched as it drove past. Her gaze was drawn immediately to the crest on the door, for it was the Fitzroy phoenix. Her lips parted, and she looked inside, catching a fleeting glimpse of an elderly gentleman wrapped up as warmly against the autumn chill as her father had been the day before. Who else could it be but Gerald's grandfather, the Earl of Cranforth, who was leaving the seclusion at Cranforth Castle in Derbyshire in order to attend his grandson's betrothal celebration?

She clutched Stephen's arm. 'Look, I'm sure that is the Earl of Cranforth!' she said, indicating the carriage.

'Eh?'

'The Earl of Cranforth,' she said again, watching as the carriage drove on down Park Lane. 'If it turns into the drive of Cranforth House, then it can indeed only be he,' she murmured.

Sure enough, on reaching the first of the Cranforth House gates, the carriage slowed and turned in through them.

Stephen grinned at her. 'So, the old boy has arrived to give his blessing to your match.'

'So it would seem.'

'I suppose this signals another rush of the jitters on your part?'

'Don't tease me, Stephen, for I do indeed feel wretchedly nervous about all this.'

He put his arm gently around her shoulder. 'Don't fret so, Sis, for you'll make an excellent Lady Kane, and when the time eventually comes for you to become the Countess of Cranforth, you'll carry the day with all the aplomb of the Rutherfords. And by then, I vow you'll have your husband eating out of your dainty hand.'

Emma said nothing. She would never win Gerald's heart, not when the ghost of his adored Margot would always be there to trounce her.

6

THAT AFTERNOON, WHEN Stephen was out and Mr Rutherford was still in his bed, Emma sat at the escritoire in the drawing room, endeavoring to write some letters to her friends in Dorchester. Her hand trembled a little as she wrote, and the words did not flow easily from her pen, for she was far too preoccupied. She wore a delicate pale-pink woolen gown with a lace-filled neckline and long sleeves that were frilled at the wrists, and her glossy dark hair was tied loosely back with a pink ribbon, for she found it comfortable and a little more relaxing that way. A headache had threatened for some time now, and Dolly had prepared a marjoram balm which she had applied to her forehead and temples. To be as certain as possible that all had been done to stave off the headache, the maid had also provided her mistress with an infusion of primula tea, but still the dull pain lingered close by, as if just waiting for an idle moment in which to pounce. Emma knew that the headache was born purely and simply of nerves, and that nothing would really ward it off unless she suddenly underwent a metamorphosis and became filled with confidence.

She had finished one letter, and was about to embark upon the next, when Saunders suddenly announced that Gerald had called. Startled, and again caught at a disadvantage, this time with her hair not pinned at all, but simply held back with ribbon, she left the escritoire and prepared to receive him. Why had he called now, when they would see each other that evening anyway?

He was shown into the room, and bowed to her as the butler closed the double doors behind him. He wore a dove-gray coat and cream breeches, and the crimson brocade of his waistcoat was echoed by the gleaming ruby pin in his neckcloth. His dark hair was a little ruffled, and the color on his cheeks told her that he hadn't come in his carriage, but had driven in his curricle. 'Again, I must beg your forgiveness for calling without warning, Miss Rutherford,' he said, coming toward her and bowing over her hand.

His touch affected her, and she had to swallow. 'Of course you are forgiven, Lord Kane, especially if you will make allowances for my rather undressed appearance. I fear I have had a headache, and that the thought of pins in my hair was a little intolerable.' How lame it sounded!

'You look quite charming, Miss Rutherford, so please do not concern yourself about such a trifling matter as the absence of pins. Hair such as yours will always look beautiful, however you choose to wear it.'

'You are very kind, sir.'

'And you are unnecessarily anxious, Miss Rutherford,' he replied candidly, looking into her green eyes. 'May I speak honestly?' he asked then.

'By all means, Lord Kane,' she replied, wondering what he was about to say.

'I have taken the liberty of calling like this because I hoped to find you alone. Yesterday it seemed to me that even allowing for my poorly timed call, you were still rather ill at ease in my company. I know that we are barely acquainted, and, forgive me, that this match is far and beyond any which you would normally have hoped to make. It must be very unsettling for you, especially now that you are here in London and have begun to realize how very different things will be from now on. Am I right?'

She lowered her eyes. 'In part, yes.'

'In what part am I wrong?'

'It isn't that you are wrong, sir, it's simply that you haven't considered my bewilderment that you should have selected me.'

He gave a short laugh. 'Bewilderment? Why do you say that?'

'Because you could have had your pick of grand brides, but instead you've chosen me. When set beside the daughters of dukes and earls, I am a nobody from nowhere, and my fortune simply isn't large enough to explain your odd choice. Why do you want to marry me, Lord Kane?'

'You underrate yourself, Miss Rutherford.'

'Do I? Now perhaps it is my turn to speak honestly. I cannot help but know that you must always be comparing me with your first wife, and that I come out very badly in the comparison. I—'

'Please do not compare yourself with my first wife, Miss Rutherford,' he interrupted quietly.

She drew back a little. 'I fear I cannot help it, Lord Kane,' she said.

'I have chosen you because you are everything I could wish for, Miss Rutherford, and if I have shunned the daughters of dukes and earls, perhaps it is because on the whole I find them a little tiresome. You are refreshingly new and different, and I think that we will do very well together. If you do not feel the same, then—'

'I'm simply out of my depth, Lord Kane,' she said, and the painful honesty of the words shone in her eyes as she looked at him.

'A condition that will be very transient, I promise you,' he said gently. 'London will take to you, Miss Rutherford, and you will soon learn how to go on in even the most exclusive of circles.'

'Will I? Forgive me if I cannot be so certain, Lord Kane, but if you only knew how I'm dreading tonight, and how positively terrified I am about the assembly at Manchester House on Friday, when I may find myself in the company of the Prince of Wales—'

'Miss Rutherford, the Prince of Wales is not an ogre, indeed the very opposite is the case, and you will not only be under Lady Castlereagh's kindly and capable wing, you will also be with me. I will be at your side, and I promise you that I will support you throughout. Nothing you have said or done since I have met you has given me even the slightest cause to fear I am making a mistake. I wish to make you my wife, and I am here now to reassure you if I possibly can.'

She loved him so much in that moment that it was all she could do not to blurt out the truth. Tears stung her eyes, and she turned quickly away.

He took out his handkerchief and pressed it gently into her hand. 'If this really is too much of an ordeal for you, then all you need do is say,' he said softly. 'The last thing I would ever wish to do is cause you pain in any way, for I hold you in too high regard for that. Do you wish to withdraw from the match?'

She tamed quickly back to him. 'No, please, don't think that. Oh, forgive me for being so weak and silly, I really don't know what has come over me.'

'Miss Rutherford, I find your nervousness and uncertainty perfectly understandable, and indeed commendable, for if you had been supremely confident and without sign of nerves, then I would indeed have begun to wonder if I was doing the wrong thing.' He smiled a little. 'So, let us be absolutely certain about everything. You wish to proceed with the match?'

She nodded. 'Yes, of course I do,' she said, putting all her doubts behind her as she gazed into his eyes.

'And so do I, which means that we are in absolute accord. Please don't ever again doubt yourself, or my commitment in the matter. I wish you to be Lady Kane, and to eventually become the Countess of Cranforth.' He drew her hand to his lips.

'I will try to be all that you could wish for, Lord Kane,' she whispered, trying to hide the tremble in her voice, for his touch threatened to melt her to her very soul.

'You already are all that I could wish for, Miss Rutherford,' he murmured, releasing her hand. 'And to prove the fact, at least in the eyes of society, I intend to make you a present of something that is usually not given to any Lady Kane until the day of her marriage.' He took a small slender red leather case from his pocket and gave it to her.

Inside she found an exquisite diamond brooch lying on a bed of crimson velvet. The brooch was very old, and fashioned in the shape of the Fitzroy double-headed phoenix, and the diamonds flashed brilliantly in the light from the window.

Emma's breath caught with admiration. 'Oh, it's beautiful . . .'

'It's called the Kane Keepsake, and has been in my family for nearly three hundred years. As I said, it is usually given to each new Lady Kane on her wedding day, but I wish to break with that tradition and give it to you now instead.'

'Why?'

'Because when society sees it, everyone will know beyond any shadow of doubt that I have gladly chosen you to be my bride. If you wear it tonight, then the message will begin to be delivered without delay.'

'But if it is such an established tradition to wait until the day of the wedding—'

'The Keepsake is mine to give as I please, Miss Rutherford.'

'Oh, yes, of course, I didn't mean . . .' She broke off in embarrassment. The diamonds winked and glittered on their bed of crimson, and the brooch felt ice-cold when she touched it with her fingertips.

Gerald smiled at her confusion. 'If you perhaps fear that my grandfather will disapprove of anything that interferes with time-honored ceremony, then please rest assured that he is fully aware of my intention and that he has given my decision his blessing. I have come here directly from Cranforth House, for I have taken luncheon with him. He arrived in London this morning.'

'Yes, I know.'

'You know?'

'Stephen and I were out walking this morning, and we saw his carriage arrive. I saw the phoenix on the door panel, and when the carriage drove into Cranforth House, I did not think there could be any doubt that it was the earl.'

'He wishes to meet you as soon as possible. I thought perhaps that we could call upon him tomorrow afternoon.'

'Yes, of course.'

'And you will wear the Keepsake tonight?'

'If that is your wish.'

'It must be your wish too, Miss Rutherford,' he said gently.

She looked up quickly into his clear gray eyes and nodded. 'Then I shall indeed wear it tonight, sir. I am very honored indeed that you should choose to give it to me now.'

'I thought it would help to reassure you.'

She managed a small smile. 'It does, my lord. Thank you.'

'I will leave you now, and will return tonight with Lord and Lady Castlereagh. Until eight o'clock, Miss Rutherford.'

'Until then, sir.'

He bowed, drawing her hand to his lips for a last time, and then he left her. For a moment she wondered if she should hurry after him and accompany him to the door, but somehow it didn't seem appropriate on this occasion.

She gazed down at the Keepsake, nestling in the exquisite red leather case. It was an incomparable jewel, fashioned by a master craftsman, and its diamonds were somehow more dazzling than any she'd ever seen before. She touched it again with her fingertips, and then closed the case. The last time the Kane Keepsake had been presented had been on the day Gerald had married Margot.

The evening came all too quickly, and as the lamps were lit in the square, Emma dressed for the theater.

Her room was on the third story of the house, overlooking the gardens and mews at the back. It was an elegant room, but at the same time comfortable and intimate, with pale-green hand-painted silk on the walls, and elaborately lacquered furniture. The four-poster bed had a very ornate golden silk canopy, and the posts were carved and gilded. The fireplace was made of white and pink marble, with a brass fender, and the two armchairs on either side were upholstered in chintz. Through an archway there was a dressing room, its interior concealed from the bedroom by a delicately painted lacquer screen, but it contained a dressing table, a washstand, numerous chests of drawers, and three immense wardrobes.

When Emma's preparations were complete, she and Dolly emerged from the dressing room and Emma went to stand for a moment before the fire. The curtains were drawn at the windows, and the only light came from the fire and several candelabra on the mantelpiece.

For this most important of occasions she had chosen to wear a green velvet evening gown that was almost exactly the same color as her eyes. The gown had small petal sleeves, a very high waistline, and a scoop neckline that plunged almost daringly low over her bosom. With it she wore long white gloves and a lacy white shawl that was knotted at the ends. The gown was the perfect choice for the Keepsake, for its dainty bodice was softly gathered immediately beneath her breasts, providing an ideal place on which to pin the brooch. The diamonds winked and flashed in the moving light from the fire, finding an echo in the jeweled comb in her hair. Dolly had taken great care with her coiffure, pinning the heavy dark tresses up into a particularly intricate knot at the back of her head and teasing down one single ringlet, which tumbled past the nape of her neck.

Emma wished that Stephen had not had a prior engagement, for in spite of the pains Gerald had gone to to make her feel better, she would still have preferred to have her brother at her side as well. But Stephen had already gone out to join his new friends at White's for the strangely named Donkey Shingleton's coming-of-age birthday party. Emma gazed into the fire, hoping that that was indeed where Stephen had gone, and that his determination to keep his prior engagement had nothing at all to do with Lord Avenley or his thrice-cursed gaming hell in Pall Mall. She drew a long self-reproaching breath. She shouldn't doubt her brother so much, for he had given her his word that he was not misbehaving at the club.

Suddenly there was a tap at the bedroom door. She turned. 'Come in.'

Saunders entered. 'Lord Kane and Lord and Lady Castlereagh have arrived, madam.'

'Very well.'

'I have already informed Mr Rutherford, madam, and he will escort you down to the hall.'

'Thank you, Saunders.'

'Madam.' The butler bowed and withdrew again.

Emma turned nervously to Dolly. 'Have we forgotten anything?'

'No, Miss Emma. Oh, your fan and evening reticule!' With a gasp, the maid hurried through into the dressing room, returning in a moment with the little painted fan and a lozenge-shaped reticule stitched with silver spangles. It was closed by a dainty drawstring, which the maid looped carefully over her mistress's wrist with the fan, and it contained a handkerchief, a vial of Emma's favorite rose scent, a comb, and some extra hairpins, should some calamity befall Emma's coiffure.

Emma was suddenly a bundle of nerves again. 'Is there anything else?' she asked, smoothing the folds of her skirts with hands that shook.

'Just your cloak,' replied the maid, nodding toward the fur-trimmed rose silk cloak that had earlier been draped over one of the fireside chairs, to keep warm for the chill evening air outside.

Taking Emma's shawl, the maid brought the cloak, placing it carefully around her shoulders, and when it was properly tied, the folded shawl was given to her to carry over her arm beneath the mantle. Then, with her heart pounding so loudly in her breast that she was sure it could be heard all over the house, she left her room to walk along the passage toward the head of the staircase, where her father was already waiting for her.

Mr Rutherford wore a charcoal-gray coat and cream cord breeches, and his muslin neckcloth had been very neatly tied and arranged by his valet. He still looked a little tired from the journey, but he smiled approvingly as his daughter approached. 'Are you ready, my dear?'

'I will be, in just a moment,' she replied softly, putting her finger to her lips and then looking tentatively over the balustrade into the hall below, where Lady Castlereagh was seated on one of the sofas by the fire, and the two gentlemen stood in conversation nearby.

Amelia, Lady Castlereagh, known to her many friends as Emily, was thirty-seven years old, and dressed in a yellow-and-white-striped taffeta gown. Her fair hair was almost completely concealed beneath a cloth-of-gold turban from which sprang a tall ostrich plume, and beside her on the sofa lay the exquisite white fur cloak that Saunders had taken as she entered. She wasn't a beauty, but her lips had a quickness about them that suggested a willingness to smile, and there was something about her that Emma liked immediately.

The two gentlemen were dressed in the formal black evening attire that was *de rigueur* for the theater, both of them in tight-fitting evening coats, lace-trimmed shirts, white satin waistcoats, and white silk pantaloons. Dress swords swung at their sides, and they carried black tricorns beneath their arms.

Robert Stewart, Lord Castlereagh, was a handsome, smooth-faced man of about forty, with soft brown hair and observant blue eyes. He was tall and loose-limbed, and his reputation for being cold and remote seemed well deserved, for unlike his wife, he gave the appearance of being unapproachable. Perhaps it was the oddly smooth face, or the rather frozen look in his eyes. Emma studied him for a long moment, thinking about all she had heard concerning his difficulties with Mr Canning. It was hard to imagine him feeling sufficiently angered and provoked to call anyone out to a duel, but from all accounts this might very well be what was about to happen.

Beside him, Gerald was as immaculately turned out as ever, and it seemed to Emma that he grew more handsome each time she saw him.

Mr Rutherford touched her arm gently. 'Emma, my dear, I think we should go down.'

She nodded, taking a deep breath to compose herself; then she accepted her father's arm, and they began to descend the stairs.

Gerald saw them first, and came to the foot of the staircase, his glance sweeping briefly over her before he met her eyes.

Mr Rutherford spoke. 'Good evening, Lord Kane.'

'Good evening, Mr Rutherford. Miss Rutherford.'

'I must say again that I wish my health permitted me more license, for nothing would please me more than to join you tonight. I do hope that my regret is sufficiently expressed.'

'It is indeed, sir,' Gerald replied. 'Come, allow me to present my friends Lord and Lady Castlereagh.'

Lady Castlereagh was as agreeable and friendly as Emma knew she would be, and could not have been more at pains to make her young charge feel at ease.

'My dear Miss Rutherford, how very charming you look tonight. I vow that I am consumed with jealousy over your hair, for it is everything that my wretched mop has never been. I doubt very much if you will ever be reduced to wearing odious turbans rather than display your locks to the eyes of the world.'

'You are too kind, I think, Lady Castlereagh.'

'Not at all, my dear, I merely give credit where credit is due. Now, then, I will look after you tonight, and on any other occasion that may arise, so please do not give propriety another thought, for all is well.'

'Thank you, Lady Castlereagh.'

Lady Castlereagh gave Gerald a stern look. 'Sirrah, you have been very remiss, for you did not tell us how very pretty she is. You have found yourself a positive treasure, and I doubt very much if you deserve such good fortune.'

Gerald smiled. 'Emily, I doubt it too, but Lady Luck has chosen to single me out, I fear.' Taking Emma's hand, he drew her to meet Lord Castlereagh. 'Miss Rutherford, allow me to present Lord Castlereagh. Robert, this is Miss Rutherford.'

Lord Castlereagh bowed over her hand. 'I'm delighted to make your acquaintance, Miss Rutherford.

'My lord.' She looked up into his blue eyes, and for the first time saw the warm kindness which he was usually at such pains to hide from the world. He wasn't the impassive, stuffy, remote man he appeared to be, and with a moment of sudden insight Emma realized how very deeply hurt he would have been to hear the foreign secretary's perfidy.

He smiled suddenly, his face transforming. 'I agree with my wife, Miss Rutherford, you are far too much of a treasure for a wretch like Kane.'

For a few minutes they all stood in polite conversation, and then Gerald murmured that if they wished to arrive in Covent Garden before the curtain rose, they had better be on their way. Saunders assisted Lady Castlereagh with her white fur cloak, and then stood at the door as she and Lord Castlereagh took their leave of Mr Rutherford before emerging into the night.

A thin mist had risen between the trees in the central garden of the square, and the light from the streetlamps seemed diffused. The air was very cold, with more autumn about it than there had been even the day before, and the impatient team drawing Lord Castlereagh's fine town carriage stamped and tossed their heads, their breath standing out in silvery clouds.

Emma said good night to her father, and then Gerald escorted her from the house. Before entering the carriage, where Lord and Lady Castlereagh were already in their seats, Gerald paused, turning Emma to face him.

'Don't be anxious about tonight, Miss Rutherford, for I know that you will carry it off splendidly.'

'I hope you are right, Lord Kane.'

'I know I'm right.' He glanced into the carriage, and then lowered his voice so that only she could hear. 'I fear that this Canning business is out in the open at last, and that Robert has taken it very badly indeed. He's putting a brave face on it, but tonight will be as much an ordeal for him as it is for you.'

'Will he do anything about Mr Canning?'

'I don't know, but I fear he well might. It is a very grave state of affairs.' Gerald smiled then. 'But what isn't grave is that tonight you and I are to face London society together. Are you wearing the Keepsake?'

'Yes.'

He drew her fingers to his lips for a moment. 'Then from now on everyone will know beyond any shadow of doubt that you are soon to become Lady Kane.'

He assisted her into the carriage and then climbed in as well. Saunders closed the door behind them, and a moment later the coachman's whip cracked, and the carriage drew away from the curb.

7

AS THEY NEARED the theater's main entrance in Bow Street, more and more private carriages choked the way, so that soon they were able to proceed at only a snail's pace. It seemed that a large proportion of society was attending the famous opening night, for the ladies and gentlemen in the carriages were all attired for the occasion, the men in black with cocked hats and swords, the ladies in their finest evening clothes, with plumes and jewels in their hair.

At last the new theater appeared ahead, its entrance brilliantly illuminated with lamps. It was a stern rather than beautiful building, and was the design of the fashionable new young architect Mr Smirke. Emma had read in the newspapers about the vast sum of money the new building had cost, and so found its exterior a little disappointing, for it did not seem possible that so plain a construction could have consumed such a fortune.

The main doors were approached up steps beneath a grand portico standing on four immense Greek Doric columns, and the building was separated from the pavement by an iron railing, along intervals of which there arose graceful wrought-iron lamps. The street echoed to the clatter of hooves and wheels, and as Lord Castlereagh's carriage edged closer and closer to the portico, Emma became aware of the sound of refined laughter and conversation.

The carriage drew to a halt at last, and two theater footmen came to open the doors. The sound of the street seemed to leap inside, and Emma became faintly aware of the orchestra playing in the auditorium. She strained to recognize the piece, and was sure it was the *rondo* from Mozart's *Eine Kleine Nachtmusik*.

Lord Castlereagh alighted, followed by Gerald, and then they turned to assist the two ladies down as well. Emma shivered, glancing up at the huge lamps that lit the portico. She could hear the orchestra more clearly now, and could tell that it was indeed playing the Mozart *rondo*.

A line of carriages was constantly moving toward the theater, and each vehicle disgorged a glittering party of ladies and gentlemen. Emma was immediately conscious of everyone's reaction on seeing Lord Castlereagh's tall figure. Meaningful glances were exchanged, quizzing glasses were raised, and fans put to lips as the unfortunate lord's problems were discussed yet again. As for Lord Castlereagh himself, he evinced supreme unconcern about everything around him, seeming to be interested only in his wife's chatter.

Emma was ashamed of herself for feeling relieved that Lord Castlereagh was attracting so much attention. It was hardly charitable on her part, but she couldn't help herself, for it meant that very few glances were turned in her direction.

Gerald offered her his arm, and they followed Lord and Lady Castlereagh up the steps into the crowded vestibule, where a sea of elegant people stood beneath dazzling chandeliers. Jewels flashed, plumes wafted, and military decorations shone as the gathering prepared to enjoy what promised to be a very entertaining evening. A number of footmen moved among them all, relieving the new arrivals of their outer garments, and several small black boys in pink brocade robes endeavored to sell programs. The orchestra continued to play in the auditorium, with more Mozartean trills echoing through the building.

From the moment Lord Castlereagh's small party entered the vestibule, a stir passed tangibly through the gathered theater-goers. Conversation died away for a few seconds, and then broke out again, but Lord Castlereagh still seemed unconcerned, as did his wife, who laughed at something he said, tapping her fan playfully on his sleeve.

A footman came for Emma's cloak, and as he took it away, it was remarked by one and all that she wore the Kane Keepsake. The phoenix brooch flashed brilliantly in the light from the chandeliers, the diamonds so sparkling that they drew everyone's gaze.

She was conscious of Lord Castlereagh's sudden eclipse as the whispered topic of conversation turned from his troubles to the surprising break with convention which had prompted Gerald to present his bride-to-be with the famous family heirloom before she even wore his betrothal ring.

Gerald assisted her by putting her shawl around her shoulders, and then smiled into her eyes as he became aware of the stir caused by the Keepsake. 'The significance of a mere trinket is sometimes hard to credit,' he murmured.

'Hardly a mere trinket,' she replied, wishing that telltale color hadn't immediately flooded into her cheeks.

'Whatever its value, its beauty is greatly enhanced by the lady who wears it tonight,' he said suddenly.

She looked up quickly. 'Thank you for saying that.'

'You think it is an empty compliment?'

She didn't reply, and he said nothing more.

At that moment two gentlemen detached themselves from another party nearby. The first one was about thirty years old, freckled, and red-haired, the second was about ten years older, slightly built, with pale skin and thin, fair hair. The red-haired gentleman was introduced to her as Lord Yarmouth, who was Lord Castlereagh's cousin, and the son of the Marquis of Hertford, whose assembly it would be at Manchester House on Friday. His companion was named as none other than the gentleman whose coming-of-age birthday celebration Stephen had professed to be attending at White's, Mr Edward 'Donkey' Shingleton, so named, it seemed, because of his immensely long ears, which he concealed as best he could by the judicious combing of his sparse hair.

Emma was startled on learning his name, and dismayed, for it was plain that he was long past the age of twenty-one, and that if he had a birthday today, he most certainly was not celebrating it with a dinner at White's. So Stephen could not possibly be doing what he'd claimed to be doing tonight, which meant that he was elsewhere. But where? Lord Avenley's wretched den of gambling iniquity?

Lord Yarmouth's appreciative glance had taken in every inch of Emma's appearance, and he grinned approvingly at Gerald. 'You sly dog, Kane, snapping up such a delightful morsel. Tell me, are you and Miss Rutherford honoring the old man's invitation on Friday?'

'We are,' confirmed Gerald.

'Excellent. Miss Rutherford, there is to be some dancing at Manchester House, and here and now I claim at least two measures with you.'

'I'm flattered, my lord.'

'And I'm determined to be one of the first to be seen with the next Lady Kane on my arm,' he replied, sketching her an elegant bow.

The two gentlemen withdrew, and she and Gerald became temporarily separated from Lord and Lady Castlereagh. Gerald drew her aside. 'Is something wrong, Miss Rutherford? You seem suddenly a little withdrawn.'

'My brother's claimed prior engagement tonight happens to be Mr Shingleton's birthday dinner at White's,' she explained.

'Ah. So Stephen has been caught out in a fib.'

'He has indeed, and if he's where I fear he is . . .'

'Avenley's?'

'Yes.'

'It may simply be that he is with a lady,' Gerald pointed out gently.

'It could be, but I don't somehow think so. In the past Stephen has always confided in me concerning his affairs of the heart.'

'Forgive me for saying this, but there are some ladies that brothers would not wish to discuss with their sister,' Gerald said, smiling a little.

'Yes, I suppose there are,' she conceded, coloring.

'Then at least give him the benefit of the doubt.'

'I'm afraid that my brother requires rather a lot of such discreet consideration, Lord Kane, at least he has in recent months.'

For the next ten minutes she had very little opportunity to think any more about Stephen's untruthfulness, for she was presented to person after person, and strove throughout to conduct herself perfectly. She bobbed graceful curtsies, inclined her head, looked interested, murmured suitable phrases, and was generally all that she was required to be. She was rewarded by the impression that most of those she spoke to found her to be not as far beyond the pale as they'd expected of the daughter of a minor Dorset landowner.

During a lull, before they had even reached the staircase that led up to the inner vestibule and the stairs to the rows of private boxes, she came face to face with the first person who was openly unfriendly and disapproving, and that person was Raine, Countess of Purbeck. It happened when Gerald's attention was temporarily diverted and Emma was stealing a few private moments to brace herself for the business of actually ascending the staircase with its throng of people.

An elegant folded fan tapped her naked shoulder, making her whirl about with a gasp. She found herself gazing once more into the sweet heart-shaped face she'd seen the day before in the open landau that had almost run her down. Raine was wearing a three-quarter-length geranium velvet tunic dress over a sheer white silk slip, and there was a little geranium velvet hat resting on her frothy golden curls. Pearls encircled her throat and trembled on the hat, and a long white feather boa trailed on the floor behind her. Her magnificent lilac eyes were cold, and there was a false smile on her lips.

'Well, if it isn't the famous Miss Rutherford. Allow me to introduce myself—'

'I already know who you are,' Emma interrupted, conscious of an immediate feeling of intense and implacable dislike for this ravishingly beautiful but unpleasant creature.

'Ah, yes, no doubt your dear brother told you yesterday.'

Emma said nothing. She wished she knew what all this was about, but no doubt she would soon find out, for the countess was not the sort of woman to be coy about speaking her mind.

Raine smiled coolly. 'Well, you aren't quite the provincial mouse I'd been led to expect, but you're not exactly the hot-house bloom either, are you? I've no doubt that the London atmosphere will soon prove too much for you.'

'Really? And why should it?'

'Because you quite patently haven't the slightest notion of how to go on. Put you at a hunt ball, and no doubt you'd shine well enough, but a London gathering is something else. You'll make a hash of being Lady Kane, if you get that far.'

'What do you mean by that?'

'Come now, surely you know that Gerald's grandfather is against the match? Oh, don't be fooled by the Keepsake, for it signifies nothing, and can be taken back as easily as it is given. The old earl doesn't want you in the Fitzroy family, my dear, and what he wishes becomes law.'

Emma stared at her, but then, quite suddenly, Raine's lovely eyes softened, and she looked beyond her victim toward someone else. 'Why, Gerald, I was just introducing myself to Miss Rutherford. She really is quite sweet, is she not?'

Gerald took Emma's arm and began to draw her away.

Raine smiled. 'Surely you don't mean to cut me, sir?'

'Good evening, Raine.'

'I commend you on your choice of bride. And as to the Keepsake, well, it really is quite charming that you should present it so early in the proceedings.'

'The proceedings are hardly in their early stages, Raine, for the business is entirely settled, as I think you already know.'

'Is it, Gerald? Are you quite sure of that?' Raine murmured, giving him another sweet smile and then flicking her sheer silk skirts aside as she walked past him.

He immediately turned Emma to face him. 'What did she say to you?'

'Nothing that I would wish to repeat.'

For a long moment he searched her eyes, and then he relaxed a little. 'Keep her at a distance.'

'I mean to.' She longed to ask him about Raine, but somehow she just couldn't. There was something going on about which she knew nothing, but others seemed to know a great deal. With part of her heart she wished to find out what it was, but with the other part she preferred to remain in ignorance. One thing disturbed her very much, however, and that was Rain's warning about the Earl of Cranforth's attitude toward the Rutherford match. Was he really opposed to it?

The thought still occupied her as Gerald led her to rejoin Lord and Lady Castlereagh to ascend the staircase. She was introduced to more and more people, and a bewildering succession of names washed over her, but all she could really think about was whether or not Gerald's grandfather approved of her as the next Lady Kane.

They were delayed in the anteroom, and then in the inner lobby on the next floor, but at last they mounted the narrow staircase that led to the tier of boxes containing that taken by Lord Castlereagh. A passage lay behind the row of mahogany doors that gave onto the boxes themselves, and there was a doorman to usher them inside. As they entered, the noise of the auditorium itself seemed to suddenly leap at Emma, startling her a little. There was a loud babble of voices, and the orchestra was now playing Haydn, a dashing piece that rippled brilliantly over the theater.

The auditorium was horseshoe-shaped, with three tiers of gray-fronted boxes resting on slender golden columns. Gray partitions separated the boxes, so that the occupants could not see their neighbors, and the seats were light blue, but otherwise the predominant color was pink. High above, the ceiling was painted to resemble a temple dome, and just beneath it were the alcoves containing the highest seats of all, where servants were pressed uncomfortably together. Down below there was the pit, known as 'Fops' Alley' because it was there that the gentlemen of fashion displayed their persons, lounging elegantly, talking in loud tones, rattling their canes, and snapping their snuffboxes open and closed.

On the stage, a partially lowered gold-fringed curtain made of crimson velvet revealed a fully lowered canvas drop curtain depicting a temple dedicated to Shakespeare. Bright lamps illuminated everything, including the orchestra, in its well just before the stage.

The appearance of Lord Castlereagh's party caused another stir, and Emma was careful to keep her eyes lowered as she sat in the blue chair Gerald drew out for her. She felt as if the Keepsake was brighter even than the lamps on the stage, drawing all attention to her, but she was still preoccupied with the Earl of Cranforth. If he was against the match, it would surely become clear tomorrow afternoon when Gerald took her to Cranforth House to meet him.

The two ladies were soon seated, but before the gentlemen joined them, something in the pit caught Gerald's attention. He touched Lord Castlereagh's sleeve. 'I say, Robert, do you notice anything odd down there?'

'Odd? In what way?'

'The fifth row back, about halfway along. Do you see that piece of paper that is circulating?'

Emma sat forward, peeping over the edge of the box. Sure enough, there was a piece of paper being passed from person to person. Each gentleman read it carefully, nodded at the one who'd passed it to him, and then gave it to his neighbor on the other side. And so it moved along the row, and at the end was passed to the row behind, where it proceeded from person to person in the same way.

Lord Castlereagh's brows drew together in puzzlement. 'What is it, do you think?'

'I don't know, but I fancy it signifies trouble in the offing. I know that there is a great deal of resentment about the inflated prices being charged for this rebuilding.'

'A planned demonstration, d'you think?' murmured Lord Castlereagh.

'It's possible. If anything happens, I think we should beat a prudent retreat straightaway, don't you?'

'Agreed,' Lord Castlereagh replied, glancing down at the intriguing piece of paper once more, and then taking his seat.

Gerald sat down as well, and then smiled reassuringly at Emma's rather alarmed expression. 'Don't be anxious, Miss Rutherford, for we will show a very clean pair of heels if anything starts.'

There were only a few minutes to go now, and the orchestra prepared to play the songs made famous by Madame Catalini. An air of expectation passed through the audience, and there was less conversation and laughter as everyone prepared for the rising of the curtain.

No one in Lord Castlereagh's box was aware of the door opening softly behind them, or of the silent entry of a tall, elegant gentleman with a black velvet patch over one eye. He was about thirty-five years old, lean, and coldly good-looking, with his fair hair combed back from his high forehead. The patch concealed his left eye completely, but the other was dark and shining, like that of a cunning dog. He wore the same formal evening clothes as both Gerald and Lord Castlereagh, and he paused just inside the box, surveying the occupants without their knowing he was there.

Emma suddenly sensed his presence, and turned with a quick gasp to find his gleaming eye upon her. There was something so speculative and calculating in his gaze that her heart missed a beat, and it was not an agreeable sensation. She was immediately on her guard, disliking him as intensely as earlier she had disliked the Countess of Purbeck.

8

GERALD HEARD HER gasp, and looked sharply behind. In a moment he was on his feet, his eyes very hard and cold as he faced the intruder. 'What do you want, Avenley?' he demanded tersely.

Emma stared at the newcomer. So this was the infamous Lord Avenley.

Lord Castlereagh had also risen to his feet, his expression less than welcoming when he realized who had entered the box. Lady Castlereagh's lips parted in dismay, and she busily employed her fan, her eyes determinedly averted to the stage, to avoid any possibility of having to acknowledge a gentleman who was quite obviously not a friend.

The moment Gerald had risen, Lord Avenley tore his glittering gaze from Emma and sketched him a rather contemptuous bow. 'Kane.'

There was nothing amiable in his manner, indeed everything about him suggested that his sole purpose was to cause mischief of some sort. Stephen's opinion of him echoed in Emma's ears. *He's a splendid fellow, friendly and agreeable.* To Emma's mind, Lord Avenley was none of these things.

Suddenly his single bright eye was turned upon her again. 'Miss Rutherford, I presume?'

'Sir,' she replied coolly, for she liked him less and less with each passing second.

He smiled, glancing at the Keepsake. 'Ah, the seal of approval, no less,' he murmured.

Gerald stiffened. 'Why have you come here, Avenley? The theater is hardly your usual haunt.'

'I abhor the theater, Kane, but occasionally there are attractions to be viewed.' Again Lord Avenley's eye was fixed solely upon Emma.

'Avenley—'

'Kane, I pray you not be so damnably touchy, for I mean no offense. I merely wish to make the acquaintance of your bride-to-be. Is that so heinous a crime?'

Lord Castlereagh endeavored to take the sting from the situation. He went to the door of the box, holding it pointedly aside. 'I'm sure you have other things to do, Avenley,' he murmured.

Lord Avenley gave him the thinnest of smiles. 'I trust you mean to defend your honor where Canning is concerned, my lord, for if you do not, then I fear I shall lose a rather large wager.'

'Please leave, sir,' Lord Castlereagh replied, a nerve flickering at his temple.

Lord Avenley bowed to him, and then to Emma. 'Farewell for the moment, Miss Rutherford, but I am sure that you and I will meet again. I will be sure to tell your brother that we've met, for I shall be seeing him at my club in Pall Mall in about . . .' He took out a golden fob watch, glanced down at it, and then closed it with a snap. 'About half an hour,' he murmured, then turned and left.

Lady Castlereagh breathed out with relief. 'Oh, what an odious, odious reptile that man is,' she muttered, still employing her fan to full effect.

Lord Castlereagh put his hand briefly on Gerald's arm. 'Pay him no heed, Gerald, for he simply isn't worth it.'

'That is easier said than done.'

'It's past, and should remain as such.'

'Maybe, but it's unresolved past,' replied Gerald.

Emma glanced from one man to the other. What were they thinking about? She remembered what Stephen had said concerning the dealings between Gerald and Lord Avenley. *They despise each other, it's a well-known fact.* It was something that she now knew to be true, for their mutual loathing had been almost tangible.

She looked toward the stage, her thoughts moving on from Gerald and Lord Avenley to the now disagreeable realization that Stephen had lied about his activities tonight, and had gone to Lord

Avenley's exclusive private gaming hell!

Gerald resumed his seat next to her, and now leaned a little closer. 'I must ask you to forgive that unpleasant interlude, Miss Rutherford.'

'The only thing that was unpleasant was the presence of Lord Avenley, Lord Kane,' she replied.

'I trust you now understand to the full why I advise you so strongly to do all you can to steer your brother away from him.'

'I understand to the full, sir, but I fear that so far my pleadings have fallen on the stoniest of ground. Stephen gave me his word that he was merely an onlooker at the club, but now that I have found him out in a monstrous untruth about his whereabouts tonight, why should I believe anything he has said to me?'

'Miss Rutherford—'

Whatever Gerald may have been about to say to her remained silent, for at that moment the orchestra began to play the opening bars of Madame Catalini's best-known song, and the canvas drop curtain was raised to reveal the renowned singer standing in the center of the stage. A burst of approving applause drowned her first notes, but then the audience fell silent, its attention fully upon the shimmering bejeweled figure of the world's most famous *prima donna*.

Madame Angelica Catalini was possessed of an extremely rich and powerful voice, and this, together with her penchant for wearing scarlet and diamonds, made her very impressive, indeed almost intimidating. Audiences adored her, but behind the scenes she was known to be a grasping, temperamental virago, much given to fits of rage and jealousy. She sang with a constant smile on her face, even in tragic roles, and it was murmured that this was entirely due to her satisfaction with the huge sums she could demand for her services. The management of the new theater was rumored to have paid her an exorbitant amount for her present contract, and this had added to the general public displeasure about the new prices that had been imposed.

As she launched wholeheartedly into the song, there came the first hint that a disturbance had indeed been planned, just as Gerald and Lord Castlereagh had feared. It began in the pit, where the circulation of the mysterious piece of paper had apparently primed the gentlemen to begin a demonstration. They erupted into a cacophony of noise, stamping their feet, whistling, and shouting, while some of them waved banners, blew whistles, and even produced some drums to beat. There was absolute uproar, and it wasn't long before the trouble spread to the rest of the theater, for missiles began to rain down from the alcoves near the ceiling. Rotten tomatoes and eggs pelted the stage, a snow of torn-up programs fluttered in the air, and someone even threw an old boot, which landed on the stage at Madame Catalini's feet.

The singer faltered, for even a voice as powerful as hers could not hope to be heard above such a din. For a moment she was too nonplussed to do anything but stand there, but then her Latin temperament boiled over, and she waved her fist and launched forth into a torrent of Italian abuse, which Emma guessed to be anything but ladylike.

Gerald and Lord Castlereagh were already on their feet, as were many gentlemen in the boxes, for the new Covent Garden theater was suddenly no place for their ladies. The boxes were emptying quickly, and as Gerald took Emma's hand to lead her along the passageway toward the inner lobby and the staircase, there was such a crush of departing theatergoers that they became separated from Lord and Lady Castlereagh. The grand staircase was a positive melee, and still there was no sign of the Castlereagha, who seemed to have disappeared into thin air.

Emma caught a glimpse of the Countess of Purbeck, her geranium tunic dress a vivid splash of color in the vestibule, but then she too vanished from sight in the press. Gerald managed to retrieve their outdoor garments from the cloakroom, and then he and Emma emerged beneath the portico into the cold night air, where a mist had begun to creep across the city from the Thames.

The line of carriages was in some chaos; for few of the coachmen had expected their services to be required just yet. The footmen were calling out the names of the ladies and gentlemen who were leaving, and various vehicles endeavored to maneuver toward the steps. Gerald looked around for any sign of Lord and Lady Castlereagh, but they were nowhere to be seen, and their carriage was not there either.

Someone touched Gerald's sleeve suddenly, and they turned to see Lord Yarmouth. 'I say, Kane, are you looking for Castlereagh?'

'Yes, have you seen him?'

'He and his wife have already left, I fear. La Purbeck approached them a short while ago, to tell them she'd seen you both leaving with someone else. She said that Miss Rutherford was close to the vapors on account of the riot.'

'Did she, indeed?' Gerald murmured.

Lord Yarmouth drew a long breath: 'No doubt it's Raine's notion of an amusing jape.'

'No doubt.'

'Look, I came in my carriage, but I've just been invited to go on somewhere with friends. I was about to send my vehicle home, but you and Miss Rutherford are most welcome to use it, for I am sure you wish to escort her safely home.'

'I would indeed, and if you're quite sure you don't require the carriage yourself, I'd be most grateful,' Gerald said.

'Oh, I'm quite sure, Kane. Come with me, and I'll show you where it is.' He led them down the theater steps toward the line of vehicles, halting when they reached a particularly handsome maroon barouche. 'Just send it back to my address in Seamore Place when you've finished with it,' he said, holding the door open himself so that Gerald could assist Emma inside.

She took her place on the mustard velvet upholstery, shivering a little, for the evening was very cold, and then she glanced out at the brightly lit façade of the theater. Why had the Countess of Purbeck done something so petty and spiteful? What did she hope to achieve?

Beside the batouche, Lord Yarmouth and Gerald were speaking for a moment.

'I'm in your debt for this, Yarmouth,' said Gerald.

'Think nothing of it, Kane. Besides, I think that you and I are about to see a great deal of each other in the next few days.'

'Because of Castlereagh?'

Lord Yarmouth nodded. 'He's my cousin and I know him well enough to realize that he can't possibly let this Canning business drift. He's too proud a man for that, and so I think he'll issue a challenge.'

Gerald drew a long breath. 'I think you're right.'

70

'He'll ask us to be his seconds, you know.'

'I know.'

'It's a rum do, and no mistake,' murmured Lord Yarmouth. Then he turned to Emma, doffing his tricorn and bowing. 'Good night, Miss Rutherford.'

'Good night, Lord Yarmouth. And thank you.'

He smiled. 'It's a pleasure, my dear. As to the fact that you and Kane are now compelled to travel entirely alone, you may rest assured that no word of it will ever pass my lips.'

Inclining his head to Gerald, he turned and left them. Gerald instructed the coachman to drive to Grosvenor Square, and then climbed into the barouche, slamming the door behind him. As he took his place opposite her, he smiled a little, his eyes shining in the light from the theater portico.

'Propriety cannot always be strictly observed, I fear.'

'I quite understand that, Lord Kane.' She hesitated. 'Will you answer a question, sir?'

'That depends upon what the question is, Miss Rutherford.'

'Why would the Countess of Purbeck do such a thing?'

'I really have no idea, Miss Rutherford,' he replied lightly, his eyes still meeting hers.

She did not believe him, but felt there was no point in pursuing the matter. She said nothing more, and looked out at the street as the barouche drew slowly away from the curb, endeavoring to thread its way though the incredible jam that now choked Bow Street from one end to the other.

As Lord Yarmouth's carriage conveyed them away from the scene, a shadowy figure moved from beneath the theater portico and stood watching the maroon barouche until it passed from his sight.

Lord Avenley smiled a little, pushing his hat back with the tip of his cane. How very fortunate that the future Lady Kane was so very much to his taste, for it made his plan so much more agreeable and satisfying to carry out. He had always had a penchant for a profusion of dark curls, and the delightful Miss Rutherford had them in plenty.

His own carriage at last halted at the foot of the steps, and Lord Avenley whistled softly to himself as he entered it. He leaned his

71

head back against the leather upholstery, still whistling softly. The past was about to be avenged, and if poor Miss Rutherford was to be the pawn, then that was simply her misfortune.

Very little was said in Lord Yarmouth's barouche as it bowled west across London toward Mayfair. Emma would have liked to make more use of these unexpected minutes alone with Gerald, but his suddenly rather aloof manner prevented her. Earlier he had gone to a great deal of trouble to reassure her by giving her the Keepsake, but now she felt strangely further away from him than she had before.

By the light of passing streetlamps she could see his withdrawn expression as he gazed silently out of the barouche. She could also see how he toyed with his wedding-ring finger, as if the ring were still there. It was as if a barrier had been erected between them. Her doubts, eradicated when he gave her the Keepsake, now returned anew.

The barouche entered Piccadilly and then had to halt before turning into Bond Street. On the southern side of Piccadilly, its windows cluttered with open volumes, was Hatchard's, the most famous bookshop in London. Gazing at it, the thought suddenly entered Emma's head that it would be good to purchase an entirely unsuitable, farfetched Gothic novel of the type adored by ladies but scorned by so many men. Lord Bagworth's library was very worthy and serious, and she needed a silly diversion, something to distract her for a while.

Gerald had been observing her as she looked at the bookshop windows, and he spoke suddenly. 'You seem deep in thought, Miss Rutherford.'

She collected her thoughts. 'I . . . I was merely thinking that I would like to visit Hatchard's as soon as I can.'

'What sort of book do you enjoy?'

'The sort you would not, I fancy,' she replied.

'You cannot know that for sure.'

'I think I can be fairly certain, Lord Kane, for I enjoy gothic novels.'

He smiled a little. 'You have judged me accurately, Miss Rutherford, for gothic novels aren't at all to my liking.'

She looked at him. 'I cannot judge you at all accurately, Lord Kane,' she said quietly. 'Indeed, I think I know you less now than I did when we set out this evening.'

His gray eyes shone in the light from passing streetlamps as the barouche drove north up Bond Street. 'Miss Rutherford, I promise you that you know all you need to about me.'

'Do I?'

He smiled again. 'Yes, you do.'

She lowered her eyes and said nothing more. She didn't know him at all. She didn't know what his feelings really were toward her, or if he compared her with Margot. She didn't know why there was such ill feeling between Lord Avenley and him, or why Lord Avenley should make such a point about meeting her. And she didn't know why the Countess of Purbeck was behaving as she was. But Gerald knew all the answers, she could see it in his eyes, just as she could see that he had no intention at all of telling her.

The barouche left Bond Street and struck west through Mayfair toward Grosvenor Square, coming to a halt at last at the door of Lady Bagworth's house. Gerald alighted and turned to hand her down.

She hesitated before accepting. 'Would you care to come inside for a while, Lord Kane? Perhaps you and my father could share a glass of cognac?'

'I fear I most decline, Miss Rutherford. I have many papers to attend to at the moment, things which I meant to work on after the theater, and which would have kept me busy well into the night. Now they can be dealt with at a more civilized hour, and so I think I should return directly to St James's Square. With your permission, I will simply see you to the door and then go, but I do thank you for the kind invitation.'

Awkward color touched her cheeks as she slipped her hand into his and allowed him to assist her down to the pavement. Then she turned to face him. 'Good night, Lord Kane.'

Now he hesitated, as if realizing that he had brought the already shortened evening to a rather abrupt close. 'Tonight may not have gone to plan, Miss Rutherford, but I promise that for you it was a victory.'

'A victory?'

'Those who met you approved of you.'

'Except for the Countess of Purbeck.'

A light passed through his eyes. 'There will always be exceptions to prove the rule,' he murmured.

'Is your grandfather such an exception?' she asked suddenly.

He seemed surprised. 'Why on earth do you ask that?'

'I . . . I just wondered if he would have preferred you to find a bride from an aristocratic family.'

'He has never expressed a preference. Miss Rutherford, what is all this about?'

'It doesn't matter.'

Suddenly he put his hand to her chin, forcing her to look directly at him. 'You are everything I wish for in a bride, Miss Rutherford, and I am quite certain that when my grandfather meets you tomorrow, he will be charmed by you.'

She said nothing.

His hand remained where it was. 'I have no wish to ever hurt you,' he said gently, 'indeed it is still my desire to reassure you as much as I can that this match means a great deal to me. I know that I am not without fault, and that I am occasionally less than communicative, but you must never think that it is because I am having second thoughts about our marriage.' For a moment his thumb moved softly against her skin. 'May we dispense with strict formality and be forward enough to address each other by our first names? I confess that I would much prefer to call you Emma instead of Miss Rutherford.'

She stared up into his eyes. When he spoke gently, and when he smiled so winningly, all her doubts began to recede again, like an ebbing tide. 'If that is what you wish, my lord—'

'My name is Gerald,' he prompted.

'Gerald.'

For a heart-stopping moment she thought he was about to kiss her on the cheek, but then he drew away. 'I must leave now, for those damned papers beckon me, but I look forward to tomorrow afternoon. I will call for you at three, if that is acceptable?'

'It is very acceptable.'

'Good night, Emma.'

'Good night . . . Gerald.' She couldn't help stumbling over his name.

Her awkwardness amused him, but he said nothing more as he returned to the waiting barouche.

Saunders had detected the arrival of the carriage, and now opened the door to admit her. She paused on the doorstep, turning to look at Gerald again, and she was just in time to hear the last part of his quietly uttered instructions to the coachman.

'. . . House in Upper Brook Street, if you please.'

'Yes, my lord.'

Emma's lips parted in surprise. Upper Brook Street? But he had just insisted that he was driving straight back to his residence in St James's Square to attend to some urgent papers.

The barouche drew away, and she watched as it drove around the misty square before vanishing from sight in the gloom as it entered Upper Brook Sheet in the northwest corner. She stared after it. If only she'd heard the full address. Something House. But there were so many fine mansions in that particular street, and he could be going to any one of them.

'Madam?' Saunders was waiting at the door.

She turned and went inside.

9

MR RUTHERFORD WAS at first a little alarmed to hear of the unseemly demonstration at the theater, but was relieved that Emma had not come to any harm. Over a cup of chocolate in the library, he listened to her account of the evening and expressed his full approval of her conduct. She did not tell him about her brush with the Countess of Purbeck, about Lord Avenley, or about Stephen's deception, for she saw no point in worrying him unduly.

Stephen had not returned by the time she and her father retired to their beds, and Mr Rutherford fell asleep still believing that his son was attending Donkey Shingleton's birthday celebrations. Emma lay awake, staring up at the gentle shadows cast by the fire. She had so very much on her mind that sleep was quite impossible, even though she was tired.

Midnight had long since passed, and London was quiet in the small hours of the night. The clock on the mantelpiece began to whir and chime once more, and suddenly Emma couldn't lie there any longer. She flung the bedclothes aside and slipped from the bed. Drawing on her blue-and-white floral wrap, she went to the window, holding the curtains aside to look out.

The mist had thickened a little, obscuring the lights of all but the nearest streets and the lamp in the mews lane. The garden was in darkness, the trees very still and ghostly, and the little wrought-iron gazebo looked very lonely in the sunken area where in the height of summer Lady Bagworth's roses were a glory to behold and where the Michaelmas daisies were just coming into full bloom.

She wondered when Stephen would return. Oh, how angry she

was with him for his deceit. She'd actually believed him about tonight, and now she felt she couldn't trust him at all. What if he'd lied about his activities at Lord Avenley's club? What if he wasn't merely a spectator at the green baize tables, but a participant?

As she looked out, a shadowy figure moved by the little postern gate that gave access from the mews lane to the house and garden. There was a lantern on the corner of the coach house, and by its light she recognized her brother. His hat was pulled low over his forehead, and the collar of his greatcoat was turned up against the chill of the night, but there was no mistaking him as he made his way along the garden path toward the house. Why on earth was he returning by the back way? Even as she wondered, Emma knew why. Their father's bedroom was at the front of the house, and he might hear if a carriage drew up on the cobbles at the door. If ever there was a guilty conscience abroad, it was Stephen Rutherford's.

She left the window, moving to the bedroom door to hear her brother pass, but the minutes went by and there was no sign of him. Puzzled, she opened the door and peeped out into the candlelit passage. It was deserted. She listened, but she couldn't hear anything either.

Quickly she left her room, hurrying along to the gallery above the staircase and entrance hall two stories below. There was still no sign of Stephen, but as she looked she heard a soft sound from the library, the door of which stood slightly ajar. The sound was the unmistakable chink of a decanter on a glass.

Gathering her skirts, she went silently down the staircase. As she neared the ground floor, she saw her brother inside the library, his figure dimly lit by the fading glow of the fire. He was slumped dejectedly in one of the armchairs, a glass of cognac in his hand. His hat and greatcoat lay on a table, and he'd undone his neck-cloth. Alarm crept through Emma, and her steps faltered, for she could tell that he was very troubled indeed.

Suddenly she heard a door open on the bedroom floor above, and she turned quickly to see the flickering light of a candle approaching the top of the staircase. Her father appeared, protecting the candleflame with his hand. He wore his warm paisley dressing gown, with a thick shawl around his shoulders, and there was a tasseled night hat on his head.

Emma fled to the morning room, slipping safely out of sight inside just as her father began to descend the staircase. She left the door open a little, and watched her father as he reached the hall. In the library, Stephen at last became aware of his father's approach, and he got up quickly from the armchair, draining the glass of cognac and replacing it on the tray next to the decanter. Then he emerged from the library, assuming an air of lighthearted unconcern.

He halted as he saw his father. 'Father, what on earth are you doing up at this time?'

Mr Rutherford surveyed him for a moment. 'One might ask the same thing of you, sir.'

'I'm afraid the junketing went on a little longer than I expected.'

'And Mr Shingleton is now well and truly his new age?'

'Oh, most definitely.' Stephen grinned.

Mr Rutherford nodded. 'Well, young men will be young men, I suppose. As to why I am prowling the house so late, it so happens that I slept so much during the day that I'm quite restless now. I finished the book I was reading, and decided to come down and look for another.'

'So that you can sit up all night reading it, and be too tired to get up in the morning?' Stephen asked lightly.

'Don't be impudent,' his father retorted, but with a wry smile. 'To bed with you, sirrah, before I feel obliged to chastise you.'

Stephen grinned again, and then went up the staircase, taking the steps two at a time, again as if he didn't have a care in the world.

Shaking his head at the folly of the young, Mr Rutherford proceeded into the library, where he could soon be heard, but not seen, rummaging along one of the shelves.

Emma seized her moment, slipping from the morning room and hurrying up the staircase before her father could see her. She'd have to confront Stephen another time, but confront him she would, especially now that she knew something was wrong. He may have fooled their father with his lightheartedness, but she could see through the act. Something had happened tonight, and if her gravest fears were correct, then that something was a heavy loss at cards.

Mr Rutherford was at the breakfast table in the morning, and so once again there was no opportunity to speak to Stephen. Emma decided therefore to make an opportunity.

She smiled across the table at him. 'Stephen, I have a favor to beg of you.'

'A favor?' He looked up from the newspaper he was reading.

'I wish to go to Hatchard's bookshop after breakfast, and hope you might be able to escort me.'

He was horrified. 'Hatchard's? But that's at the other end of Piccadilly!'

'It isn't all that far.'

'It's a positive route march!'

She looked reproachfully at him. 'But, sir, you were the one who said that brisk walks in the fresh air were the very thing to restore one.'

'Yes, but—'

Mr Rutherford looked at his son over the top of his spectacles. 'Your sister is quite right, sir, and if you had returned to the house at a civilized hour last night, I have no doubt that you wouldn't find the prospect of a walk quite as wearisome as you apparently do. You will escort Emma to Hatchard's.'

'Yes, Father,' Stephen replied, giving her a dark look before returning his attention to the newspaper.

Just over an hour later, brother and sister set off for Piccadilly. Emma wore a chestnut velvet spencer over a gown of brown-spotted cream muslin, and her dark hair was pinned up beneath a high-crowned straw bonnet tied beneath her chin with wired brown satin ribbons. Stephen had on a sky-blue coat, oyster marcella waistcoat, and white kerseymere breeches, and his high-crowned beaver was worn at a rakish angle. They discussed her visit to the theater and her invitation to meet the Earl of Cranforth that afternoon, and it wasn't until they entered the elegant but crowded confines of Bond Street that she made it known that she'd found him out in his lies about the night before.

'Your Mr Donkey Shingleton is a most remarkable fellow, is he not?'

'Eh? I don't follow.'

'Well, there he was at the theater last night, looking almost twenty years past his coming of age, and yet according to you he was wining and dining the night away, celebrating that very thing.'

Stephen halted, unlinking his arm from hers. 'What are you saying?'

'That you are an infamous fibber, sir. Not only did I speak to Mr Shingleton last night, but also to your odious Lord Avenley, who was very careful to inform me that within half an hour of our speaking, he would be seeing you at his club. *His* club, not White's,' she added.

'Avenley didn't say anything about meeting you.'

'He said he was going to. But what does it matter now that you have been found out?'

'In what? All I did was go to Avenley's place and watch the play. That is hardly a crime to end all crimes,' he replied defensively.

'I saw you in the library last night, Stephen, just before Father came down, and you didn't exactly look the picture of joy, did you?'

'My, my, how crowded it was down there last night,' he murmured, looking away.

'You didn't just watch the play last night, did you? You took part in it, and you plunged in over your foolish head.'

'Leave it, Sis, I beg of you.'

'I want the truth, Stephen.'

'It isn't any concern of yours.'

Her green eyes flashed. 'How dare you say that!'

'It's my business, and mine alone, Emma. I don't wish you to pry into it, and I certainly don't wish Father to—'

'I'll warrant you don't.'

'If I tell you, you will promise not to tell him?'

'I promise not to go unnecessarily to him,' she replied in a qualified tone.

He removed his hat and ran his fingers agitatedly through his hair. 'Very well, Sis,' he said at last, 'I admit that I broke my word last night. I didn't mean to, but it happened. I lied to you about Donkey's birthday, and went to Avenley's club instead. Avenley wasn't there at first, but when he arrived he seemed intent upon

80

luring me to try a hand or two, something he's refrained from doing before. In the end, to my shame, I gave in. I joined him at one of the tables, and at first I won handsomely. Naturally I thought I was on the proverbial winning streak, and so I continued, but of course I began to lose. Convinced that I would soon recoup my loses, I played on and on, but I merely succeeded in losing more. Much more.'

'How much?' Emma hardly dared to ask.

He drew a long breath. 'Ten thousand guineas. Avenley holds my IOU's.'

Emma stared at him. 'Ten thousand!' she gasped.

'I fear so.'

'Oh, Stephen . . .'

'Don't rebuke me, Emma, for I've felt dreadful ever since. Avenley says he does not mean to press me, so I'll be able to manage somehow. But you must promise not to tell Father, for I could not bear him to be disappointed in me, and I certainly could not do without my allowance.'

'But, Stephen, ten thousand guineas—'

'I'll manage somehow,' he said again, looking urgently at her. 'I'm trusting you to keep my secret, Sis.'

'What if Lord Avenley calls the debt in?'

'That's a chance I'll have to take, but he says he will give me time.' He ran his fingers through his hair again. 'I'm sorry I've let you down so badly, Emma, truly I am.'

She couldn't bear to see him look so wretched, and she slipped her arms around him, resting her head against his shoulder. He hesitated, and then held her tightly for a moment.

'Stephen, I have some jewelry that Father would not miss,' she suggested tentatively.

'This scrape is of my own making, Sis, and so I'll get myself out of it without being low enough to use your jewelry.'

'Yes, but—'

'No, Emma, not your jewels.' He kissed her on the cheek, and then drew back. 'Let's be on our way, or we'll never get to Hatchard's.'

They walked on south toward the corner of Piccadilly, and the noise of London seemed to grow even louder. Bond Street was where the finest tailors made the clothes that were famous throughout the world, and it was also a street of gentlemen's lodgings and hotels, so that the pedestrians were predominantly male. There were some ladies, however, and as an open landau passed by, Emma thought for a horrid moment that it was the Countess of Purbeck's, but to her relief it wasn't.

Stephen followed her gaze and guessed her thoughts. 'It isn't the *chienne*, Sis,' he said.

'No, thank goodness,' she replied with feeling. She glanced at him. 'I met her last night at the theater.'

'The countess?'

'Yes.'

He pursed his lips for a moment. 'What did she have to say?'

'She made it plain that she doesn't like me.'

'Keep well away from her, Sis.'

'I intend to, just as I trust you intend from now on to keep well away from Lord Avenley.'

He nodded. 'Last night taught me a lesson, Emma.'

'I hope so, Stephen.'

When they reached Piccadilly, there was such a flow of traffic that for several minutes it was quite impossible to cross to the far side. Emma found it all almost overwhelming, for it made Dorchester, Dorset's county town, seem like a mere hamlet.

Directly opposite where they stood was the remarkable building known as the Egyptian Hall, which resembled a temple from ancient Egypt. It housed the Museum of Natural History, and there was nearly always a small queue of people waiting at the doors. Two doors further on, with a private dwelling in between, was Hatchard's, and this morning there were three carriages drawn up at the curb.

A break appeared in the traffic, and Stephen seized Emma's hand, making her run across the street. They reached the other side in safety, and then walked along the pavement to the bookshop. The doorbell tinkled as they entered.

Their visit to the bookshop had not passed unnoticed, however, for one of the three carriages drawn up outside bore the arms of the earls of Purbeck, and Raine was seated alone inside, waiting for some friends who were already in the shop.

She looked breathtakingly beautiful in a dove-gray silk pelisse trimmed with narrow black fur, and there was a curling black ostrich plume trembling in her gray silk hat. Her lilac eyes glittered spitefully, and there was a thoughtful twist on her lips, as with sudden decision she alighted from the carriage, following Emma and Stephen into the shop.

10

IT WAS VERY quiet and dark in the bookshop, and the smell of coffee hung in the air, for it was fashionable for young gentlemen to be seen lounging at Hatchatd's, discussing literature with their friends. A small group of modish young men were gathered at one end of the counter, deliberating rather pretentiously over the finer points of a volume of poetry, while at the other end an elderly male assistant was assuring a fussy matron that the book she wished to buy was in every way suitable as a gift for a daughter who also happened to be the wife of a bishop.

There were shelves stretching from floor to ceiling, all of them crammed with books, and ladders were provided so that the topmost shelves could be properly examined. Two writing desks stood in a dark corner, providing all the implements necessary for letters, and a fat, rather wheezy gentleman with a red face was seated at one of them, scowling as he penned a communication that did not augur well for the recipient. Part of the shop stretched away toward the rear of the building, and several ladies and gentlemen could be dimly observed perusing still more shelves that were filled to capacity with all types of publications.

The young gentlemen sipped coffee as they argued over the merits of a particular poem in the book on the counter before them, but then one of them noticed Stephen.

'Rutherford! I say, do come and join us.' He gestured warmly, and waved the coffeepot.

Stephen hesitated, but then Emma smiled at him. 'Join them if you wish, for I'm sure you have no desire to watch me choose a book.'

'If you're quite certain—'

'I can manage perfectly well without you.'

He grinned, and then hurried over to join his friends, who welcomed him with obvious pleasure. Emma watched for a moment, thinking how strange it was that her brother had so taken to the ways of the more dandified section of London society. In Dorchester he hadn't bothered at all with the vagaries of fashion, but here it seemed that he was like a duck to water. There was nothing at all effeminate about him, or about the friends he was with, for the glances they directed toward a rather pretty lady with bronze hair and a curvaceous figure were ample proof of that, it was simply that they enjoyed indulging themselves in the art of being fashionable.

Emma went to inquire of an assistant where she might find all the latest novels, and as she was directed to the furthest and least well lit part of the shop, she remained unaware of Raine's presence.

Raine had slipped quietly into the shop, not wanting to attract any attention, and to this end she drew back behind some shelves, pretending to examine a book of botanical illustrations. She watched as Emma made her way toward the back of the shop, and after a moment she slipped along behind her, waiting until Emma was alone and at her mercy.

The other ladies and gentlemen in this part of the shop had now gone elsewhere, and Emma had the shelves of novels to herself. She selected one with a particular melodramatic title, and began to glance through the pages.

'Well, well,' said a feline voice behind her, 'how very vulgar the lady's taste appears to be.'

With a gasp, Emma whirled about, almost dropping the book. She found herself gazing into Raine's malevolent eyes.

Raine gave a venomous smile. 'I trust you've begun to make arrangements for a swift return to the rustic homestead from whence you so unwisely chose to emerge, for if you have not, then I fear you're going to suffer a great deal of humiliation, Miss Rutherford.'

Emma began to recover a little. 'I have no wish to speak to you, my lady,' she said.

'Oh, I'm sure you haven't, my dear, but I'm not about to give you any choice in the matter. You are patently unsuited to the role of Lady Kane, and as for presuming that you can eventually carry off the role of countess, well, the mere thought is laughable. When the Earl of Cranforth sees you this afternoon—'

'You appear to be well informed concerning my social diary,' interrupted Emma, wondering how she could possibly know about the visit to Cranforth House.

Raine gave a soft laugh. 'My dear, I know everything there is to know, and what is more, I have the information on the very highest authority.'

'What do you mean?'

'I have Gerald's confidence, my dear.'

'Indeed?' Emma met her gaze as steadily as she could.

'Oh, yes, which is why I know that he is beginning to have second thoughts where you are concerned. He knows that his grandfather has set himself against the match, and he has also witnessed the flaws in your veneer of refinement. You are a provincial creature, Miss Rutherford, and I fear that there is something of the farm about you.'

'A preferable fault to yours, my lady, for I. fear that you have about you something of the kennel,' Emma replied.

Rain's oyes flashed with loathing and fury, and it was all she could do not to strike Emma's face. 'How dare you!' she breathed.

'You have not given me any cause to be civil to you, Countess.'

'I'll make you pay dearly for your insolence, missy.'

Emma raised her chin defiantly. 'Please leave me alone, my lady, for I have no desire to have your society forced upon me.'

'Oh, do not concern yourself that that will ever be the case again, Miss Rutherford, for you will not know my society, or the society of any other lady of consequence, you have my promise upon that. If you persist in your willful determination to cling to this match, I will see to it that you are snubbed. No one will send out invitations to you, and there will be a great many changes of heart concerning attendance at your betrothal ball, should it by some miracle still take place.' A thin, malicious smile played on Raine's lips. 'I don't want you here in London, Miss Rutherford, and what I want, I always get. Go back to the country, my dear, before you discover exactly how spiteful and cruel I can be when I'm crossed.'

With that she turned and walked away, the plumes in her gray silk hat streaming and her little shoes tapping coldly on the floor of the shop. Emma stared after her, too upset for a moment to do anything but stand there in wretchedness. Then she slowly replaced the book on the shelf and pressed her shaking hands to her cheeks. She was trembling from head to toe, for the previous few minutes had been the most disagreeable of her life. Never before had she encountered such virulent hatred, or been threatened in such a way.

There was a burst of laughter from Stephen and his friends, and it aroused her from her silent torment. Taking a long breath to compose herself, she took the book from the shelf once again and then made her way toward the front of the shop.

Stephen glanced around and saw her approaching the counter with the book, and he got up to excuse himself from his friends. One of them caught his eye again. 'I say, Rutherford, you will join us this afternoon, won't you? It promises to be an excellent diversion, provided you have sea legs. The Thames may be the Thames, but it can still be quite choppy, and Jerry Warburton's yacht is disgustingly small.'

One of the others, evidently the Jerry Warburton concerned, looked up indignantly. 'She's a damned fine vessel, I'll have you know,' he protested.

The first young gentleman grinned impishly and leaned across to ruffle Jerry's rather spiky sandy hair. 'She'll bob around like a walnut in a bathtub, and you know it,' he teased.

Jerry scowled, and then looked at Stephen. 'You'll soon know better than to believe a word he says. Join us this afternoon, for you'll be most welcome. We'll be at Old Swan Steps at three, when the tide should be just right.'

'I'll be there,' Stephen promised, then picked up his hat, gloves, and cane, and went to rejoin Emma, who was just picking up her book, neatly wrapped in brown paper and string. 'That didn't take you long, Sis,' he said, taking the book to carry for her.

She gave him a light smile. 'I happened upon the very work almost straightaway,' she said, having decided not to say anything at all about her confrontation with Raine.

They left the shop, and Emma did so gladly, determining that whatever happened, she would never again set foot into Hatchard's. She glanced both ways along the pavement, but there was no sign of Raine, whose carriage had departed.

As Emma walked back to Grosvenor Square with Stephen, she tried to push the whole incident from her mind, but it was impossible. Try as she would, she could only dwell miserably upon all that Raine had said.

Stephen was not unaware of the change in her. 'What is it, Sis? You seem a little quiet.'

'Mm.'

'Is something wrong?'

'No, of course not,' she replied lightly.

'Forgive me if I question that, for I can't help noticing that you are oddly thoughtful.'

She managed a smile. 'I'm just looking forward to reading the book, that's all.'

'I thought perhaps you were beginning to work up a lather about meeting the earl this afternoon.'

'I'm trying not to think about that,' Emma said with some feeling, for facing Gerald's grandfather was something from which she now shrank, for fear that Raine had spoken the truth, in spite of Gerald's assurances to the contrary.

'It won't be as bad as you fear.'

'No, of course not,' she murmured.

He glanced at her. 'I rather fancy that my activities this afernoon will prove more torturous than your little excursion to Cranforth House.'

'Oh?'

'I've been invited to go sailing on the Thames.'

'I seem to recall you went a peculiar shade of green when you went sailing in Lyme Bay,' she pointed out.

'That was then.'

'And now is different?'

He pulled a face at her. 'How tedious older sisters can be at times,' he said with a long-suffering sigh.

They were nearing Grosvenor Square now, and the elegant

mansions of Mayfair rose all around. Emma glanced at the exclusive doors and windows, and the gracious gardens with their tints of autumn. It was all so very beautiful, but increasingly alien. She was beginning to feel too out of place here, and to think longingly of the home she'd left behind in Dorset.

As they entered the southeast corner of Grosvenor Square, Emma knew that she had to do something, for it was out of the question that things could be left as they were. She had to know exactly what Gerald's position was, and she had to know before they left for Cranforth House. She would confront him when he called that afternoon, and this time she would not shrink from telling him exactly why she was so troubled. He would learn what the Countess of Purbeck was saying and threatening, and he would have to put his bride-to-be's mind completely at rest, or she would withdraw from the match.

Stephen had already set off for Old Swan Steps and his sailing friends, and Mr Rutherford was dozing in the library, having succumbed yet again to the vicious circle of nighttime insomnia and daytime sleep that his son had predicted. There was an hour to go before Gerald was due to call, and Emma walked in the garden for a while before going to her room to change for the meeting with the Earl of Cranforth.

The September sun was bright, but lacked warmth, and she was glad of her shawl as she strolled in the sunken garden near the gazebo. She wore a long-sleeved apricot wool gown, and there was a lace-trimmed day bonnet on her head, its ribbons fluttering prettily free as she paused to touch one of the roses which still bloomed in this sheltered place. There were doves in the garden next door, and they cooed gently in a cherry tree. A church clock struck the half-hour, and she made her way back toward the house, where Dolly would be waiting with the clothes they had both selected for this all-important meeting with Gerald's grandfather.

She entered the house through the French doors of the library, and as she emerged into the hall, having tiptoed past her slumbering father, she heard a knock at the front door. Surely it couldn't be Gerald already!

The butler opened the door, and Emma peeped out to see that

the caller was Lord Avenley, not Gerald. Her heart sank, and she watched him with distaste. She had disliked him at the theater, but after what had now happened to Stephen, she loathed him more than ever.

Saunders bowed to him. 'My lord?'

'Is Mr Stephen Rutherford at home?'

'I fear he is not, my lord. He went out a little earlier, I believe to go sailing on the Thames.'

'When will he return?'

'I do not know, my lord, for he did not say.'

Emma did not realize that she could be seen reflected in the wall mirror in the inner hall, but Lord Avenley's sharp eye had very swiftly perceived her hiding just inside the library. And now he made her start guiltily by addressing her.

'Good afternoon, Miss Rutherford,' he said.

She was horrified, and remained immobile for a moment.

The moment Lord Avenley spoke to her, Saunders stood aside to admit him, and Emma's heart sank still further as it became clear that she had no option but to receive him. Angry with herself for having been so silly as to let herself be seen, she stepped reluctantly into the hall, waiting there as the butler relieved the caller of his hat, gloves, and cane.

Toying with his cuff, Lord Avenley approached her, his eye raking her deliberately from head to toe. 'How very fortunate that you should be at home, Miss Rutherford,' he murmured, taking her hand and drawing it to his lips.

It was all she could do not to shudder visibly at his touch, for she found him everything that was repellent. His voice was soft and smooth, and his single eye shone with too bright and reptilian a light.

He smiled a little. 'I am glad of this opportunity to speak to you again, Miss Rutherford, for it seems that our meeting last night may have set us off on a rather unfortunate foot.'

'I cannot agree, sir, since I cannot imagine that anything fortunate could ever adhere to our dealings with each other,' she replied coolly.

He raised an eyebrow. 'Indeed? How very frosty you are, to be sure.'

'Can you wonder at it? I am hardly likely to regard you in a favorable light, Lord Avenley, for you have led my brother into a great deal of debt.' Remembering that her father was still asleep in the library, the door of which was open, she lowered her voice a little. 'You must have known that Stephen was in no financial position to play for such high stakes, but still you let him plunge further in. I find that totally despicable, my lord, and I will certainly never regard you in a favorable light.'

The ghost of a smile played on his thin lips. 'How very delightful you are when you are angry, Miss Rutherford. I vow I find you quite irresistible.'

She recoiled with a mixture of distaste and startlement. 'I beg your pardon?'

'I merely paid you a gallant compliment, Miss Rutherford, so pray do not look so wide-eyed and alarmed.'

'I do not care for your compliments, Lord Avenley.'

'Maybe not, but I am sure you care about your brother's debts.'

She searched his face. 'What do you mean by that?'

'Mean? My dear Miss Rutherford, you should not seek a hidden purpose in every sentence, for I am all that is open and honest.'

Her eyes flickered. Open and honest? Pigs would fly at Portland Bill before that would apply to him!

He affected to look offended at her disbelieving expression. 'I am of a mind to take offense, Miss Rutherford, for in truth I do not mean any harm. If you are concerned that Stephen's IOUs will be difficult to redeem, let me assure you that it will prove a remarkably simple process.'

'I don't understand. In what way will it be simple?'

He glanced at his fob watch. 'Good heavens, is that the time? I fear I must go now, Miss Rutherford. It was very pleasant indeed to speak to you again. I was afraid that my first impression at the theater might have been erroneous, but I know now that it was not. *Au revoir.*' Sketching her an elaborate bow, he turned to the console table, where Saunders was waiting to hand him his hat, gloves, and cane. Then he bowed to her again, before strolling out, the cane swinging in his hand.

Saunders closed the door behind him and then returned to where she stood. 'Is there anything you wish, madam?' he inquired.

'Yes, Saunders, I trust that you will not mention my brother's debts in the kitchen, for if Jacob should hear of it, and see fit to carry tales to my father . . .'

'I will not say a word, madam.'

She nodded. 'Thank you, Saunders.'

'Madam,' he replied, bowing.

She turned to go to the staircase, but then paused again. 'When Lord Kane calls shortly, you will be sure to show him up to the drawing room, won't you? It is important that I speak privately with him before we leave.'

'Very well, madam.'

She went slowly up the staircase, her eyes downcast to the marble steps. What would the outcome be of this confrontation with Gerald? Maybe it would not go well, and not only would there be no visit to his grandfather at Cranforth House, but maybe she would soon be on her way home to Dorchester, the match a thing of the past.

11

THE KANE KEEPSAKE glittered on its bed of crimson velvet. Emma gazed at the symbol of her forthcoming match, and then she quietly closed the leather case, hiding it in the depths of her brown fur muff.

Taking a deep breath, she turned to Dolly. 'How do I look?'

'You look beautiful, Miss Emma,' replied the maid, her satisfied glance taking in her mistress's stylish figure. For the visit to Cranforth House, Emma wore a sage-green woolen mantle, fitted tightly at the waist by a wide self-belt with an oval gold buckle. The mantle was lavishly trimmed at the hem and collar with soft dark-brown fur, and there was more of the same fur adorning the brim of her brown velvet hat. On her feet there were neat little brown kid ankle boots, and she carried a reticule that was small enough to conceal in the capacious muff. Her hair was dressed up into a knot beneath her hat, with a frame of soft curls around her face. Surveying her with much gratification, Dolly was content that there was not a maid in the whole of London whose mistress would be better turned out than Miss Emma Rutherford.

Without another word, Emma left the room to make her way down to the drawing room, where Gerald was waiting. At the elegant double doors she paused for another moment; then she opened the doors and went inside.

Gerald was standing facing the fireplace, his face aglow with fiamelight, and he turned swiftly as she entered. He wore a wine-red coat, cream brocade waistcoat, and tight gray breeches, and a discreet pearl pin adorned the knot of his softly tied neckcloth.

His penetrating gray eyes met hers without any hesitation, and he smiled. 'Good afternoon, Emma,' he said.

It came as something of a shock to hear her first name on his lips. She'd quite forgotten their agreement on last parting, and the lapse of memory on her part robbed her of her carefully summoned impetus. 'G-good afternoon,' she replied, unable to bring herself to say his name.

He looked curiously at her. 'Is something wrong? Is your father—?'

'My father is quite well, my lord,' she said quickly.

He raised an eyebrow. 'My lord? Is convention to be imposed after all?'

'It may be that it has to be, Lord Kane. I have something to say to you.'

'Something serious, it seems,' he murmured, studying her closely. 'Well, do proceed, Miss Rutherford, and by all means let us be formal, if that is what you wish.'

Dull color had begun to seep into her cheeks, and she felt dreadful, but she had no choice, she had to confront him. 'Lord Kane, I know that you have gone to some lengths to reassure me that your heart is fully in this match, but—'

'There are no buts about it, Miss Rutherford, my heart is fully in the match.' He came a little closer. 'What has happened to make you again doubt my commitment?'

She lowered her eyes. 'At the theater last night—' she began.

His eyes sharpened. 'Avenley?' he interrupted brusquely.

'No, my lord, not Lord Avenley. The Countess of Purbeck.'

His gaze was intense. 'What did she say?'

'She simply made it plain that she disliked me, but she also hinted that the Earl of Cranforth is set against me as your second bride.'

'That isn't true, as I believe I have already said.'

Emma met his eyes again. 'Then, this morning, when Stephen accompanied me to Hatchard's bookshop, the countess singled me out again. She repeated that your grandfather is against the match, and she also said that she was your confidante, and that she had it on your own authority that you are beginning to have second thoughts about me.'

'And you are prepared to take her word on such an important

matter?' His tone was more than a little clipped.

'The countess is very convincing, my lord.'

'So it seems. Well, Miss Rutherford, what exactly do you wish me to say? I've already promised that I intend to proceed with the match and that I will treat you honorably. I've endeavored to assure you that I will do all I can to make ours a happy marriage, and by giving you the Keepsake I had hoped to allay your under-standable fears. As to my grandfather's opposition, let me say again that it simply does not exist, nor does my so-called confi-dence in the Countess of Purbeck. That particular, lady is no longer a friend of mine, indeed my dealings with her have become barely civil, owing to certain aspects of her conduct. What she is doing to you now is nothing more or less than spitefulness, and I have to say that I am more than a little disappointed that you should take her word before mine.'

Emma lowered her eyes. 'Surely you understand my position, Lord Kane. I am fresh from the country, I know nothing about you, and nothing about your life here in London, and that places me at a great disadvantage.'

'Disadvantage?' There was a sudden flash of anger in his eyes. 'Miss Rutherford, you are soon to become Lady Kane, and in the due course of time you will be the Countess of Cranforth, with all the privilege and position that that rank entails. What in God's name is disadvantageous about that?' Realizing that his tone had been too harsh, he looked apologetically at her. 'Forgive me, I did not mean to sound—'

'Perhaps I deserve it, my lord,' she interrupted, raising her glance to his again. 'Maybe I am entirely in the wrong in allowing the countess to upset me.'

'She is a woman of experience, and knows full well how to go about such things. I only wish you would realize that she is moved solely by malice, and that the truth plays very little part in her philosophy.'

'Why is she so bitter toward me?'

'I would prefer not to answer that,' he replied after a moment.

'Please tell me.'

He exhaled slowly, running his fingers through his dark hair. 'If I tell you what you wish to know, I fear it will mean a very embarrassing admission on my part.'

'Embarrassing?'

He smiled a little ruefully. 'I may have been a widower for some time now, Miss Rutherford, but I have to confess that I have not been living a particularly cloistered and monkish life. I have enjoyed a number of brief dalliances, none of them amounting to anything of any seriousness, but only on one occasion have I broken a very strict rule that has always governed my conduct, that of never toying with other men's wives. That single fall from grace on my part took place one night last spring with the Countess of Purbeck, and it is something that I have regretted ever since.'

Color flooded into Emma's cheeks.

He gave another rueful smile. 'Forgive me for telling you such things, Miss Rutherford, but since the truth was a requisite in these proceedings, then the truth is what you must have. I am not proud of myself for having broken the rule, and if I could turn the clock back, believe me I would, for the countess has proved to be a veritable thorn in my side ever since. She will not accept that our brief encounter was a single event, never to be repeated, and she has not ceased to try to win me back ever since. She did not take kindly to learning of my impending betrothal, and she is doing her utmost to see that it never takes place. That is why she is so very unpleasant toward you and Stephen.'

Emma turned away. Suddenly so much was explained, and she could see Raine clearly. The venom and spite were jealousy, nothing more and nothing less. The unparalleled Countess of Purbeck was jealous of plain Emma Rutherford!

Gerald drew a long breath. 'I didn't want to tell you something that revealed me in a shabby light, Miss Rutherford, and I certainly did not wish to speak of matters which a gentleman should never mention in front of a lady, least of all the lady he hopes to marry.'

'I may be fresh from the country, sir, but I am not entirely green,' she replied. 'I do know that there are very few monks in this day and age.'

'I regret now that I did not explain the situation a little earlier, but I will do all I can to ensure that the countess does not approach you again.'

'I do not think that she intends to approach me again, my lord, for she has told me she means to have me ostracized by society.'

He seemed amused. 'Does she indeed? Well, influential she may be, but not that influential. Not even the Prince of Wales has the power to decree that any particular person is to be snubbed by the entire *beau monde*. She may have her own coterie of friends, and she may be the toast of London, but she is most definitely not the be-all and end-all of society's existence. I can tell you that all she is trying to do is make you cut and run.'

For a long moment Emma was silent, but then she took the Keepsake and its case from her muff and laid it on the table beside her. 'If that is her intention, then she has come very close to succeeding,' she said softly.

He looked at the red leather case. 'You meant to return it to me and end the match?'

'If you had not told me the truth.'

'It is the truth, I promise you. And when I say that I deeply regret having broken my own rules where the countess was concerned, that also is the truth. I have very particular reasons for wanting to avoid other men's wives, for I know only too well . . .' He broke off, turning away. 'Because I know only too well the pain of being a betrayed husband,' he finished quietly.

Emma stared at him. Margot? Margot had been unfaithful to him?

He glanced at her again. 'My marriage was not the joyous thing it appeared to be, and was already effectively at an end when Margot was killed. Oh, I was grief-stricken afterward, grief-stricken that I had been taken for such a fool, and if I continued to wear my wedding ring, it was as a reminder never to rush blindly into another match.'

Emma was so startled by these revelations that she could only stand there.

He smiled a little, and faced her properly again. 'I have never told anyone about this, apart from my grandfather, but it is something else that I think you now have the right to know. You asked me once if I compare you to Margot and find you lacking. Well, perhaps now you realize that there is absolutely no comparison between you and Margot, and that if anyone is lacking, then it is she.

'I . . . I had no idea.'

'The facts of my previous marriage are hardly such that I would wish them spread around London. I would prefer to forget I ever knew Margot.' His glance moved to the red leather case on the table. 'What do you wish to do, Emma? Does the match stand, or would you prefer to cry off?'

She could hear her own heartbeats. A huge weight seemed to have been lifted from her. She didn't have to fight the ghost of his first wife! Margot was not the flawless angel she'd feared, but had had feet of clay! Her lips trembled so much that she could barely manage to smile at him. 'I wish the match to stand, Gerald,' she whispered. Nothing else mattered now. Let the Countess of Purbeck do her worst, let her try her utmost, for she would not succeed!

Gerald came to her, putting his hand briefly to her cheek. 'I'm glad, Emma, for I truly wish to make you my wife.' He looked into her green eyes. 'Please don't doubt me again, for there is no need.'

'Forgive me.' Her skin burned beneath his hand.

'There is nothing to forgive.' He took his hand away, turning to look at the clock on the mantelpiece. 'Well, since we are to proceed with everything, I think it is time we left for Cranforth House, otherwise we will be late.'

Dolly was waiting outside the drawing room doors, for she was to accompany them in order to satisfy propriety, and Emma quickly told her to return the Keepsake to her room before rejoining them in the hall. Several minutes later, followed by the maid, she and Gerald emerged from the house to enter the waiting carriage, which immediately conveyed them to Park Lane.

Cranforth House was bright in the September sunshine as the carriage swept in between the phoenix-decorated gates and came to a standstill beneath the grand porch.

Gerald alighted, his boots crunching on the freshly raked gravel as he turned to hold his hand out to Emma. He paused before assisting her down. 'Please don't be nervous, because I promise you faithfully that my grandfather is not in any way opposed to our match. You do believe me, don't you?'

She smiled into his eyes. 'Yes,' she answered. She was so happy that she felt as if she were floating. He had confided in her, and she was closer to him at last.

'Are you quite certain of that?' he asked lightly.

'Quite.'

'I'm relieved to hear it,' he murmured, assisting her down. Then he was thoughtful enough to help Dolly as well, and the maid's cheeks became instantly pink, for it was not often that a gentleman of rank concerned himself with the welfare of a mere maid.

A footman in splendid green-and-gold livery admitted them to a vast marble entrance hall, where a black double staircase rose to the floor above. The staircase's rail was golden, and its newel posts were gilded likenesses of the Fitzroy phoenix. The phoenix appeared again and again, in the marble tiles on the floor, in the gilded plasterwork adorning the walls and doorways, and was woven into the upholstery of the exquisite sofas and chairs against the walls.

Their reflections looked back at them from the mirror above the marble fireplace as the footman conducted them toward the rear of the ground floor, where the earl had elected to receive them in the conservatory that overlooked the famous gardens.

To reach it, they had to cross the glittering ballroom, where on Halloween their betrothal ball would be held. The walls were paneled alternately with mirrors and murals of classical scenes, and from the lofty golden ceiling there was suspended a positive battery of fine crystal chandeliers. Tall French windows opened into the conservatory, which was adjacent, and as they followed the footman across the ballroom's polished parquet floor, the smell of tropical foliage drifted toward them.

The sun streamed in through the glass, and the air was filled with the gentle splash of water from the ornamental fountains that played among the shrubs and palms. Everything smelled of warm, damp earth, but not of flowers, even though there were some very exotic blooms among the leaves.

The Earl of Cranforth was seated on a cushioned cane chair of surprisingly large proportions, its curved back framing his frail figure almost like the decoration on a Russian icon. He had a volume of botanical illustrations on the table before him, and he was poring very diligently over it, gazing shortsightedly at the exquisite paintings, and then at a sprig of greenery in his bony hand. Emma remembered him well from the brief glimpse she had had of him when he drove past her in Park Lane. His fine-boned, aristocratic face was a little pale, and, like her father, he wore a tasseled day cap and a number of warm shawls around his thin shoulders, even though it was stiflingly hot in the conservatory. Everything about him reminded her irresistibly of her father, even to his chosen reading matter.

He became suddenly aware of their approach and looked up quickly from his book, removing his spectacles from the end of his nose. 'Ah, there you are, m'boy,' he said, his watery blue eyes moving swiftly to encompass Emma.

'How are you, Grandfather?' Gerald inquired.

'Tolerable, m'boy, tolerable. I loathe traveling almost as much as I loathe London, but I am content that it is all in a good cause.' The old man's gaze returned to Emma, and he rose shakily to his feet.

Gerald hastened to effect the important introduction. 'Grandfather, I would like to present Miss Rutherford. Miss Rutherford, my grandfather, the Earl of Cranforth.'

The earl's hand was like a claw as he took her fingers and drew them to his lips. 'We meet at last, m'dear,' he murmured, his glance sharp and shrewd.

'I am honored to make your acquaintance, my lord earl,' she replied, sinking into a graceful curtsy.

'Let me look at you properly.'

She stood there awkwardly as he surveyed her slowly from head to toe, and then he looked into her eyes for a long moment. At last he smiled. 'You have a steady gaze, m'dear, and I like that in a woman. I cannot abide fluttering eyelashes and coyness, of which faults you seem thankfully free. I confess I was somewhat taken aback to learn that my grandson's choice was someone of whom I had never even heard, but now that I've met you, I can see that he is most certainly not a fool. Sit down, m'dear, sit down.' He gestured toward a second cane chair. A third awaited Gerald.

The earl looked intently at her when she was seated. 'Would you care for some refreshment, m'dear? Some tea, perhaps?'

'That would be most agreeable, sir,' she replied, her glance drawn to a decanter and glasses on the table before him. 'But please do not feel compelled to drink tea with me, for I am sure you would prefer your cognac,' she said.

He looked at her with thorough approval. 'Upon m'soul, a wench with consideration for an old man's failings! Gerald, m'boy, I thought such wonderful beings were extinct, but it seems that you have found one!'

Gerald smiled. 'And not before time?' he murmured.

His grandfather pursed his lips. 'You know full well what I think of your hitherto questionable taste. A suitable decision on your part is most certainly long overdue.'

Gerald glanced at him, and then lowered his eyes to the open volume on the table. 'Sir Joseph's gift?'

The earl pursed his lips again. 'I'll warrant it provides an excellent topic to which to change the conversation,' he muttered. 'Yes, it is indeed the book kindly sent to me by Sir Joseph Banks. I am quite sure that its pages contain an illustration of this wretched weed, but I fear I cannot find it. There was an earlier volume of Sir Joseph's expeditions, but I fear it came to grief in that disastrous fire at Cranforth Castle, and now I begin to think that it was the source of the illustration concerned, and not this later publication.'

Emma had been looking at the book, and it seemed very familiar to her. 'My lord, I am sure that the library in Lady Bagworth's house contains a volume very like this one, but bound with a green leather cover.'

The old man's eyes lit up. 'Indeed? If so, it is the very book I wish to examine.'

'I am sure there would be no harm in sending it around to you, sir.'

'Excellent. Well, that old reprobate Bagworth had one redeeming feature, his library, but in everything else he was quite beyond the pale.'

Tea was brought for Emma, and for a very agreeable half-hour they all three sat conversing. They spoke of a variety of things, but Emma felt quite relaxed and comfortable throughout.

At last it was time to leave, and the earl rose from his chair once more, taking Emma's hand and drawing it to his lips. 'It has been a pleasure to meet you, m'dear, a very great pleasure indeed. You will make a delightful Lady Kane, and I confess that although I was a little perturbed when Gerald expressed a wish to present you with the Keepsake before you were officially betrothed, I can quite understand his desire to do so. You must not doubt your position, m'dear, for it is quite secure.'

Emma smiled at him. 'You are very kind, sir.'

'Nonsense, it's simply that I'm very pleased indeed to discover that you are everything my grandson said you were.'

Her eyes moved fleetingly to meet Gerald's, and then she smiled at the earl again.

The old man cupped her hand gently in both his. 'I trust we will meet again soon. Perhaps at Manchester House this Friday. I have received an invitation from the Marquess of Hertford, and I may stir myself to toddle along. Hertford and his circle can be very tiresome at times, but they will do, I suppose. At the moment I am in two minds, for Manchester House assemblies are always such a press that pleasure is the last thing one feels when enduring them.'

'I hope you will be there, my lord,' she replied.

He patted her hand and then released it, resuming his seat at the table as Gerald prepared to escort her out again. He called after them, 'Miss Rutherford, you will not forget that volume, will you?'

'I will see to it as soon as I return, sir,' she said, pausing to smile back at him from the French doors into the ballroom.

As she and Gerald retraced their steps through the house, he glanced at her. 'That was not so bad, was it?'

'No.'

'He liked you very much.'

'He reminds me of my father.'

'There are many similarities,' he agreed. 'May I change the subject for a moment?'

'By all means.'

'Have you spoken to Stephen about Avenley yet?'

'Yes, and I do not think my brother will be having anything more to do with him. At least, not anything beyond certain unavoidable contact.'

'Your persuasion was effective?'

'He did not need persuading, for he saw the error of his ways,' she said, recalling how guilty and remorseful Stephen had been since Lord Avenley had acquired his IOUs.

'You don't know how relieved I am to hear it, Emma, for Avenley is the devil himself, and no spoon could possibly be long enough when supping with him.'

She nodded, thinking about her own recent meeting with Lord Avenley.

Dolly was waiting for them in the entrance hall, and soon they were all there in the carriage once more, being conveyed back along Park Lane and Upper Grosvenor Square. As the coachman drew up at the curb in Grosvenor Square, Gerald glanced at Emma.

'It occurs to me that we have no plans to meet again before Friday evening and the Manchester House assembly. I would like to see you before then.'

'And I would like to see you,' she replied honestly. See him again? She wished she could spend every moment with him, every moment of every day of every week. . . .

He smiled. 'I would have suggested this evening, but I am afraid it is out of the question. Before I left St James's Square, I received a message from Castlereagh, summoning me to call upon him tonight. I gather that Yarmouth will also be there, which does not bode well for the foreign secretary, I fear.'

'There is to be a duel?'

'It is the only conclusion I can reach. By the way, Lady Castlereagh was most upset to learn that they had been misled at the theater, and she wishes me to reassure you that they would never have knowingly left us in the lurch. She is at pains to emphasize that there will be no repetition of such a regrettable occurrence.' He smiled then. 'I digress, I fear, for we were discussing our next meeting. If this evening is out of the question, tomorrow afternoon surely is not. Perhaps a drive in the country would be agreeable? I believe that the ornamental gardens at the Sadler's Wells theater are well worth a visit.'

'I would like that very much.'

'At two o'clock?'

'Very well.'

He alighted, and then assisted both Emma and her maid down as well, again to Dolly's pink-cheeked confusion. Saunders had already opened the door of the house, and Dolly hurried on inside, but Gerald paused again for a moment on the pavement.

'Emma, please do not ever doubt me again,' he said softly, ignoring Saunders, who still waited at the door.

'I'm sorry that I ever—' she began, the words dying on her breathless lips as he suddenly bent his head to kiss her on the cheek.

Her heart stood still for a moment, and then began to pound wildly in her breast. She quickly lowered her gaze, for she was sure that her emotions were written as clearly in her eyes as words upon a printed page.

Gerald did not seem to notice her disarray, for he had already turned to reenter the carriage, which a moment later drove smartly away.

Emma watched it leave and was suddenly startled by Saunders's rather anxious and urgent voice from the doorway behind her.

'Madam, it's imperative that I speak with you without delay.'

She turned, instantly alarmed. 'What is it?'

'Master Stephen has met with an accident, madam. I fear it may be serious, and I do not know what to tell Mr Rutherford.'

12

EMMA HURRIED INTO the house, waiting in the inner hall as Saunders closed the door and then came quickly toward her. 'An accident, Saunders? Is he badly hurt?'

'He fell overboard into the Thames, madam, and unfortunately it was several minutes before his companions could rescue him. Both the water and air were very cold, and he received a great soaking.'

'Where is he now?' She glanced instinctively up the staircase.

The butler shook his head. 'He hasn't been brought back here yet, madam. A carriage is bringing him, and one of his companions rode ahead to give warning that a physician should be sent for without delay. I have taken the liberty of dispatching a footman for Dr Longford of North Audley Street. The message arrived here only a minute or so before you returned, and Mr Rutherford is asleep in his room. I did not know what to do for the best, madam, for imparting such distressing news . . .'

'You were right to withhold the information for the moment, Saunders. I will tell him myself once the doctor has examined my brother. How long will it be before the carriage arrives?'

'The gentleman who rode ahead said that it would be only minutes behind him, madam,' the butler replied, and as he did so, they both heard a carriage drawing up outside.

Saunders hastened to open the door again, and Emma recognized the two young gentlemen who swiftly alighted. from the vehicle, for they had been at Hatchard's that morning. That morning? It seemed as if several days had passed since then.

Stephen was assisted carefully into the house. His face was

drained of color, his hair was still damp, and beneath several coats borrowed from his anxious friends, he still wore his wet clothes. There was an ugly bruise on his forehead, and he seemed a little dazed. He shivered so much that his teeth were chattering, and Emma knew that it was as much from shock as the icy drenching he had received in the Thames.

His friends helped him up the staircase, and Saunders dispatched a footman to see that hot water was brought from the kitchen. Dolly joined Emma outside Stephen's room as the two gentlemen, assisted by Stephen's valet, Frederick, at last divested him of his wet clothes, and put him in a warm, dry nightshirt. Emma paced anxiously up and down, wishing that they would finish so that she could speak to her brother.

At last the two young gentlemen emerged, and the one named Jerry Warburton, whose boat the party had been sailing in, spoke to her. 'I cannot apologize enough for this, Miss Rutherford. I wouldn't have had it happen for the world.'

'Is he badly hurt, do you think?'

'He's very shaken and cold, but I don't think the blow he received to his head is very serious. I'm no expert, of course, but I feel reasonably confident that he will soon recover. I wouldn't hesitate at all if it were not for this wretchedly unseasonable September, which has made the Thames intolerably cold. I vow there was a bite to the river air that would have done justice to January. We did what we could, and brought him back here without delay, and now we can only hope that he was not too greatly affected by the bitter cold.'

'I thank you for acting so promptly, sir.'

'I wish our first meeting had taken place under more pleasant circumstances, Miss Rutherford, especially as you are soon to become a member of my family.'

She was surprised. 'You are related to Lord Kane?'

'I'm his second cousin. May I take this opportunity to wish you every happiness for the future?'

'Thank you, sir.'

They turned to leave, and Dolly stood aside for them to pass. As their carriage drove away again, the doctor arrived, thrusting his hat and gloves into Saunders's hands and then following him up the staircase, where Emma was still waiting, for his arrival had been so prompt upon the others' departure that she had not as yet had a chance to go in to see Stephen.

Dr Longford was a stern-faced, superior man with thinning brown hair and a pale, rather horsey face. He was about forty-five years old, and dressed in the elegant style that would be expected of a successful Mayfair physician. His blue coat had velvet facings, and there was a plain golden pin in his neck-cloth. The chain of a fob watch dangled from his brocade waist-coat, and he carried a capacious black leather bag embossed with his initials. There was an arrogant air of self-importance about him, and Emma took a swift dislike, which she was at some pains to disguise.

He inclined his head to her. 'Miss Rutherford, I presume?'

'Dr Longford.'

'I will examine the patient and then consult with you,' he said imperiously, inclining his head once more and then following Saunders to the bedroom door.

The door closed behind him, Saunders withdrew discreetly toward the back staircase, and Emma resumed her anxious pacing. From time to time she heard the murmur of voices in the room, but the minutes passed and there was no sign of the doctor's examination coming to an end.

She was beginning to think that the consultation would go on forever, when suddenly the door opened and Dr Longford emerged to speak to her. He drew her to one side, so that their voices would not carry into Stephen's ears.

'I have given Mr Rutherford a thorough examination, Miss Rutherford, and I can assure you that he is in no immediate danger and that if he follows my instructions he will not suffer any lasting ill effects.'

Relief flooded through her.

'Do not be misled into a false sense of well-being on the matter, Miss Rutherford, for there are certain problems.'

'Problems?'

'To begin with, he struck his head during the accident, and while the blow does not appear to be serious, it is my experience that reaction can be delayed, and therefore he must be watched closely during the next few days. I must also inform you that he has cat-

107

egorically refused to allow me to proceed as I feel best, by which I mean that he has not permitted me to bleed him. Bleeding is essential in such cases, for it reduces the risk of inflammation of the lungs, but it has proved impossible to reason with him, and so I am forced to resort to the less effective remedy of castor oil and hot baths. At all costs we must guard against inflaming the lungs, and so I have also prescribed an excellent tonic infusion of red wine and the leaves of the vinca minor plant. As to food and drink, I must insist that hot beverages are continually administered, together with nourishing broths, but until the patient is manifestly well in every respect, he is not to have any solid food, cold drinks, or alcohol in any form. Do I make myself clear, Miss Rutherford?'

'Perfectly clear, sir.'

'The patient is not to leave his bed, and his room is to be kept as warm as possible. I must also emphasize that drafts are a very real hazard at this time, and so the window must not only be kept closed, it must also be sealed. Should a feverish ague ensue in spite of all these precautions, then you must administer one hundred drops of laudanum every three hours. If the ague should then worsen, you must send for me without delay.'

'I will see that your instructions are adhered to, Doctor.'

'I trust that you will, Miss Rutherford. That will be one guinea.'

Emma glanced along the passage, to where Dolly was waiting in readiness with her reticule. She beckoned to the maid and then selected a guinea coin from her purse.

With an alacrity that was hardly to be commended, the doctor pocketed the coin and then hurried away down the staircase. Emma gazed after him, hoping that they would not have to send for him again, for she did not like him in the least.

At last she was able to see Stephen herself, but as she entered his room, she was startled and dismayed to see him standing by the roaring fire with a large glass of cognac that his valet had just handed to him. He wore a peacock paisley dressing gown over his nightshirt, and the firelight flickered on the gold threads in his Turkish slippers. His hair was quite dry now, and there was only a slight sign of the daze he'd been in when his friends had first brought him back to the house. There was a bandage around his forehead.

She stared in astonishment 'You are supposed to be in bed!'

He sighed irritably, swirling the glass and draining it in one swallow. 'It's all a fuss about nothing, and Longford is without a doubt the most pompous ass in creation.'

'I agree with you about the doctor, but not about the fuss being about nothing. Stephen, you fell in the Thames and struck your head, and you should therefore be obeying the doctor's orders.' She went to him, removing the glass from his hand and giving it to the valet. 'Take the decanter away, Frederick,' she said.

Frederick was reluctant to obey her when he knew his master wished the cognac to remain in the room, but at the same time he did not like to defy his master's sister. He stood there unhappily glancing from one to the other. He was forty years old, a wiry former postboy whose riding career had ended when his leg had been broken in an accident, leaving him with a stiff knee and a pro-nounced limp. His easygoing nature and ability to learn quickly had commended him to Stephen, whose thoroughbred horse he had ridden several times in matches against other blood horses, and the position of valet had been accepted the moment it was offered.

Emma fixed him with a cross look. 'That will be all for the moment, Frederick,' she said, pointedly nodding toward the decanter.

Without another murmur, the valet picked up the decanter and removed it from the room.

Stephen was indignant with her. 'Oh, don't be tiresome, Sis! I received a slight knock on the forehead and a brief dunking in the Thames, neither of which events requires me to be treated like a chronic invalid!'

'Stephen, when you came back here you were trembling and shaken.'

'Because I was cold, that's all,' he interposed. 'Oh, why on earth did you have to send for Longford? It really wasn't necessary.

'Saunders sent for the doctor because he was given a message that that is what he should do. Stephen, your friends believed a medical examination was of paramount importance, and I happen to agree with them. You struck your head, and you were in the water for a long time, and—'

'A few minutes.'

'Very well, you were in the water for a few minutes, but the water was very cold, and so was the air when you were pulled out. You were then brought back here still in your wet clothes. Dr Longford is right to fear inflammation of the lungs if you do not adhere to his instructions.'

Stephen sighed again, giving her a grumpy look. 'You can be incredibly overbearing at times, Emma Rutherford,' he grumbled.

'Then do not give me cause,' she replied, pointing firmly toward the bed.

With a theatrical sigh he untied the dressing gown and flung it on the bed. Then he kicked off his slippers with decidedly ill grace and climbed into the bed, where he lay back on pillows, scowling at her. 'Will this do?'

'For the moment,' she replied. 'You are to remain in bed, sir, for if I hear that you've been disobeying the doctor's orders, then I will deal very firmly with you.'

'Poor Kane. He is undoubtedly about to acquire a dragon of the first degree,' he replied. Then he leaned back, surveying her a little speculatively. 'And how did the great meeting go? Was the old boy human, or a monster?'

'Human.'

'You liked him, I take it?'

'Yes, and I believe that he liked me.'

Stephen smiled. 'Another ordeal that did not live up to expectations?'

She sat on the edge of the bed, milling as well. 'Yes, I suppose so.'

'You seem different,' he said, observing her. 'Have things warmed between you and Kane?'

She hesitated. 'I understand more now. I know about the Countess of Purbeck, for instance.'

Stephen's lips parted in astonishment. 'You do?'

'Yes. He told me himself.'

Stephen sat up. 'You do not seem exactly upset,' he said.

'Why should I be? Now that I know the truth, I can understand why she is behaving as she does. I can also understand why you and she are so at odds. It is on account of me and the match, isn't it?'

'Yes.' He sat back again, a rather bemused expression on his face. 'I must say, your composure is quite astonishing,' he murmured.

'I'm not totally without knowledge of the world, Stephen,' she replied a little crossly.

'Yes, but all the same—'

'I would rather know than be surrounded by mysteries,' she said, getting up and going to the window.

Stephen's room, like hers, looked out over the rear gardens toward the mews lane behind the house. The September sun was still fairly high in the sky, but the shadows were beginning to lengthen. In the neighboring garden the doves fluttered prettily and somewhere nearby a dog was barking. Mayfair stretched away in perennial elegance, its grandeur only slightly spoiled by the views of the rears of the houses. The symmetry of the front elevations may have been missing, but the luxury and quality were still there, and there were the gardens, so leafy and beautiful.

Stephen watched her. 'Are you happy, Sis?'

'Yes,' she replied, remembering the moment Gerald had taken leave of her. Oh, how sweet it had been when he had kissed her cheek.

'Well, at least one of us is,' Stephen mused.

She turned quickly.

He smiled a little ruefully. 'I have my debts to face up to, a fact which I wish I could conveniently forget.'

'Oh, Stephen . . .' She went back to the bed, sitting down and taking his hand. 'You can still have my jewelry, you know.'

'That will be my very last resort. I will have to ask Avenley how long he will give me.'

She released his hand. 'Lord Avenley called here when you were out.'

'He did? What did he want?'

'I don't know, exactly, but I had no option but to receive him. Stephen, I find him totally abhorrent.'

Stephen nodded reluctantly. 'I have to confess that I am no longer quite as enamored,' he conceded. Then he looked at her again. 'Did he mention my IOUs?'

'Among other things.'

111

'What did he say about them?'

'That they would be very simple to redeem.'

Stephen's eyes brightened. 'He did? Are you sure?'

'As sure as I can be.'

He closed his eyes, exhaling with relief. 'If he will only let me pay up piecemeal.'

'He didn't say what he meant. By the way, to change the subject a little, it seems that all the speculation about Lord Castlereagh challenging Mr Canning to a duel may be on the point of becoming fact.'

'There is going to be a duel?'

'Gerald and Lord Yarmouth have been summoned to Lord Castlereagh's house this evening.'

'Then it must indeed mean a duel,' Stephen murmured. He glanced at her. 'So it's "Gerald" now, is it? Things have indeed progressed.'

She colored, and ignored the remark. 'I hope there isn't a challenge, for dueling is so very hazardous.'

'Women never understand these things. Sis, men must always defend their honor, and the honor of their families. If anyone were ever to insult or injure you, I would not hesitate to call him out for his pains.'

'I would rather be insulted than have to arrange your funeral,' she replied with feeling.

There was a tap at the door, and at Stephen's call, Dolly came in.

She curtsied. 'Master Stephen, Miss Emma, I thought you would like to know that Mr Rutherford is now awake. He doesn't know about the accident, and so I've come straight to you.'

Emma nodded and got up. 'I'll go to him right now.' She looked down at Stephen. 'I'm going to be very firm with you, sir, and I'm going to insist that you obey Dr Longford's orders. I know that you feel all right at the moment, but that doesn't alter the fact that you were far from well when your friends brought you home. A dunking in the Thames and a blow to the head are not to be shrugged off lightly, and so you are to do as you're told.'

'But, Sis—'

'Stephen, I'm not open to persuasion on this. Father will agree with me, as you well know.'

'Father *has* to do everything doctors tell him to do. I don't.'

'In this instance you do, sir,' she replied. 'Try to sleep now, for sleep is an excellent restorative.'

'Except that there is nothing to restore, because I'm perfectly well, apart from a slight bump on the head,' he grumbled, touching the bandage and then wincing a little because it hurt.

'You see? It isn't just a slight bump, it's quite a nasty blow.'

'Oh, very well, I concede that I'll have a lump there for the next few days.'

She smiled. 'If I hear from Frederick that you've been out of that bed for anything other than necessity, I shall tell Father about your IOUs.'

'You wouldn't!'

'Try me.'

He glared at her. 'You've made your point.'

'Good.' Turning, she left the room.

13

EMMA WAS STILL fast asleep when Dolly brought her her morning
cup of tea the next day. The maid placed the dainty gold-and-white
porcelain cup and saucer on the table next to the bed and then
went to draw the curtains back to allow the morning light in. It
was bright outside, the sun shining down from yet another clear
blue sky.

Emma stirred in the bed, her dark hair dragging on the lace-
edged pillow. Her eyes flickered and opened, and she smiled up at
Dolly as the maid came to the bedside.

'Good morning, Miss Emma. It's another lovely day,' said the
maid, waiting until her mistress had begun to sit up and then
plumping up the pillows behind her.

'Good morning, Dolly. How is my brother?' Emma asked,
accepting the cup of tea.

'I believe he had a rather restless night, Miss Emma.'

'Restless?'

'Yes, miss.'

'Is he otherwise all right?' Emma feared the onset of a fever.

'I think so, miss.'

'I'll go to see him directly I've dressed.'

'Yes, Miss Emma. Which gown will you wear today?'

'Oh, the cream sprigged muslin, I think.'

'Yes, miss.' Dolly bobbed a curtsy and then hurried through into
the dressing room, where she again drew back the curtains. As the
maid went to select the gown from one of the three large
wardrobes, Emma called after her.

'How is my father this morning?'

'He slept well, miss, and has sent word down to the kitchen that he intends to get up for breakfast.'

When Dolly had laid out the gown and its accessories, she returned to the bedroom to do what she could to encourage the fire into life. A housemaid would shortly come to attend to it, but in the meantime it had almost gone out.

Emma replaced her cup and saucer on the table and then lay comfortably back on the pillows. She wondered what had transpired at Lord Castlereagh's house the evening before. Was a challenge to be issued to the foreign secretary? She hoped not, for she liked Lord Castlereagh and did not like to think of him facing an adversary in a duel.

The door of the bedroom was flung unceremoniously open, and Stephen strode briskly in. He was dressed in his pine-green riding coat, cream cord breeches, a rose armazine waistcoat, and shining top boots. A diamond pin glittered in the folds of his neckcloth, and he carried his top hat, gloves, and riding crop. He had removed the bandage from his head, revealing a very ugly bruise that had swollen since the day before. His face was a little flushed, and his eyes were oddly bright. Perhaps too bright.

Emma sat forward in astonishment. 'Stephen. What on earth. . . ?'

'We agreed to ride in Hyde Park one day soon, and since this morning is so fine, I thought there is no time like the present. I've told Saunders to send someone for two suitable horses, and all you have to do is get up. We can be there and back before breakfast.'

She stared at him.

'Well, don't just look at me, Sis. Get up and get dressed.'

'Stephen, you are supposed to be in bed. You know what Dr Longford said.'

'A plague on Longford. Emma, there's nothing wrong with me, I had an excellent night, I feel as fit as the proverbial fiddle, apart from a slight headache, and I would very much like you to accompany me on a ride in the park.'

'But—'

'Don't coddle me, Sis. Look at me, I'm absolutely fine.' He spread his arms and grinned at her.

She was disturbed. He seemed well, and yet at the same time he didn't seem quite himself. 'Stephen, let's leave the ride for another

115

day, when we are certain beyond any doubt that you have recovered from yesterday.'

'That quack really knows how to earn his guinea, doesn't he? Emma, there is nothing wrong with me, and I intend to go for a ride whether or not you accompany me, so you might as well indulge your passion for riding and give in to me.' He grinned again.

She suddenly found herself returning the grin. 'Oh, very well, since you do indeed look remarkably hale and hearty. I'll be ready in fifteen minutes.'

'That's more like it.' He left the room again, but as he closed the door behind him, he paused for a moment, closing his eyes as everything swam slightly. Then he recovered, and hurried on down to the hall to wait for her.

If Emma had witnessed his momentary dizziness, she would never have complied with his wishes, but she saw nothing, and so remained convinced that he was quite well. She even decided that her own doubts about him were imagined, for surely someone could not be ill and behave as he was behaving? He seemed in such good spirits, and certainly did not lack energy.

In less than fifteen minutes she hurried down the staircase in her aquamarine velvet riding habit, which had a jacket trimmed with black military braiding. Her little hat resembled a soldier's shako, complete with festoons and tassels, but was at the same time very feminine indeed, with a dainty net veil that concealed her face. Dolly had pinned her hair up into a knot beneath the hat, without even a single ringlet or curl protruding.

Stephen smiled approvingly. 'How very stylish, Sis. I vow that you look every inch the fine London lady.'

'Thank you.'

'Come on, then.' He offered her his arm, and together they proceeded out into the sunshine.

The morning air was still very cold, and it seemed to Emma that the leaves in the square were more golden, as if the overnight cold had burnished them. The riding stable had provided two very fine mounts, a pretty dapple gray for Emma and a large red bay for Stephen.

Stephen assisted her to mount, and then turned to climb onto the bay. Emma was arranging her skirt and did not see how once again her brother had to pause. He closed his eyes for a moment, for the world seemed to be slowly revolving, but then it all became steady again, and he mounted. They rode toward the beginning of Upper Grosvenor Street, only to find it blocked by an accident at the far end, and so they rode north around the square to use the Upper Brook Street route instead.

Emma hadn't given Upper Brook Street any further thought at all, but now she found herself wondering what its significance was. She glanced at Stephen, half-inclined to press him again to explain to her, but then she decided against it. It could not possibly be anything of great importance, and she had surely learned the lesson now that she must stop questioning everything where Gerald was concerned.

Their horses' hoofs echoed along the elegant street, where everything was very quiet. But then a large dog began to bark at them from behind some closed wrought-iron gates, and Emma's horse shied. Stephen reined in, waiting to see that she could control her mount. For a moment the dapple gray continued to dance around and toss its head, but gradually Emma soothed it, for she was an excellent horsewoman. She patted the animal's neck, and was about to urge it on again when something drew her attention to the large white mansion on her right. As she looked, a bright-red curricle she had seen before was brought around from the stables at the rear of the mansion. The team of two black horses was very fresh indeed, and had obviously only just been harnessed.

Emma stared, for the curricle was Gerald's.

Stephen followed her glance, and then pressed his lips together a little pensively as he looked at Emma again.

She straightened slowly in the saddle, still gazing at the curricle. It was far too early for a social call, and besides, the team was obviously fresh after a night's rest. There was only one conclusion to reach, and that was that Gerald had spent the night at the mansion. As she looked, the door of the house opened and Gerald himself emerged. He was dressed in formal evening wear, and he didn't glance at the groom as he climbed lightly into the curricle, urging the team swiftly into action.

117

Emma maneuvered her horse a little further along the street as he drove away from the mansion, turning the curricle toward Grosvenor Square. He didn't glance at the two riders, but even if he had, it was doubtful he would have recognized them. Stephen's hat cast his face in shadows, and his coat collar was turned up, and Emma's face and hair were hidden by her hat and veil.

She turned in the saddle, watching the curricle drive swiftly away and vanish into the square; then she looked at her brother. 'Whose house is it, Stephen?' she asked quietly.

He was a little perplexed. 'Surely you know already?'

'If I did, I would not ask,' she replied.

'Look, Sis, yesterday you told me that you knew all about Kane and the Countess of Purbeck.'

Emma stared at him. 'Yes, but—'

'Then why should you be so surprised to see him leaving her residence after spending the night there?'

Behind her veil, Emma's eyes widened and her lips parted on a stifled gasp. 'What are you saying?' she whispered, her gaze fleeing to the house again.

Stephen was silent for a moment, and then he drew a heavy breath, tilting his hat back. 'What exactly did Kane tell you yesterday, Sis?' he asked gently.

'That he had had a very brief affair with her in the spring, an affair that he deeply regrets, but which she wishes to revive.'

'Oh Emma . . .'

Her green eyes were very large and unhappy as they searched his face. 'Are you telling me that that is not the truth?'

He nodded slowly. 'Sis, the countess has been Kane's mistress for months now, and everyone in London accepts that if it were not for the fact that she is already married, then she would by now be the second Lady Kane.'

Tears stung Emma's eyes, and she strove to blink them away. Oh, what a gullible fool she'd been! How could she have been so witless as to believe Gerald's tale of a single repented night?

Stephen maneuvered his horse a little closer and leaned across to put his hand over hers. 'Emma, I—'

'Why didn't you tell me? Why did you let me remain in ignorance?' she cried.

'Because I hoped the affair was ending and that you would therefore never need to know about it. Emma, yours is an arranged match, and the world knows that such matches do not require faithfulness on the part of the husband, or on the part of the wife until she has produced the required heir. I confess that I was a little taken aback at your attitude yesterday, for you seemed to have taken it all so amazingly well, and I thought that you really were approaching it all with commendable calm.'

'Well, now you know that I have simply been a gull,' she whispered.

'You love him, don't you?'

She didn't reply, but snatched her reins to urge her horse back along the street toward the square. There were tears in her eyes, and her breath caught on a sob.

Stephen remained where he was for a moment. The strange dizziness of earlier had swept over him again, and he clung to the pommel of the saddle until it had passed; then he urged his mount after his sister.

She reached the house and dismounted, pausing only long enough to loop the reins over the iron railings before hurrying into the house. Saunders was in the ball, and he went quickly to the table near the front door, picking up a letter that lay with the various calling cards.

'Miss Rutherford, Lord Kane called very briefly to leave this letter.' He looked curiously at her, for she could not conceal her distress. 'Is something wrong, madam?'

'I'm quite well, thank you,' she replied, accepting the letter. Stephen entered, and spoke briefly to the butler. 'Saunders, have the horses returned to the stables, if you please.'

'Very well, sir.' The butler walked swiftly away to instruct a footman.

Stephen hesitated again, for the weakness had returned, and was more confusing this time. He felt suddenly very hot, and had to lean his hands on the table, his head bowed.

Emma saw nothing, for she was opening Gerald's letter. Her hands trembled, and she struggled to quell the bitterness and emotion that filled her. Then she read:

My dear Emma

I fear that I must cry off our drive this afternoon, for my duties as Lord Castlereagh's second have intervened. As you will have gathered, Lord Yarmouth and I were indeed summoned last night to be asked to act in the unfortunate matter of a duel. Lord Castlereagh has written a very long letter, setting out his grievances, and it has fallen to me to deliver it to the foreign secretary, who is at present at South Hill, near Windsor. The letter conveys to him that nothing short of a duel will suffice, and suggests a meeting at dawn tomorrow, Thursday, the twenty-first, near Lord Yarmouth's cottage at Putney Heath.

Knowing that the drive to South Hill will take some time, and wishing to return to London in time to see what else I can do in support of my friend, I have taken the precaution of writing this explanatory letter to you, which I will leave, as it is most unlikely that you will be up at such an early hour.

Seconds are required to do a great deal of negotiating, and I therefore doubt very much if I will be able to see you again before the duel, but I expect to call upon you directly it is over. I also trust that the outcome will be favorable to Lord Castlereagh.

Please forgive me for failing to keep our appointment this afternoon, but I know that you will forgive and understand.

Gerald

Slowly Emma folded the letter again. Oh, yes, she could forgive and understand his loyalty to Lord Castlereagh, and she would not expect him to behave otherwise, but she could never forgive or understand his lies and deception over the Countess of Purbeck. For all his protestations the day before, he had that morning risen from his mistress's bed, and that was something Emma Rutherford could not accept.

Stephen watched her in concern. 'What does it say, Sis?'

'Read it if you wish,' she replied, giving it to him.

He glanced through it and then looked anxiously at her. 'This is not the letter of a man who cares nothing for you, Emma. Please consider the matter very carefully, and don't do anything rash.'

'Stephen, at this moment I really don't know what I want to do. On the one hand I think that the marriage could still work, because there is sufficient warmth between Gerald and me, but then I am faced with his lies and the fact the countess is his mistress.'

'But if you love him . . .'

She lowered her eyes, and the tears wended their sad way down her pale cheeks.

Stephen tilted her chin, making her look at him. 'You do love him, don't you?'

Biting her lip, she nodded. 'Yes,' she whispered, 'yes, I love him with all my heart.'

'Then don't do anything you may regret. As his wife, you will hold all the trumps.'

'How can I possibly fight someone like the countess? She has everything, and she is a woman of the world, whereas I am little better than a country bumpkin.'

'Oh, Emma Rutherford, you sell yourself very short indeed. Kane likes you and wants to marry you. If he doesn't love you yet, then surely there is an excellent chance that he will come to love you. The countess may be beautiful and fascinating, but above all she is a *chienne*, as even Kane will eventually realize.'

'Stephen, he has lied to me about her, and I no longer trust him.'

'Please, Sis, give it a great deal of thought before you act. If you love Kane, then he's worth fighting for. Dammit, you'll be Lady Kane, you'll share not only his name but also his bed! I'd back you with such odds, Emma, believe me I would. Promise me that you won't do anything just yet.'

She swallowed. 'I don't know, Stephen—'

'Please, Emma. If not for yourself, then for Father. You know how delighted he is about the match. Promise?' He looked intently into her tear-filled eyes. 'Don't give in without a fight, Sis, for if you do, then you are simply handing her the victory. I know that Kane is at fault in this, but there is something about his letter which makes me feel he must be given another chance. It's the letter of a man of honor.'

She broke away at that. 'I'm tired of hearing about men of honor!' she cried, hurrying to the staircase.

'Emma . . .' Stephen took a hesitant step after her, but suddenly everything began to spin sickeningly around him. A fierce heat rushed over him, and the light began to fade, as if he were falling into a dark pit. A low moan escaped his lips as he lost consciousness and fell heavily to the floor.

Emma halted, whirling about as she heard him moan. 'Stephen?' Her eyes widened with alarm, and she ran back to his unconscious figure. She knelt beside him, putting her hand to his cheek. His skin burned to the touch, and his eyelids fluttered, but she couldn't arouse him.

Fresh tears stung her eyes, and she scrambled fearfully to her feet. 'Saunders! Saunders, come quickly!'

14

THAT EVENING, EMMA and her father waited anxiously outside Stephen's room, where Dr Longford was once again carrying out a thorough examination. Stephen was now in the grip of a fever, and muttered unintelligibly as he tossed on the bed. Emma felt dreadfully guilty, blaming herself for what had befallen her brother. If only she'd been more firm that morning, and had refused to let him get up or set out on the ride, and if only the physician had come immediately, but he had been out on another urgent call that had detained him for hours.

At last the doctor emerged, and his baleful glance fell immediately upon Emma. 'I can only presume that my instructions were ignored, madam.'

'Not exactly—' she began.

'I ordered that the patient was not to leave his bed, and yet it seems that not only was he encouraged to do this, but he was also allowed to leave the house itself! Perhaps I did not make myself perfectly clear after all, Miss Rutherford, for I cannot imagine that you would be remiss enough to permit all these things to happen when you knew what my instructions were, or that you—'

Mr Rutherford interrupted. 'Sir, I am more concerned now with how best to look after my son from this point on, rather than hold an inquest into what should or should not have been done previously. Now, then, what is your judgment of his condition?'

'My judgment is that he is suffering the effects of the blow to his head and that he has also contracted a very grave inflammation of the lungs. I have already administered some antimony powder to reduce the fever, but I shall also prescribe a strong dosage of willow bark. He must not be left alone, someone must sit with him at all times in order to continue giving him one hundred drops of laudanum every three hours, and also to be at hand should he enter a crisis. It is a very savage distemper, aggravated by the blow he received to the head at the time of his accident. His pulse is thin, low, and weak, but I am still confident that he will successfully throw off the ague. It will take time, however, and great care must be observed at all times to see that he does not suffer another setback. He is a healthy young man in every other respect, and should possess the physical strength and stamina to emerge safely from his grave difficulties. I have other patients I most attend now, but I will return in the morning to assess his progress. Should anything particularly untoward occur in the intervening time, then you must send for me immediately. Should I be unavailable, then I suggest that, depending upon the urgency of the situation, you contact either Dr Baillie of Conduit Street or Dr Farquarson of Berkeley Square.'

Mr Rutherford nodded. 'We will do that, Doctor.'

Dr Longford gave a cool bow, his disapproving glance encompassing Emma again for a moment, and then he again accepted a guinea coin, this time from Mr Rutherford.

As the doctor was going down the stairs, he paused as something else occurred to him. 'One thing more. It has always been my experience that toast water is a sovereign remedy for inflammation of the lungs. Instruct your cook to take dried crumbs of wheaten bread, it must be wheat, and boil them with a little butter and salt. The strained liquid is then to be given to the patent.' With that he went on down the staircase to the entrance hall, where Saunders was waiting to give him his hat, gloves, and cane.

As the front door closed upon him, Emma looked unhappily at her father. 'I'm so very sorry about this, Father—'

'You must not blame yourself, my dear.'

'If only I'd been more firm with Stephen—'

'Emma, I know only too well how insistent and willful your brother can be, and I am also aware of how unpredictable people are after a blow to the head. I have spoken to Dolly, and to Saunders, and so I know how difficult your position was. Maybe, with the benefit of what we know now, you should not have decided as you did, but it is always easy to say that after the event. You thought he was well, and no one blames you for that.'

Tears stung her eyes, and she hugged him. 'Thank you, Father.'

'Not at all, my dear,' he murmured, patting her trembling shoulder. 'Now, then, let us go in and see the patient.'

Stephen stirred restlessly in the bed, his cheeks aflame with fever as his head tossed deliriously from side to side. His valet was leaning anxiously over him, patting his fiery skin with a cloth dipped in cool lavender water. The room was very hot and stuffy, for the fire had again been banked up, and fresh flames were licking eagerly around the coals and logs.

Outside, the evening sun was beginning to sink toward the western horizon, for the day was drawing to a close. The sky was ablaze with crimson and gold, and thin horizontal clouds floated like islands in a flame-colored sea. It was going to be a cold night, and as Emma glanced out at the sprinkling of fallen leaves in the garden, she felt that autumn was advancing almost tangibly.

Mr Rutherford sat on the edge of Stephen's bed and took his hot hand. 'Stephen, my boy?'

Stephen's lips moved, but he didn't speak. His eyelids flickered, almost as if he were about to look at his father, but nothing happened.

'Can you hear me, my boy?'

Still there was no response.

The valet shook his head. 'He's out for the count, sir, and no mistake. The doctor said he might come around by dawn, or thereabouts.'

'Dawn? I see.' Mr Rutherford got up wearily and looked at Emma. 'I think we should divide the time we sit with him, my dear. I will remain with him now, for I slept all afternoon again, and am feeling relatively fresh at the moment. You, on the other hand, appear to be somewhat tired and over-anxious, and so I suggest you retire to your bed for a while.'

'But, Father—'

'Do as I say, Emma,' he insisted quietly, putting a firm hand on her arm. 'I perceived earlier that you were distressing yourself over this, and so I took the precaution of dispatching a footman to purchase valerian root from the apothecary. It will assist you to relax and sleep.'

'I don't want to sleep, Father.'

'I intend to sit with Stephen now, my dear, and I will be sure to send Dolly to awaken you when it is your turn. What point is there to us both sitting up with him, when it will only result in us both becoming tired at the same time? So do as I say, Emma. Dolly has already been instructed to prepare the valerian root for you, and I wish you to go to your bed now.'

Reluctantly she gave in. 'Very well, Father. You do promise to send for me if anything happens?'

'Of course.'

She kissed his cheek and then went to the bed, bending down to kiss Stephen. He muttered something unintelligible, but again made no other sign that he was closer to regaining consciousness.

With a heavy heart she left the room, walking slowly along the passage. A footman was lighting the chandeliers down in the entrance hall, holding up a candle on a long handle. The crystals jingled softly together, and the new flames flickered gently, setting soft shadows swaying on the walls and columns.

Dolly was waiting in her room, and the crushed valerian root was in a little dish on the bedside table. A silver spoon lay beside it.

Emma said very little as the maid helped her to undress. She sat before the dressing table, watching in the looking glass as the hair-brush crackled through her long dark curls. The curtains were drawn, but the sunset pierced a crack, falling in a narrow shaft across the floor and the wardrobes.

Wearing her lace-trimmed nightgown, Emma slipped reluctantly into her bed and accepted the valerian root.

'Shall I sit with you, Miss Emma?' asked the maid.

'No, that won't be necessary, Dolly.'

'You mustn't blame yourself, miss, for anyone would have done what you did.'

'Would they? I can't believe that I was so utterly foolish as to be taken in like that. I knew he wasn't well, and I knew what the doctor had said, but still I went out on that ride. I'll never forgive myself. Never.'

'Master Stephen will soon be quite well again, Miss Emma, and you'll be able to put all this behind you. He won't let you blame yourself, you may be sure of that.'

Emma smiled at the maid's sturdy support. 'What would I do without you, Dolly Makepeace?'

Dolly smiled as well. 'You try to sleep now, Miss Emma. And try to think of something pleasing, like Lord Kane.'

Emma's smile faded a little. 'Dolly, I'm afraid that Lord Kane is not a pleasing subject.'

'Miss Emma?' The maid was concerned.

'Good night, Dolly.'

'Miss Emma.' Dolly bobbed a little curtsy and then withdrew from the room, leaving a lighted candle by the bed.

Alone, Emma stared up at the canopy of her bed. With all that had happened since the early morning, she had been able to push thoughts of Gerald from her mind, but now those thoughts returned, causing her more pain than she could bear. She loved him so much, and she'd believed everything he said. How cruel, then, to know that the Countess of Purbeck had been his mistress all along, and that last night, at least, he'd been in her arms at the mansion in Upper Brook Street.

The tears were wet on Emma's cheeks, and she turned away to hide her face in the pillow. The happiness she had glimpsed so fleetingly now seemed to have been dashed into nothing. Raine, Countess of Purbeck, was a powerful adversary, perhaps even an invincible one, and to struggle against her was surely a futile exercise. Stephen said that society knew Gerald would have married his mistress had she been free, which meant that the second Lady Kane would never be more than a cipher. She couldn't proceed with the match, and when next she saw Gerald, she would tell him so. She would also tell him exactly why.

It was some time before her tears subsided and the valerian root lulled her into sleep. Her heart felt as if it had been torn in two, and the pain ached endlessly through her, so much so that when she slept, her dreams were a continuation of the heartbreak she was enduring at Gerald's hands. She could hear her heartbeats and see him as he faced her. His gray eyes were cold, and there was a cynical smile twisting his lips. He reminded her that he had never promised her a love match, and he called her a fool for ever presuming that he might regard her in anything other than a practical light.

The city was dark, and the clocks were striking two in the morning as a shadowy male figure slipped silently into the garden from the mews lane behind Grosvenor Square. It was a stealthy figure, stocky and broad-shouldered, and was dressed in an old brown boxcoat that had seen better days and a wide-brimmed beaver hat that kept his face completely in shadow. Not that his face could be seen anyway, for he wore a mask that left only his unshaven chin exposed.

As he reached Lady Bagworth's rose garden, he paused to tie some pieces of sacking over his boots so that they made no sound at all as he then continued toward the house, making his way toward the French doors of the library. When he reached them, he paused again, glancing up at the windows of the house. It was at Emma's windows in particular that he looked, and as he saw the telltale glow of a tiny light, he smiled.

He inserted the thin blade of a knife into the lock of the library windows, and after some careful and skilled manipulation was able to open them without a sound. Pocketing the knife, he stepped into the house, closing the French doors quietly behind him.

Crossing the dark, deserted library, he stealthily opened the door into the entrance hall. Everything was quiet, and he knew that the house was asleep. The sacking on his feet deadened all sound as he left the library and made his way up the staircase to the bedroom floor, pausing only to get his bearings before slipping along the passage to Emma's door.

He hesitated as he neared it, for there was a bright light shining from beneath another door nearby. He did not know that it was Stephen's room and that Mr Rutherford was reading while he kept vigil; he only knew that the light signified someone to be awake. The man listened at the door, but all was quiet beyond, and after a moment he continued past it.

He listened again at Emma's door, but was sure that she was asleep. Holding his breath, he gently turned the handle, peeping very cautiously inside as the door opened. The soft light from the night candle moved very gently, and he could see Emma lying

asleep, her dark hair in a tangle on the pillows. The man's lascivious gaze moved appreciatively over her, taking in the soft curve of
her bosom, outlined by the thin folds of her nightgown. Then he
drew a long breath, for he wasn't there to ogle the lady, he was
there to relieve her of the Kane Keepsake.

Closing the door behind him, he glanced swiftly around the
room, and then he went into the adjoining dressing room. Now,
then, where would she keep her jewels? He went to the dressing
table and opened the jewelry casket, but he saw immediately that
the particular red leather case wasn't there. He hoped she hadn't
taken the precaution of locking it away in a safe, for that would be
most inconvenient.

His glance fell upon the chest of drawers, and he went to it. A
smile broke out on his lips as he immediately espied the leather
case. He took it out and looked inside. The diamonds of the
Keepsake winked and glittered in the semi-darkness as he took the
Keepsake from its bed of velvet and pushed it into his pocket Then
he carefully replaced the leather case in the drawer, so that the
theft would not be realized until the moment someone actually
opened the case.

Quietly he retraced his steps to the bedroom door, listening
carefully before emerging into the passage. There wasn't a sound
in the house as he went back down to the entrance hall and out
through the library, closing the French doors so carefully behind
him that they looked as if they had never been forced.

A moment later his shadowy figure could be seen hurrying
silently back down the gardens toward the mews lane, and soon he
had vanished into the nearby streets. Behind him, no one in the
house was aware that he had ever been there, and no one was to
realize for some time that the Keepsake had been stolen.

The first fingers of dawn were lighting the eastern sky as Dolly
came to awaken Emma, who sat up sharply in the bed. 'Is everything all right? Is Stephen—?'

'Master Stephen is sleeping quietly, Miss Emma. Mr Rutherford
says I am to tell you that he thinks the delirium has gone and that
maybe the very worst is over.'

'I'll go to him now.' Emma flung back the bedclothes, shivering a little as she slipped from the bed.

Dolly brought her wrap, and then quickly brushed and combed her hair, leaving the dark curls to fall loose about her mistress's shoulders.

Before going to her brother, Emma went to the window to look briefly out at the dawn. This was the time Gerald had mentioned in his letter, when, unless Mr Canning apologized suitably for his odious conduct, the duel would take place on Putney Heath. There hadn't been any word the previous day to suggest that such an apology had been received, and so she could only guess that at this very moment the two protagonists were facing each other in some concealed dell. If they were, then she hoped that Lord Castlereagh would emerge the victor and unscathed.

Gerald had promised to call upon her when the duel was over, and when he did she would inform him that she was withdrawing from the match. This time there would be no hesitation; she would do what she had to in order to preserve her own dignity and pride.

15

EMMA SAT WITH Stephen all that morning. The fever and delirium had abated, and now he slept quite quietly. His cheeks were still fiery, and it was clear that he was far from well, but it seemed that he was responding to Dr Longford's medication. He had not opened his eyes at all, and he hadn't spoken intelligibly, but from time to time Emma felt that he was close to consciousness.

She sat by the window, for it was too hot by the fire. The September sun shone in on her neat light-green woolen gown with its long sleeves and frilled neck and cuffs. There was a golden locket around her throat, and she wore peridot earrings that caught the sunlight. She had discarded her white woolen shawl because of the heat, and it lay on the floor beside her chair as she turned another page.

There was a tap at the door, and Dolly peeped in. 'Begging your pardon, Miss Emma, but I thought you would like to know that there is a boy selling newsheets in the square, and he's calling out that Lord Castlereagh won the duel and that both gentlemen survived.'

'Are you sure?' asked Emma gladly.

'Quite sure, miss. Would you like me to purchase one of the sheets?'

'No, that won't be necessary. If Lord Castlereagh was the victor, that is all I really wish to know.'

'Yes, Miss Emma. Oh, and the cook wishes to know if she may discuss today's meals with you.'

'Would you tell her that I will leave the choice in her capable hands. I am sure that she knows best and that I would only be following her advice if we were to discuss it.'

'Yes, Miss Emma.' Dolly gave a quick curtsy and then withdrew again.

Emma sighed, closing the book. At Foxley Hall she had always discussed the meals with the cook, and she was far from ignorant about such things, but somehow she just didn't feel like considering such mundane matters as whether to serve fish or meat, or whether one combination of vegetables was preferable to another. And as to whether she and her father would rather have a syllabub or meringue and cream. On a day like this she really could not have cared less.

She glanced out the window. How lovely Lady Bagworth's garden looked, the autumn flowers so bright and cheerful. She wished she could take more pleasure in them, but she felt too empty and wretched inside to feel delight about anything. In the hours she had been sitting with Stephen, she had had time to think, and was sure that now she had found out about his long-standing affair with Raine, there was only one course she could take; she had to withdraw from the match with Gerald. Her father had been very tired when she had taken over from him at Stephen's bedside earlier that morning, and somehow the moment had not been appropriate to tell him of her decision, but she had to tell him soon, for she could hardly present him with a *fait accompli* by telling Gerald first. He would soon be awake again, and the first thing he would do would be to come to see how Stephen was faring. She would tell him then.

But unknown to her, her father was already awake, and was at that very moment going down the staircase to greet Gerald, who had arrived on the promised call to tell Emma how the duel had progressed.

MrRutherford's walking stick tapped on the marble staircase. 'Lord Kane, may I say how pleased I am to see you yet again, and how delighted I am to learn that Lord Castlereagh has vanquished his despicable opponent.'

Gerald returned the smile, coming to the foot of the steps. 'Maybe "vanquished" is a little too strong a word, sir, but the foreign secretary has certainly come off worse.'

'Was Mr Canning wounded?'

'A flesh wound in the thigh. Lord Castlereagh suffered the indignity of having a button shot from his coat.'

'The loss of a button is hardly a grave blow, sir, especially if the result of the entire matter is to restore Lord Castlereagh's honor.'

'He considers it in some way restored, sir, but is naturally still offended to have been so poorly used, and to know that it all took place with the knowledge of his fellow ministers in the government. However, I trust that today's encounter was the last we will hear of the matter.'

'I trust so too, sir.' Mr Rutherford smiled again. 'I cannot imagine that you have called to see me.'

'I promised Miss Rutherford that I would come to tell her about the duel.'

'Then tell her you shall. She is at present sitting with my son, whose condition has improved a little, but—'

'Condition?' interrupted Gerald quickly. 'Has something happened?'

'But of course you cannot possibly have heard. I fear that my son had an unfortunate accident in the Thames at the time you and my daughter were at Cranforth House. He was in the water for some time, and was then exposed to the cold air while being brought home here. It all resulted in a severe inflammation of the lungs, and we have been most concerned about him. I am told that this morning he appears to be much improved, although he has yet to awaken.'

'I'm very sorry to hear of this, Mr Rutherford.'

'I believe that the worst is now over, Lord Kane.' Mr Rutherford paused. 'Lord Kane, may I beg a favor of you?'

'By all means. I will do whatever is in my power.'

'It is but a small favor, and it concerns Emma. I fear that she blames herself for Stephen's condition—'

'Blames herself? But if he fell overboard from a boat—'

'On the morning after the accident, when Stephen had yet to fully show signs of his illness, he persuaded Emma to go for a ride with him. The ride came to a swift end, I know not why, but immediately on his return to this house, Stephen collapsed. Emma is convinced that if she had only stopped the ride from taking place, then her brother would not have been taken so ill. Maybe the ride was indeed a little unwise, but he was already very poorly, and the ride cannot have made any real difference. I would be most grateful if you could persuade her that she was not the cause of his condition.'

'I will do all I can, sir.'

Mr Rutherford nodded, content. 'Yes, I am sure you will, just as I am sure that you will succeed in your purpose, for it is clear to me that you and my daughter have hit it off. Arranged matches are of necessity hazardous affairs when it comes to how well the pair get on, but it was always my fervent hope that you and Emma would strike a perfect note.'

'She has most certainly struck that note with me, sir, and I can only hope that I have been similarly fortunate where she is concerned.'

'Oh, I'm sure you have, my boy,' Mr Rutherford replied. 'Come, let me take you to her. By the way, I dispatched the volume of Sir Joseph Banks's work to the earl the moment Emma informed me. I trust it is the book he seeks.'

'I believe it is, sir.'

Gerald accompanied Mr Rutherford up to the bedroom floor, and Mr Rutherford had to pause at the top of the second flight of steps, for he was a little out of breath. 'Plague take my health,' he grumbled. 'It is a constant irritation to me that my mind is as nimble as ever it was, but my wretched body grows ever more feeble. I vow that inwardly I am the same young man I ever was, but outwardly I am fast becoming a Methuselah.'

After a moment they walked on, and after the briefest of knocks on Stephen's door, Mr Rutherford ushered Gerald in.

Emma rose swiftly from her chair, her book falling to the floor. She was once again caught completely off guard by Gerald's arrival, just as it seemed she had been so frequently during their brief acquaintance. The last thing she had wished was to again be at such a disadvantage for this most vital meeting, but that was what had happened. Her feeling of having been cornered before she was ready increased as she saw how well he and her father were getting on.

Mr Rutherford came swiftly over to her, kissing her on the cheek. 'Lord Kane has come to tell you all about the duel, my dear,

and so I took the liberty of bringing him up here. How is Stephen?'
He left her to go to the bedside, looking down at his sleeping son.

'He is comfortable, Father,' she replied, glancing briefly at
Gerald. His gaze was upon her, his gray eyes dark and warm. She
felt her heartbeat quicken, and knew to her dismay that in spite of
all she had now learned of his deception and untruthfulness, she
still loved him. His closeness affected her, and to look into his eyes
was to fall deeper under his spell. She tore her glance away, going
to stand with her father at the bedside.

Mr Rutherford looked sadly down at his son. 'If only he would
speak to us, then I would feel that he is indeed on the road to
recovery.'

'I'm sure he is, Father, for he is responding well to the laudanum
and willow bark.'

'Have you been able to give him any of the toast water?'

'Just a spoonful or so.'

Mr Rutherford drew a long breath. 'As you say, he does appear
to be responding to the medication. He's certainly sleeping more
soundly.'

Emma didn't say anything, for as she looked down at her
brother, her sense of guilt returned. If only she'd stopped him
from going out on that ride. . . .

Mr Rutherford noticed her silence, and then glanced pointedly
at Gerald, who nodded slightly to indicate that he understood.
Emma's father then gave her a brisk smile. 'I'll leave you now, my
dear, for I'm sure you and Lord Kane would prefer a few moments
alone, and I was just about to go down for my breakfast.'

As her father withdrew tactfully from the room, Emma
remained at the bedside. Now that the moment was upon her and
she was alone with Gerald, she really did not know what to say.
She tried to remind herself that she had seen him leaving his
mistress's house after having spent the night there, but all she
could think now was that he was only a few feet away and that if
she reached out she could touch him.

He watched her as she stood by the bed. 'The fact that you went
out on that ride will not have made any difference, Emma,' he said
gently.

'I wish I could be certain of that. All I know is that I permitted him to go out into the cold morning air . . .' She broke off, remembering that cold air and the sound of a curricle's wheels on the cobbles of Upper Brook Street.

'He is ill because he fell in the river and because he was cold for some time after that.' Gerald went a little closer to her. 'Please don't blame yourself, for there is nothing you could have done to prevent this happening. If he did not appear as ill as he really was when you went out on that ride, you may be sure that he would still have collapsed even had he remained in his bed.'

She turned toward him. 'My father has obviously asked you to reassure me.'

'Yes, he has, but I am not saying anything that I would not have said to you anyway. It isn't your fault, Emma.' He put out his hand suddenly, as if to touch her cheek, and she moved quickly away, going to the window and looking out over the garden.

He could not have mistaken the action, for it was obvious that she had avoided the contact. 'Is something wrong, Emma?'

'I . . .' She bit her lip, for she couldn't bring herself to say what she planned. Instead she found herself asking about the duel. 'I understand that Lord Castlereagh was the victor at the duel,' she said.

For a moment he didn't reply, because he knew that that was not was really on her mind, but then he nodded. 'Yes, he was.'

'Please tell me about it.'

He went to the fireplace, leaning a hand on the mantelpiece and looking down into the roaring flames. 'Castlereagh, Yarmouth, and I arrived at the appointed place on Putney Heath at six o'clock in the morning. Castlereagh was surprisingly relaxed, indeed he hummed some of Madame Catalini's songs. I endeavored to reason with the foreign secretary's seconds, but they would not move. The distance was fixed at twelve paces, and the two gentlemen took up their positions. There was quite a crowd around the clearing, for word had more than got out. Avenley was there, of course.'

'Why do you say "of course"?'

'Because he can be guaranteed to turn up for anything upon which he has placed a wager, and judging by his smirk at the outcome, I can only imagine that his money was on Castlereagh.'

Emma said nothing more, for she could envisage Lord Avenley's look. She could see his single shining eye, and the cold smile on his thin lips.

Gerald continued. 'The first shots were exchanged, and neither man was struck. Yarmouth suggested to Castlereagh that a single exchange was sufficient, but Castlereagh would have none of it. The foreign secretary showed considerable courage, stating that he had come to give Castlereagh satisfaction and that it was therefore entirely up to Castlereagh when a halt should be called. The two opponents then took aim for a second time. Canning fired first, and his bullet took a button from Castlereagh's coat. Castlereagh then took aim, and wounded the foreign secretary in the fleshy part of the thigh. Castlereagh deemed his honor to be thus satisfied, and Canning was removed to Yarmouth's cottage nearby, where a surgeon attended his wound. I then accompanied Castlereagh back to London, where he was able to reassure Lady Castlereagh that all was well and that the matter was concluded.'

'I can imagine Lady Castlereagh's great relief.'

'She fell into floods of glad tears,' Gerald replied, smiling a little as he recalled.

'And that really is the end of it?'

He glanced at her. 'Except for the dividing of the spoils by the lucky wagerers. Avenley was especially gloating, which leads me to believe that he had a considerable amount resting on it. Not that he ever plays for low stakes, of course. Nothing that man does is ever for mere pennies,' he added, almost as an aside.

Emma turned from the window. 'Why do you and he despise each other so much?' she asked.

He straightened. 'It is an entirely personal matter, Emma, and the original cause is most definitely in the past.'

'I am not to be trusted with the facts?'

He met her eyes. 'That isn't what I said. Emma, something is quite obviously wrong, and I think you should tell me what it is.'

She steeled herself. 'It concerns the Countess of Purbeck,' she said.

To her surprise, he gave a brief laugh. 'Has she been dripping her poison again? Well, let me assure you that it will not happen again, at least not for some time. When you and she next encounter each other, you will be firmly ensconced as my betrothed, and soon after that you will become Lady Kane.'

'I . . . I don't understand . . .'

'She has left town for her husband's family seat in Sussex, and it is extremely unlikely that she will return to London for at least two months.' He smiled a little. 'And should you be wondering how I know all this, let me tell you that it is because I called upon her the evening before last, after Yarmouth and I had been summoned to Castlereagh. I was angry with her because of her conduct toward you, and I meant to speak to her in no uncertain terms. She was not at home when I called, but was expected at any moment, and so I waited, kicking my heels in her drawing room. The hours passed, and I knew that it would soon be too late for me to see you about having to cancel our plans for a drive because of my duties as Castlereagh's second. I was still determined to see the countess, however, and so I decided to write a letter to you while I waited. After the letter, I helped myself to a glass or two of the earl's good port, and then made the grave mistake of sitting down in a comfortable armchair. I fell asleep, and was only awoken the next morning by the sound of the countess's rather hasty return. She was in a panic because she'd caught wind of the momentous return from the dead of her stepson, who was believed to have been lost at sea two years ago. The Earl of Purbeck is apparently overjoyed to have his son restored to him, but the countess is anything but delighted, for she and the son loathe the very sight of each other, and she has lost no opportunity in the past to blacken his name. There is no doubt that the son will now seek to redress the balance, and will do all he can to persuade his father to divorce her. She dares not take this possibility lightly, for if there is one person the earl dotes on more than she, it is his son. I left her in the middle of her panic-stricken preparations for the journey to Sussex, and I said nothing to her about you, for there seamed no point. She was hardly aware of my presence, she was so taken up with alarm that ruin was looming on the horizon. I therefore drove straight here to leave the letter, and then proceeded the thirty miles to Windsor, to the foreign secretary's residence.'

Emma stared at him, not knowing quite what to say, for she hadn't expected him to volunteer what sounded like a very plausible explanation indeed. A flicker of hope stirred within her. 'Is that really why you were at her house?'

He studied her carefully. 'Yes. Why do you ask?'

She lowered her eyes. 'Because Stephen and I saw you leaving.'

He was silent for a moment. 'And you concluded that I had been there for much more improper reasons?'

She colored, unable to meet his eyes. 'Yes. Stephen said that it is all over town that you and the countess—'

'Emma, the countess has been spreading all manner of wishful thinking over town, but none of it is based on fact. I can quite believe that your brother may have heard whispers, but I promise you that the story I told you is the truth of it. My dealings with her amounted to one much-regretted night last spring, no less, and certainly no more.' He left the fireplace and came to her. 'Have you been worrying over this?'

'I didn't want to believe it, but it seemed that I had the evidence of my own eyes, and then when Stephen told me what he'd heard—'

He stopped her words by putting his hand to her cheek. 'This is one occasion when the smoke of scandal has no fire at all behind it.'

'Stephen was told that if it were not for the fact that the countess is married already, then she would by now be Lady Kane.'

'That is what the countess wishes, but I promise you it has never been my wish.' His thumb moved against her skin. 'I'm not in love with her, Emma, and I would never be taken in by her, for she is too clear an echo of Margot. My lapse with Raine was a moment of madness, one I sometimes cannot credit I surrendered to, and certainly one which I would never repeat.' He lowered his hand. 'I married Margot because I was head over heels in love with her, so infatuated that I could not see her as she really was. I learned a very painful lesson, and in the end I despised her.'

'Oh, Gerald . . .'

His eyes were dark and warm. 'Emma, you are more fascinating and enchanting than Margot ever was, or Raine ever will be, and I would never be unfaithful to you.'

Before she knew it, he had bent his head forward to kiss her lingeringly on the lips. His arm slid around her waist, drawing her closer, and for a breathless moment she could feel his heart beating close to hers. A thousand and one emotions seized her, making her feel weightless, as if she would float away if he did not hold her. Her lips trembled beneath his as she returned the kiss.

He drew back then, his eyes even darker. 'Do you trust me now, Emma?' he asked softly.

Had a spell been cast over her, she could not have been more under his influence. 'Yes,' she whispered, 'I trust you.'

'It would be so easy to fall hopelessly in love with you, so very easy . . .' He kissed her again, his warm lips moving luxuriously over hers, and this time her senses stirred eagerly to meet him. She linked her arms around his neck, giving in to all the passion he had aroused from the first moment she had seen him. Love and desire swirled together through her veins, and from the depths of her former misery she was now raised to the dizzying heights of ecstasy.

Slowly he released her. 'I think it is time I left,' he said softly. 'By conducting myself in this manner, I have almost taken monstrous advantage of your father's discretion and hospitality.'

'When will I see you again?' she asked, her voice barely above a whisper.

'I do not think it can be before tomorrow evening's assembly. Tonight I am dining at Carlton House, and tomorrow morning my lawyer has countless tiresome documents for me to examine and sign, concerning the sale of some of my Scottish land. I am free tomorrow afternoon, but I rather think that you will wish to rest in readiness for the night, which I can guarantee will be very long and tiring.' He smiled. 'In my experience, ladies usually resort to a little previous sleep rather than trust to their stamina for a lengthy and very noisy social occasion.'

Even his smile caressed her. She was so happy that she felt lightheaded, as if she had had several glasses of champagne. Was it really possible for everything to change so completely? Only a few minutes ago she had been sad and heartbroken, but now she felt as if she could dance on air. The following evening seemed a lifetime away. 'I am sure you are right about resting, and so I will take your advice.'

'I will come here at about nine o'clock, and I will enlist Lady

Castlereagh's assistance again.' He drew her hand to his lips, kissing her palm, and then he went to the door, but there he paused again. 'I almost forgot to tell you that my grandfather has now elected to definitely accept the Manchester House invitation, and so I think it would be entirely appropriate if you wore the Keepsake.'

'I will do that.'

'Until then.'

She nodded. 'Until then.'

The door closed behind him, and Emma suddenly hugged herself with joy, turning around several times so that the hem of her gown fluttered around her ankles and the ribbons of her day bonnet danced against her hair. Her lips still tingled from his kisses, and his tender words rang in her ears. *It would be easy to fall hopelessly in love with you, so very easy. . . .*

A weak voice behind her brought her dancing to a standstill. 'Hello, Sis.'

She whirled gladly around to see Stephen smiling wanly at her.

16

STEPHEN WAS STILL very frail indeed, and he slept for most of the afternoon and evening, but he was able to take a little broth and drink a good draft of the toast water. He complained of a searing pain in his chest, and both Emma and her father remained alarmed about this until Dr Longford called again and could assure them that this was only to be expected with severe inflammation of the lungs. He insisted that the willow bark and laudanum should continue to be administered, and declared that in his opinion the patient would soon show signs of steady progress, provided he was not foolish enough to leave his bed before the medication had had time to assert its beneficial effect. The doctor laid great emphasis upon this, eyeing Emma as he did so, thus making it clear that he had very little faith in the household's ability to observe even the most simple of instructions. Then, with another guinea safely in his pocket, he again departed.

Emma and her father slept well that night, and both of them for the same two reasons: Stephen's turn for the better and Emma's happy new understanding with Gerald. Mr Rutherford, who knew nothing of how close the match had come to ending, could not have been more delighted that things were progressing so well, and before retiring declared that if only he could arrange a similarly successful contract for Stephen, he would be a very happy man.

The beautiful September weather continued, albeit still with that chill of autumn that was so fast turning the leaves to russet and gold. In other years such endless days of sunshine would have meant a prolonging of summer, but this year was different. Emma awoke and left her bed to look out the window at the gardens of Mayfair. Oh, yes, she thought, this year was so very, very different, for it had changed her life completely. She was filled with happiness, and now, even though she was still alarmed at the possibility of being presented to the Prince of Wales, she could not wait for the evening to come, so that she could be with Gerald again.

She dressed in a lemon wool gown, and Dolly pinned her hair up into a simple knot. Then, with a green-and-white floral shawl around her shoulders, she went to see Stephen. She found that her father was already there.

Stephen had had a comfortable night, but was still very weak and suffering a great deal of pain in his chest. Propped up on his pillows for a while, he had managed to drink some more of the cook's nourishing beef broth. He was a little drowsy from the laudanum, but was obviously making the steady progress predicted by the physician. His sense of humor surfaced from time to time, especially when Emma tried to persuade him to drink some more of the toast water.

'I'd prefer not to, for it tastes like gnats'—'

Mr Rutherford looked sternly over his spectacles. 'That will do, sir.'

'Well, it does taste like it.'

'No doubt. Nevertheless, it is prescribed for you by the physician, and so you will drink it.'

Stephen pulled a face, but made no more protest as Emma put the spout of the posset cup to his lips.

She smiled. 'There, that isn't so bad, is it?'

'Just wait until you are ill, sister mine, and I'll make you drink some foul concoction like this.' He leaned his head back on the pillows. 'Oh, how I long for a generous measure of cognac.'

'All in good time,' she replied, putting the posset cup down again and then sitting on the edge of the bed.

Mr Rutherford came to stand beside her. 'And how are you this morning, missy?'

'I'm very well.'

'Yes, so I see. I vow I haven't seen your eyes sparkle so much for far too long.'

'I couldn't be happier.'

143

He patted her shoulder fondly. 'Nor could I, my dear, nor could I. By the way, I have to announce that I am venturing forth tonight.'

She looked up quickly. 'You're coming to Manchester House with me?' she asked hopefully.

'No, my dear, for I fear that would prove too arduous. As it happens, I am only going two doors away from here. I looked out of my bedroom window this morning and I saw a well-remembered face alighting from a carriage just along the pavement. It was none other than my old school crony Algie Winchester. I haven't seen him for twenty years or more, but I'd know that hook nose and stooping posture anywhere. I sent a footman out immediately, and as a result I am to dine with Algie this very evening. I do not think that a few seconds in the night air will do me any harm, and I can wrap up as warmly as possible. Oh, I am looking forward to it, for we have so many old times to remember.'

'Just take care, Father,' said Emma.

'Don't fuss, my dear, for I promise you won't have two invalids to take care of. I am feeling much restored after the journey here, and I hardly think that dining *à deux* with an old friend is likely to cause a crisis.' He patted her shoulder again. 'Come now, let us go down for breakfast, and leave Stephen to rest again.'

After breakfast, encouraged by the sunshine and by the decision to rest that afternoon in readiness for the long night ahead, Emma decided to go for a walk around the square. Wearing her orange wool pelisse trimmed with brown braiding, and her gold-tasseled brown beaver hat, she emerged from the house with Dolly, and they set off to make a circumambulation of the square.

They passed the junctions of Charles Street and Grosvenor Street in the southeastern corner, and then walked north toward the junctions of Brook Street and Duke Street. Then they walked west, toward the junctions of North Audley Street and Upper Brook Street. Emma felt nothing as she gazed toward the street that had first held such mystery and then such misery for her. She wondered how the countess was progressing at the Earl of Purbeck's family seat. Was her newly returned stepson doing all he could to dislodge her? Emma was uncharitable enough to hope so, for nothing could have been more unpleasant or spiteful than the countess's recent conduct.

In the square's central garden, the equestrian statue shone brightly in the sunlight, and the light breeze rustled through the trees. Some men were raking the gravel paths, and another was painting the wrought-iron railing. The flower girl was seated in her usual place, and everything was very calm and peaceful, but suddenly there was a clatter of hoofs, and Emma glanced along Upper Brook Street again to see a party of fashionable gentlemen returning from a ride in Hyde Park. They were very stylish indeed, mounted on Arabian horses that were kept solely for rides in the park. The horses had long manes and tails, and stepped high as they trotted. The gentlemen had their greyhounds with them, rangy, lean beasts that padded silently in the wake of the horses.

The horsemen and the two women reached the corner of the square at the same time, and while his companions rode on, accompanied by the greyhounds, one of the riders reined in. 'Good morning, Miss Rutherford.'

The remembered voice struck a cold note, and Emma looked up swiftly into Lord Avenley's single shining eye. He was dressed in a sage-green riding coat and white kerseymere breeches, and his hat was worn at a rakish angle. A jeweled pin reposed in the folds of his neckcloth, and he carried a gold-handled riding crop. His horse was a prancing, glossy-coated chestnut, and he maneuvered it in front of her as she and Dolly made to cross the junction to the western side of the square.

Emma drew back. 'Please let us pass, sir,' she demanded.

'So unfriendly? Come now, Miss Rutherford, at least be civil enough to observe the courtesies.'

'I have no reason or need to oblige you with courtesy, sir,' she replied.

'Indeed? I would be careful what you say, my dear, for I promise you that I hold all the trumps.'

She was so anxious to escape that she didn't really hear what he said. 'Please allow us to pass,' she said again, walking further along the pavement.

He turned his horse, and again blocked her way. 'How very determined you are to escape from me, I vow I am most disappointed. Was it maybe something that I said?' His tone was taunting and cool, as if he found her reactions irritating as well as foolish.

She halted, unable to keep the loathing from her eyes and voice. 'You know full well that I have every reason to despise you, sirrah, and by your conduct now you prove more and more that you are most definitely not a gentleman!'

Suddenly he was unsmiling, and his eye became very cold. 'Have a care, my dear, for it would not do for you to go too far. As I have already warned you, I hold all the trumps.

At last his words were borne in on her. 'What trumps?' she asked warily.

'Well, to begin with, there is the small matter of your brother's IOUs. Offend me too greatly, and I will not hesitate to call them in immediately.' His smile was made even more menacing by the black velvet eye patch. 'And then there is the matter of your regard for Kane. I can only imagine that you wish to cling to your extraordinarily fortunate match.'

'My match has nothing whatsoever to do with you, sir, and as to your threat to call my brother's debts in, I suppose there is nothing I can say to make you change your mind.'

'On the contrary, my dear, there is a great deal you can say.'

He frightened her a little, and she wished he would leave her alone. 'Please allow us to pass, my lord,' she requested again.

'Pass by all means, Miss Rutherford,' he replied, maneuvering his horse aside, but as she and Dolly made to hurry by, he spoke again. 'You will hear from me again soon, Miss Rutherford, and when you do, you would be well advised to respond without any foolish delay. As to tonight's little jaunt to Manchester House, I don't think you should count upon going, for I rather fancy you will find yourself otherwise occupied.'

Her steps faltered, and she turned quickly to look up at him, but he urged his horse away, riding swiftly in the wake of his companions, who had already left the square again.

Dolly moved closer to her mistress. 'What did he mean by that, Miss Emma?'

'I don't know, Dolly. I only wish I did.' Emma shivered suddenly, for the breeze stirred more strongly across the open square, and there was a chill in it that seemed to reach through her clothes to touch her skin. Some leaves scuttered dryly over the cobbles, and Emma began to walk on, her steps quicker than before. A feeling of impending danger settled chillingly over her, and there was no longer any pleasure to be had from the morning sun.

At the door of the house, she turned to Dolly. 'I don't intend to mention this to anyone, Dolly, for if it should reach my father's ears, then it would alarm him unnecessarily.'

'Unnecessarily? But, Miss Emma, what if Lord Avenley was really threatening you?'

'And what if he was merely amusing himself by worrying me? I think it best to opt for the latter possibility, don't you?'

Dolly nodded reluctantly. 'Yes, miss. I suppose so.'

They went into the house, but in spite of her brave words, Emma felt very uneasy indeed. Lord Avenley was up to something, and she wished she knew what it was.

She rested that afternoon, but could not put Lord Avenley from her thoughts. She tried to extract enjoyment from the preparations for the evening, languishing in a rose-scented bath and washing her hair so that she would be sure it shone for the assembly. She and Dolly then spent an agreeable hour discussing exactly which gown and accessories she would wear, but at no time did either of them go to the chest of drawers to take out the Keepsake, which Emma had promised Gerald she would wear.

They decided at last upon a gown that would have been considered far too daring in Dorchester, but which was entirely acceptable in London. It was a sleeveless white silk slip with a low scoop neckline, and over it was a gown of the most delicate, transparent green-and-silver plowman's gauze. The sleeves were long and diaphanous, and gathered with silver strings at the wrists. The sheerness of the gauze was quite breathtaking, for it hid nothing of the flimsy slip beneath, and the slip was in turn so fine and dainty that it outlined her figure to perfection. Yes, indeed, very daring for Dorset, but ideal for a high-society assembly in London, as she had very swiftly realized when she had attended the theater.

An hour before Gerald and the Castlereaghs were due to arrive,

Emma sat before the dressing-table mirror while Dolly combed and pinned her hair. Emma knew that her hair was one of her best features, and so was always loath to conceal it in tight, rather unbecoming knots, even though such things were the height of fashion. She preferred to show off the length and thickness of her dark curls by allowing at least one ringlet or tress to fall. For tonight she asked Dolly to make that single ringlet very heavy indeed, and to twine it with a string of silver spangles that she had discovered so unexpectedly in the Dorchester haberdashery she frequented most. There was something so very French and stylish about the spangles, that finding them in a small shop in an English country town was really most astonishing. Now, as Dolly twined them around the thick ringlet, Emma knew that she had purchased very wisely indeed, for they set off her hair as nothing else would. Her coiffure was completed by a tall comb that sparkled with tiny diamonds, which would in turn complement the Keepsake when it was pinned to her shoulder.

Her evening cloak was in readiness over the fireside chair, and her shawl was already folded inside her muff. The clock on the bedroom mantelpiece whirred and then began to chime nine. As it did so, there was a knock at the door.

Dolly went to answer it, and Saunders was admitted. He had come to tell her that Gerald and Lady Castlereagh had arrived and that a running footman had also just delivered a note for her. The butler held out a silver tray, on which the sealed note lay.

Emma took the note and then glanced at him. 'Did you say Lord Kane and Lady Castlereagh? Isn't Lord Castlereagh with them?'

'No, madam. It seems that he is detained on government business, and will be going direct to Manchester House when it is completed.'

'Very well. Would you inform Lord Kane and Lady Castlereagh that I will be only a moment or so?'

'Madam.' He bowed and began to withdraw.

'Oh, Saunders, has my father left already?' she asked.

'Yes, madam, he went about half an hour ago. Master Stephen is asleep, and the cook says that he drank a goodly bowl of broth a short while ago.'

She smiled. 'Thank you, Saunders.'

He bowed again and went out.

She glanced at the note, wondering who could have sent it, and as she broke the seal, Dolly suddenly remembered the Keepsake.

'Oh, Miss Emma, we almost forgot the Keepsake!' she cried, hurrying to the chest of drawers.

Emma began to read the note. *If you wish to retrieve certain property, including IOUs, and if you wish to save your match, you will call upon me immediately. Forget Manchester House, for I still hold all the trumps, and will not hesitate to play them. Tell no one of this.*

An icy chill settled over Emma as she read it. It wasn't signed, and was written in a disguised hand that was far too clumsy to be Lord Avenley's, but he it was who had sent it, for who else would write of trumps?

Behind her, Dolly's breath caught with dismay. 'Miss Emma! The Keepsake isn't here, the box is empty!'

Emma whirled around, suddenly realizing what the note had meant about retrieving certain property. The Keepsake had been stolen, and Lord Avenley had it! Her mouth ran dry as she read the note again. What should she do? Should she ignore the final words, and tell Gerald without delay? This was her first and natural instinct, but then she thought again. What did Lord Avenley mean about saving her match? He had the Keepsake and Stephen's IOUs, so did he also possess something that would endanger her future with Gerald? She was afraid, for Lord Avenley was not a man to make empty threats where something like this was concerned, and there was too much at stake for her to ignore the danger by telling Gerald what had happened. Her mind was made up in a moment. Somehow she had to cry off Manchester House, even at this late hour, and instead she had to find out what Lord Avenley wanted of her.

Dolly was waiting anxiously. 'Miss Emma! Did you hear me? The Keepsake has gone!'

'I heard you, Dolly.' Taking a long breath to steady herself, Emma turned to the frightened maid. 'Dolly, I have to go to Avenley House tonight, instead of accompanying Lord Kane, and so I wish you to listen very carefully to my instructions.'

'But, Miss Emma—'

'Do as I say, Dolly. Lord Avenley has the Keepsake!'

The maid's eyes widened.

'Bring my white feather boa, for it must be arranged carefully around my shoulders so that Lord Kane will not know I'm not wearing the Keepsake. Hurry!'

The maid hastened to the wardrobes, and a moment later returned with the boa, which with trembling hands she arranged around the shoulders of Emma's green-and-silver gown.

Emma looked urgently at her. 'I'm going to pretend that I'm really going to Manchester House, and you must accompany me downstairs with my cloak and muff, but then I will affect to feel faint and unwell, and I want you to beg me not to go out. You are to tell Lord Kane that I was unwell this afternoon, and that you feel it is most unwise for me to leave the house.'

'Miss Emma, I think you should tell Lord—'

'I daren't do that, Dolly, and if you don't obey me in this, I swear I'll pack you off without a reference!' Emma cried, distraught with nerves.

The maid flinched. 'I . . . I'll do as you wish, Miss Emma.'

Emma strove to calm the wild tumult of anxiety that welled up inside her. She didn't want to do Lord Avenley's vile bidding, and she certainly didn't want to deceive Gerald, but she felt she had no choice. Maybe she was acting too hastily, but she had to make a spur-of-the-moment decision, and under the circumstances she hoped the decision had been correct. Clenching her fists to dig her fingernails into the palms of her hands, a ruse she had always found concentrated her thoughts, she nodded at the maid, and they left the room.

Lady Castlereagh's tinkling laughter echoed up from the hall, two floors below, and Emma paused at the balustrade to look down. Gerald was superb in formal black, with an amethyst pin in his lace-edged cravat. His hair was tousled, and he was smiling. To Emma he had never looked more handsome, or more dear. Guilt lanced miserably through her, for she didn't want to lie to him, indeed it was the last thing she wished to do. But she felt compelled to do as Lord Avenley instructed.

Lady Castlereagh was wearing a peach silk tunic dress over a gold satin slip, and her hair was concealed by a golden turban adorned with aigrettes and strings of pearls. She was in bubbling high spirits, and evidently felt a great deal better now that the duel was over and done with. She saw Emma and Dolly descending and tapped Gerald's arm with her closed fan.

He turned, coming to the foot of the staircase to greet Emma. His warm glance took in her gown and hair, and he nodded approvingly. 'You look exquisite, Emma,' he said softly, drawing her hand to his lips.

Oh, how she hated herself. She managed a smile, but it was a weak one, and she saw how swiftly he became concerned.

'Is something wrong?' he asked, still holding her hand.

'I . . .' It was painfully easy to act as if she were unwell, for in truth she felt dreadful. She closed her eyes for a moment and swayed on her feet.

Dolly immediately carried out her instructions. 'Oh, Miss Emma, I really don't think you're well enough to go out tonight. Please stay at home.'

Gerald looked anxiously into Emma's eyes. 'You are unwell?'

'I have had a terrible headache, and now I feel a little dizzy. I fear I may have eaten something that disagrees with me.'

Lady Castlereagh came over. 'Oh, my poor dear, you look quite low. Gerald, we simply cannot take the dear creature out, not to Manchester House, which resembles a bear garden at the best of times.'

'You're right, of course,' he replied, putting his hand gently to Emma's pale cheek. 'You stay at home and rest, for it would be quite wrong to expose you to an arduous evening when you are feeling under the weather. Take care of yourself, and I will call upon you tomorrow.'

'Please extend my apologies, and tell your grandfather that I am truly sorry not to see him tonight.'

'I'll tell him.' He hesitated, glancing at Lady Castlereagh, but then he kissed Emma's cheek. 'I'll see you tomorrow,' he whispered.

A moment or so later Saunders closed the door behind than, and Emma heard the carriage drive away. She was periously close to tears, but somehow she fought them back.

She waited until the butler returned from the door. 'Saunders, I wish you to have the carriage brought around without delay.'

He blinked. 'I beg your pardon, madam?'

'See that the carriage is brought to the door without delay.'

Having really been taken in by her display of indisposition, he could not hide his perplexity. 'But, madam, I thought—'

'I am perfectly well, Saunders. Please do as I instruct.'

He recovered apace. 'Very well, madam,' he murmured, bowing and then withdrawing toward the kitchen.

Emma removed the boa and then turned to Dolly. 'Give me the cloak and muff, and then hurry to your room and put on your own mantle, for I wish you to accompany me.'

'Yes, Miss Emma.' The maid helped her with the cloak and then hurried away with the boa. Five minutes later the carriage arrived at the door, and Emma and the maid emerged from the house. Shortly after that they were on their way to Avenley House, Pall Mall.

17

STREETLAMPS SHONE IN through the carriage windows as Emma and Dolly were conveyed south down the slope of St James's Street toward Pall Mall. St James's Street was where most of the more superior gentlemen's clubs were to be found, clubs such as White's, Brooks's, and Boodle's, and as a consequence there were a number of private carriages drawn up at the curb. At the southern end of the street was the impressive red brick façade of Tudor St James's Palace, and it was here that Pall Mall began, leading away to the east at a right angle.

Named originally after the game of pell-mell, which was played with a mallet and boxwood ball along a wide wooden alley several hundred yards in length, Pall Mall was now a fine thoroughfare. Pell-mell had long since ceased to be fashionable, and the wooden alley had disappeared, to be replaced by large and elegant residences, stylish shops, and another scattering of exclusive clubs, such as that at Avenley House. It had once been as masculine a domain as Bond Street and St James's Street, but in daytime its pavements were crowded with elegant ladies eager to examine or purchase the fashionable wares that filled the shops. At night, however, respectable ladies would only drive along Pall Mall in their carriages, for the pavements had become the territory of women of a less virtuous nature.

Emma glanced out uneasily, for this was the first time she had been out alone at night with just Dolly for company. She was filled with misgivings about what she was doing, for she knew only too well that she should not be obeying Lord Avenley, but she had committed herself now, and meant to go through with it.

Avenley House stood on the south side of Pall Mall, almost opposite one of the narrow streets that led into nearby St James's Square, where Gerald's town residence was to be found, as was that of Lord Castlereagh. The carriage drew up at the curb, and Emma looked up at the beautiful seventeenth-century building that was one of the most impressive in the street. Built by a Dutch architect for a wealthy nobleman from Breda, it was constructed in three bays with a stone pediment above the central portion. There were tall symmetrical windows, and the whole was built of red brick with stone facings, and there was a stone porch jutting out on sturdy columns across the wide pavement. There were lights in all the windows, but the blinds and curtains were drawn to keep out prying eyes. Two footmen in brown-and-gold livery stood beneath the porch, and behind them the door was open to reveal a dazzling entrance hall illuminated by numerous glittering chandeliers.

Dolly looked urgently at her mistress. 'There is still time to change your mind, Miss Emma. We could go home now, and no one would be any the wiser.'

'I cannot do that, Dolly, for I have to find out what Lord Avenley wants.' Before the maid's pleading could weaken her resolve, Emma raised her hood and began to open the carriage door.

The two footmen had looked in puzzlement at the vehicle as it drew up, for it was most unusual for a lady to call at these premises, especially at night. They were galvanized into action as it became plain that Emma was about to alight. Quickly they opened the door for her, and then lowered the iron rungs so that she could step down to the pavement.

They glanced at each other, for this was no *belle de nuit*; then the nearer of them addressed her. 'May I be of any assistance, madam?'

'I believe that Lord Avenley is expecting me.'

They glanced at each other again, uncertain of what to do. Ladies simply were not admitted when the gaming club was in progress, and they did not know what to do.

A figure suddenly appeared in the doorway behind them. It was Lord Avenley himself, clad superbly in evening black, his single eye resting brightly upon Emma. 'Good evening, my dear. Do please come inside.'

The footman stood aside for her, and Emma reluctantly gathered her cloak and skirts to enter the building. Dolly followed her, her eyes huge as she glanced around the magnificent pink-and-white marble entrance hall, at the far end of which a handsome double staircase swept grandly up to the floor above.

Emma was very careful to keep the hood of her cloak over her head, for the last thing she wished was to be recognized. She could see the gaming club beyond an Ionic colonnade to her right. Lamps hung low over a number of green baize tables, where gentlemen sat engrossed in their hands of cards. There was a murmur of voices, together with the chink of coins and glasses, and now and then came a burst of laughter. The smell of tobacco smoke hung in the air, and the chandeliers' crystal droplets tinkled together softly in the draft from the open door to the street.

Lord Avenley was about to usher them both toward the staircase, when a small group of gentlemen chose that moment to leave the club, and called to him as they emerged into the entrance hall. Emma's dismay knew few bounds when she recognized among the voices that of Stephen's friend Jerry Warburton, who was also related to Gerald.

Concealing his irritation, Lord Avenley excused himself from the two women and went to speak briefly with the departing gentlemen. Emma was careful to keep her head averted so that Jerry would not see her face, but Dolly was not as vigilant, and looked openly toward them.

Before Emma could whisper a warning to the maid, Jerry suddenly turned directly toward the two women, his glance coming to rest on Dolly's face. His brows drew together as he realized that he had seen her somewhere before, and quite recently at that. 'I say,' he said suddenly, 'don't I know you?'

Dolly's breath caught, and she shook her head quickly. 'Oh, no, sir, I've never seen you before.'

'Are you quite sure?'

'Certain, sir.'

Lord Avenley began to usher the gentlemen toward the door, and Jerry glanced back over his shoulder, obviously still puzzling over why Dolly seemed so familiar, but then he and his friends were out in the street, and the footmen were hailing their carriage.

Lord Avenley returned, his bright eye upon Emma. 'Please come this way, Miss Rutherford, for you and I have much to discuss.' He indicated the staircase.

Emma shook her head. 'Lord Avenley, I am sure that you can speak to me down here.'

'As you have already discovered, this entrance hall is a rather public place, Miss Rutherford. Besides, what I have to say to you is far too important and private to be aired anywhere but in seclusion.'

'I would prefer—'

'Miss Rutherford, do you wish to retrieve the Keepsake and your brother's notes?' he interrupted sharply.

'Yes.'

'Then please be so kind as to accompany me upstairs, where we may speak in private. If you do not, then there is no point in coming here at all, for I will carry out my threat and ruin your match with Kane.'

Emma knew that he meant what he said, and without further resistance she walked toward the staircase. Dolly accompanied her, and they were both conscious of his steps on the staircase a few feet behind them. At the top they paused, and he indicated some tall, elegantly decorated double doors to their right.

'Please come this way, Miss Rutherford,' he murmured; then he looked at Dolly. 'You may remain out here, girl, for what I have to say is strictly between two, not three.'

Emma's eyes flew unhappily to the maid, but there was nothing for it but to obey his instruction. He had already opened one half of the double door, and she went inside. As the door closed upon them, Dolly hurried toward it, crouching down and putting her eye to the keyhole. She found that not only could she see a great deal of the handsome crimson-and-gold drawing room beyond, but also she could hear what was being said.

She saw her mistress in the center of the room, one hand resting nervously on the polished surface of a fine inlaid table, and she saw Lord Avenley move to the fireplace. Emma's attention was turned away from him as she glanced around the room, and Dolly saw him suddenly reach up to a clock on the mantelpiece. He took something from a hiding place at the back of the clock and put it in his pocket, before replacing the clock in its former position. Emma sensed nothing as at last she turned to face him.

'What exactly do you want of me, Lord Avenley?'

'Please allow me to take your cloak and muff, Miss Rutherford, for I am sure I find it a little warm in here,' be said softly.

'I am quite comfortable, sir,' she replied, but she did push her hood back. 'Why have you forced me to come here?' she asked.

'Why, so that you will have the opportunity to retrieve the Keepsake, spare your brother from debt, and at the same time save your match from perdition,' he said, smiling coolly.

'And how may I do all this?'

'Is it not abundantly clear to you, Miss Rutherford? I find you very desirable indeed, and if my original intent was merely to make things awkward for Kane's new marriage by luring your fool of a brother into debt, that is no longer my sole purpose. Your match can remain intact, provided you come to me. I wish to enjoy your charms, my dear, and in return for one night with you, I will give back the Keepsake and the IOUs, and I will leave your match with Kane alone in future.'

Emma stared at him, deeply shaken by his words, and outside the door, Dolly's eyes widened.

Lord Avenley gave another cool smile. 'I cannot imagine that my terms come as all that much of a shock to you, Miss Rutherford, for it must have been obvious to you that I admired you.'

'I would rather die than give myself to you,' she whispered.

'Indeed? Is that not a little extreme? Come now, I suggest that you give the matter a little sensible consideration. Is one night so disgusting a thing to contemplate?'

'Yes. Yes, it is! I refuse your terms, sirrah, for I have no intention of bowing to blackmail. I will tell Lord Kane.'

'What will you inform him, my dear?' he asked lightly.

'I have only to show him the note you sent.'

He gave a brief laugh. 'Be sensible, Miss Rutherford. The note gives no indication as to the sender, for it most certainly is not in my hand. It makes no mention of the Keepsake as such, nor does it point to the IOUs as being those belonging to your brother. In fact, my dear, it is something and nothing, conveying meaning only to you.' He came a little closer, suddenly taking the Keepsake from his pocket and holding it up so that the diamonds flashed in the light from the chandeliers. 'I have indeed had this little trinket stolen from you, Miss Rutherford, and it is indeed in my possession now, but you will find it intolerable difficult to prove the fact.'

From beyond the door, Dolly gazed at the Keepsake, suddenly realizing that it was what she had seen him take from the hiding place in the back of the clock.

Emma was staring at the brooch, and then she raised her eyes to his face. 'I will not bow to your vile threats, sir. I mean to tell Lord Kane what you are demanding.'

'Do that, and your match will very swiftly be a thing of the past.'

'You cannot—'

'Break it asunder? Oh, my dear, I rather think that I can. Believe me, it would be a very simple matter for me to suggest to Kane that you have become infatuated with me and that you are prepared to deceive him in order to attempt to win me. You've deceived him already, haven't you? You've come to me instead of accompanying him to Manchester House. What did you tell him? Did you cry off with a headache? Whatever you did, you fobbed him off, and even though you have no doubt taken care to remain anonymous since leaving Grosvenor Square, I rather fear that Jerry Warburton somehow recognized your maid a few minutes ago. He hasn't yet remembered where he's seen her before, but I could so easily jog his memory. I can only presume that he noticed her when he helped take your brother home after the sailing accident.'

Emma turned away, her mind racing. She was trapped. It was as if an invisible net was closing in around her, its mesh tightening inch by inch until she could not move.

Lord Avenley gave a cool half-laugh. 'Like all the best plots, my dear, it is really very simple, as is your way out. I promised you that Stephen would find it easy to redeem his IOUs, and I am keeping my promise. One night with me, my sweet Emma, and your brother's debts will be a thing of the past. One night, and not only will you have the Keepsake again, but you will soon be able to give yourself to Kane with all the passion I am sure you feel for him.

One night. That is all.'

Slowly she turned to meet his gaze again. 'I despise you with all my heart,' she whispered.

He seemed amused. 'I'm sure you do, but of what consequence is that? Your opinion of me is immaterial, for I do not want your regard, I want your physical charms, which I find more and more irresistible each minute I am with you.'

She recoiled, her disgust and repugnance almost tangible.

'And I find you more and more repellent,' she said. 'You still haven't told me why you're doing this. You claim now it is because you desire me, but you also admitted that originally it was only to do with ruining the match. What is this really about?'

'Do you see that miniature on the wall over there?' he asked suddenly, pointing past her to an alcove where the light from a candelabrum on a console table illuminated an oval miniature set in an ornate silver frame.

As Emma went toward it, he turned again, replacing the Keepsake in the clock. She did not see what he did, but from the doorway Dolly witnessed everything.

Emma reached the alcove and picked up the candelabrum to examine the miniature more closely. It was a likeness of a beautiful young woman with magnificent bronze hair and large hazel eyes. She had a pale but perfect face, and her rosebud lips were a little pouting, as if she was inviting a kiss. There were pearls in her hair, and around her flawless throat, and she wore a drapery of soft white silk, like a classical statue.

Puzzled, Emma turned to look at Lord Avenley. 'Who is she?'

His eye shone with a cold steadiness. 'She should have become Lady Avenley, but chose to become Lady Kane instead.'

Emma whirled about to look at the miniature again. Margot? Gerald's first wife?

'Yes, Miss Rutherford, the first Lady Kane is the reason for all this. She was mine, but Kane lured her away with his silver words and silken looks. She didn't love him, she was blinded by his charm, and when she wished to return to me, he wouldn't let her go. She died when she eventually fled in the middle of the night and her carriage overturned on Hounslow Heath.' His voice was low and almost beguiling, and he stared across the room at the little portrait as if he could never gaze too much upon Margot's likeness. 'She was mine, my dear Emma, she was always mine, but Kane stole her. When I heard that he was marrying again, I decided to destroy the match, but then I saw you.' His eye swung away from the miniature to rest upon Emma's face. 'I saw you, and I made up my mind to enjoy you, just as he once enjoyed Margot. It will please me to know that I have sampled your charms before he has, and there will be a certain piquancy in the situation, will there not? For you will become his wife, but you will have surrendered to me before his ring was even on your finger. There is poetic justice in that, Miss Rutherford.'

She searched his cold face. 'Do you take me for a fool, sir? If I give in to your blackmail, I know full well that you will inform Lord Kane of my indiscretion. What satisfaction is there for you unless he knows what you have done?'

'That is a chance you will have to take, my dear. You have a day in which to decide. If you do not indicate that you will come to me tomorrow night, I will destroy your match before it begins.'

She replaced the candelabrum on the table, glancing for a last time at Margot's lovely face.

Lord Avenley spoke softly behind her. 'The choice is yours. If you love Kane, which I believe you do, then there is only one course open to you. You have to do as I wish. Refuse me, and you will lose him, that I can promise you. He and I despise each other because of Margot, and he has only to discover that you lied to him in order to come here tonight . . .' He allowed his voice to trail away into an eloquent silence.

The atmosphere in the drawing room was suddenly so claustrophobic that she could barely breathe. The net was tightening all the time, denying her the strength to struggle free. He was so clever, so thorough, and so bitterly determined to be avenged for the past, that he had left no chink of light in the darkness that was engulfing her. If only she could clear her thought. . . . She forced herself to meet his gaze. 'You have said all you wished to say, my lord, and now I want to leave.'

He smiled. 'I trust you mean to be sensible about this, my dear. Just remember that you cannot prove I even have the Keepsake.' He spread his empty hands.

She raised her hood again and began to walk toward the door.

'Allow me to see you out,' he said, accompanying her.

Outside, Dolly had quickly straightened and drawn a discreet distance away from the door.

He escorted them both down to the entrance hall, and then out to the porch, where the carriage was waiting at the curb. There he spoke to Emma again. 'Be advised not to say anything about this, Miss Rutherford, for if you do, it will be the worse for you. Your wisest course is to bow to my demand.'

'I find you everything that is obnoxious and immoral,' she whispered, despising him with her glance.

He smiled, taking her hand suddenly and raising it almost tenderly to his lips. 'My dear, I'm flattered to have aroused such strong emotion in your sweet, virtuous breast,' he murmured.

She snatched her hand away and turned toward the carnage. As she did so, her hood fell back, revealing her face in the lamplight and causing the spangles in her hair to sparkle eye-catchingly.

A carriage was driving past at that moment, and the solitary gentleman inside glanced out in time to witness the entire apparently intimate incident. He saw the hooded lady as Lord Avenley tenderly kissed her hand, and he saw her hood fall back to reveal her identity. Lord Castlereagh sat forward in dismayed surprise. Miss Rutherford and Avenley? Surely he was mistaken. Then he saw that the carriage the lady was entering was Lady Bagworth's town vehicle. There was no mistake, it was indeed Miss Rutherford. But why on earth was she with Avenley instead of being at Manchester House with Kane?

Lord Castlereagh turned to look back along the Pall Mall pavement, wondering greatly at the scene he'd observed. Was the little Rutherford deceiving Kane behind his back? If she was, why, oh why, had it to be with Avenley, of all the men in London!

Sitting forward again, Lord Castlereagh pursed his lips thoughtfully, and his carriage conveyed him on his way to Manchester House.

18

MANCHESTER HOUSE, THE London residence of the Marquess of Hertford, presided very impressively over the northern side of Manchester Square, just to the north of Oxford Street. The house was just over thirty years old, and although very grand, was far from being the most beautiful in the capital. It comprised a three-story central block flanked on either side by two-story wings, and the roofline was marked by a plain balustrade of little aesthetic quality. A rather ponderous columned porch jutted out from the main entrance, and on top of the porch, accessible from one of the main reception rooms on the second story, was a covered wrought-iron balcony that gave a splendid vantage point, but which did nothing at all to improve the appearance of the house.

In front of the building there was a cobbled courtyard that was separated from the square by a tall iron railing. For the occasion of the assembly there were lanterns everywhere, and all the windows of the house were ablaze with lights. A crush of carriages thronged the square, and the sound of laughter and music drifted out into the cold September night. Society always flocked to events at Manchester House, for the Marchioness of Hertford was the Prince of Wales's mistress, and therefore a person of immense influence. She was rather an unlikely royal mistress, being a stately, amply proportioned grandmother,but she held great sway over the Prince, and therefore over the *beau monde* as well.

Lord Castlereagh's carriage entered the square from the south, and could not proceeed to the house because of all the other carriages that had already arrived. With a sigh, Lord Castlereagh alighted some distance away and began to walk. He pulled his hat further forward and hunched his shoulders in his fur-trimmed cloak. His thoughts were not on the assembly, but upon the mystery of seeing Miss Rutherford engaged in a seemingly fond leave-taking at Avenley House. Something was afoot, for that particular gentleman was the very last with whom she should be seen. There was some water which never flowed beneath the proverbial bridge, and the waters of animosity and bitterness between Kane and Avenley were just such a case.

The sound of the assembly grew louder as he approached the house, and he could see the people in the elegant, brilliantly illuminated rooms. He knew where he would find his wife, for if there was dancing, then that was where she would be. In the entrance hall there were footmen to take his hat, gloves, and coat, and then there were the first guests to dally with for a while. Everyone wished to speak to him about the duel, and he was cynically amused to discover that there wasn't a soul among them who had ever supported the foreign secretary's side of it. How amazing, he thought to himself, and how perfectly predictable.

It was some time before he was able to enter the ballroom, where the small orchestra was playing a country dance. Two sets of dancers were moving on the sanded floor, and he very quickly perceived his wife's golden turban. She was partnered by Kane, and they were laughing as they danced, which to Castlereagh's mind was evidence that Kane could not possibly know of his future wife's visit to Avenley House.

A footman passed with a tray of full champagne glasses, and Castlereagh removed one, sipping it thoughtfully as he watched the dancing. At last the final chord sounded, and the dancers left the floor. He had already been seen by his wife, and she and Kane came toward him.

'Robert! I was beginning to think that you had forgotten all about coming here,' she cried, stretching up to kiss him warmly on the cheek.

He smiled. 'Forget my promise to tread at least three measures with you, my dear? Now, would I be so remiss?'

'Well, you have had your moments in the past,' she murmured, tapping him with her fan.

He smiled again, and then looked at Gerald. 'And how are you this evening, my friend?'

'In fine fettle.'

'Where is the delectable Miss Rutherford?' Lord Castlereagh asked lightly.

'I'm afraid she is indisposed. She was unwell when we arrived at Grosvenor Square, and so it was felt that she should stay at home and rest.'

'I see.'

Gerald looked curiously at him. 'Is there something wrong, Robert?'

'I fear there has to be. You are certain that she is supposed to be at home?'

'Yes.'

Lady Castlereagh was becoming anxious. 'What is it, Robert?'

'Look, the last thing I wish to do is cause trouble, but I have to tell you that Miss Rutherford is most certainly not languishing at home, for a short while ago I saw her with Avenley at Avenley House. They were just saying goodbye, and I cannot describe their manner together as anything other than tender.'

Lady Castlereagh was thunderstruck, and Gerald's face had become very pale and still. 'There has to be a mistake, Robert—' he began.

'I wish that that were so, my friend, but I fear it isn't. I recognized Lady Bagworth's town carriage, and I saw Miss Rutherford's face and hair. I can even describe her coiffure, down to the long ringlet twined with spangles. Gerald, you have to face the fact that your bride-to-be has lied to you tonight.'

At that moment Jerry Warburton approached, a broad smile brightening his face as he took Gerald's hand to shake it warmly. 'It's the first time I've had a chance to congratulate you, Kane. I envy you your bride, for she is without a doubt the most charming in—'

He said no more, for Gerald was ignoring him, his angry gaze still on Lord Castlereagh. 'Robert, I cannot and will not believe that Emma was at Avenley Hoouse tonight.'

Jerry Warburton glanced from one to the other, and then his lips parted as he realized where be had seen Dolly before. She was Miss Rutherford's maid! 'I say,' he said slowly, 'I'm afraid that I think

164

the lady probably was at Avenley House, for I saw her there myself. At least, I saw her maid, for the lady herself was careful to keep her face turned away. I was just leaving with my friends, and she and the maid were about to accompany Avenley upstairs . . .' His voice died away as he realized what he was saying. Dull, embarrassed color suffused his face, and he cleared his throat awkwardly. 'I, er, think I had better be going,' he muttered, nodding briefly at Lord and Lady Castlereagh before pushing away through the crush.

Lady Castlereagh was immediately at pains to reassure Gerald. 'There must be a reasonable explanation, for I am certain that Miss Rutherford would not—'

'Do anything underhanded? Emily, I'm afraid that that is just what she has done. She feigned illness tonight, and then promptly went to Avenley House. Why would she do that? Is this to be a repetition of the past? Is she another Margot?'

Lady Castlereagh put an anxious hand on his arm. 'Don't leap to conclusions, Gerald, for I am sure that you are wrong.'

'And I am sure that your intentions are admirable, but I am afraid that I find it impossible to believe that Miss Rutherford's actions tonight are entirely innocent. She deliberately deceived me in order to go to Avenley House, and in my view that is totally unforgivable. Now, if you will excuse me, I think it is best if I withdraw from the festivities.'

Lady Castlereagh sighed as he walked angrily away; then she looked at her husband. 'Was it really wise to tell him?'

'What would you have had me do? You heard him say that the lady was at home languishing in her bed. Languishing she certainly is not, and so I had to tell him. Come on, Emily, let's join the dancing, for there is little point in dwelling upon Kane's difficulties. I pray that Miss Rutherford does indeed have an excellent reason for visiting Avenley's den, but if she doesn't, then it is well that Kane discovers the truth about her now, rather than later.'

'As he did with Margot, you mean?'

'Margot was the greatest folly of his life, and the last thing I would ever wish upon him would be a second such folly.' Taking her hand firmly, he led her on to the crowded floor, where another country dance was in progress.

Outside in the square, Gerald walked quickly toward his carriage. The coachman was caught unawares in the middle of a game of dice with some of his fellows, and hastily left them to climb on to the box of the carriage.

A footman from Manchester House had preceded Gerald, and now flung open the door and lowered the rungs before standing in readiness to close the door again once Gerald had climbed in.

The coachman touched his hat as Gerald reached the vehicle. 'Home, my lord?'

Gerald nodded. 'Yes. Home,' he said shortly.

As the carriage drew away, threading its way very slowly through the jam of other vehicles, the pain, treachery, and deceits of the past were all around Gerald. He could see Margot again, and hear her voice. He could even smell her perfume, that gentle scent of lilac that had pervaded his entire life. He closed his eyes, leaning his head back against the upholstery. Margot's face faded and became blurred, changing into Emma's green eyes and sweet lips. What a fool he'd been. A fool to end all fools.

The carriage drove swiftly to St James's Square, where everything was very quiet after the noise and crush of Manchester Square. The wheels and the horses' hoofs echoed pleasantly on the cobbles, and the light from the streetlamps shone on the lake in the center of the square. It was one of the only squares in London to boast a lake instead of a garden, but like all the others, it still possessed the almost obligatory equestrian statue of a monarch, this time of William III.

Gerald's residence was close to the southeast corner of the square, and was a four-story town house with pedimented windows on the first floor. As he alighted from the carriage, he paused in some surprise, for the windows of the drawing room, which was on the first floor, were illuminated. The house should have been in darkness except for the entrance hall.

The butler opened the door at his approach and hastened to take his hat, gloves, and cloak. 'My lord, there is something I think you should know immediately.'

'Yes? What is it?'

'The Countess of Purbeck is here.'

Gerald turned in quick surprise.

The butler cleared his throat awkwardly. 'She arrived not long after you left, my lord, and she insisted upon waiting for you. I took the liberty of showing her to the drawing room.'

Gerald glanced up the sweeping black-and-gold staircase and then nodded at him. 'Very well. That will be all.'

'My lord.' The butler bowed and withdrew.

Gerald's steps echoed on the staircase as he went slowly up to the floor above. What did Raine want? Indeed, why was she here, and not guarding her interests at Purbeck's country seat?

He flung open the doors of the drawing room, and Raine rose swiftly from a sofa close to the fireplace. She wore a shimmering pale-pink silk gown that clung to her figure and plunged low over her bosom, and there were diamonds in her bright golden hair. Her lips were parted a little, and her hand crept nervously to her throat as she faced him.

He closed the doors behind him, and then looked at her. 'Raine?'

'Hello, Gerald.'

'Why have you come here?'

'You know why I'm here,' she murmured, coming slowly toward him. Her gown whispered in the quiet of the room, and the diamonds in her hair flashed like stars. 'I love you, my darling,' she said softly, the ghost of a smile touching her lips as he did not move away. She linked her graceful arms around his neck, pressing her body against his as she raised her lips to kiss him.

For a moment he did not respond, but then his arms were around her and he crushed her close as he returned the kiss.

Emma's bedroom was in darkness, except for the dim light of the fire, and she lay on her bed, her face hidden in the pillows as she wept. Her troubles appeared to be insurmountable as she lay there, for it seemed that whatever she chose to do would prove her undoing. If she defied Lord Avenley and told Gerald what had happened, Lord Avenley would lie about her and seem to be able to prove he was telling the truth. If she did Lord Avenley's bidding, he would either hold her fall from grace over her head in the future or tell Gerald immediately. All roads led to the downfall of Emma Rutherford.

Dolly came hesitantly into the room, pausing for a moment to look sadly at her weeping mistress. 'Miss Emma?' she said gently.

'Please leave me alone, Dolly,' Emma sobbed wretchedly, for there was nothing the maid could do.

'I don't like to leave you like this, miss,' Dolly said, moving hesitantly toward the bed.

Emma sat up slowly. 'You can't do anything, Dolly,' she said, her voice low and shaking.

'You must tell Lord Kane, Miss Emma,' urged the maid.

Emma was silent for a moment, and then she accepted that this was indeed her only honorable course. 'I know, but I also know that I'm going to lose him. Lord Avenley will see to that.'

'Lord Kane may believe you, miss.'

'I don't think so, not once Lord Avenley has lied about me.'

Dolly felt close to tears herself. 'Oh, Miss Emma,' she whispered. 'I'm so very sorry.'

'It isn't your fault, Dolly.'

'If there was anything I could do, I would do it for you.'

Emma managed a small smile, her eyes tearstained in the feeble light from the dying fire. 'Thank you, Dolly.'

'Can I bring you a warm drink? Some hot milk, maybe?'

Emma shook her head. 'No, I don't want anything. You can go to bed, Dolly, for there no need for you to stay up because of me.'

'If you're sure, Miss Emma?'

'I'm quite sure. Good night, Dolly.'

'Good night, miss.'

'Oh, Dolly. . . ?'

'Miss?'

'Has my father returned yet?'

'No, miss. He sent word a short while ago that he intends to stay overnight.'

'And how is my brother?'

'When I came a moment ago there was a light under his door, Miss Emma. I know that Frederick went to him a short while ago. I'm sure all is well.'

'Thank you,' said Emma, twisting her handkerchief in her hand.

'Good night, miss,' the maid said again, going quietly out and closing the door behind her.

Dolly paused outside the door. She felt desperately sorry for her unhappy mistress, whose troubles were not of her own making. Trying not to cry, the maid began to walk away along the passage, but as she passed Stephen's door it opened suddenly and Frederick emerged.

'Dolly Makepeace? Still up and about at this hour?' he said with a grin, but then his smile faded as he saw how upset she was. 'Here, what's the matter, girlie?'

'Nothing,' she replied, swallowing because there was a lump in her throat.

'You look mortal upset for someone who's all right,' he said.

The door was opened behind him, and Stephen was sitting up in bed sipping another cup of broth. He heard the brief exchange. 'What it is, Frederick?' he asked, looking toward them.

Dolly looked urgently at the valet, shaking her head, but he turned to his master. 'It's Miss Emma's maid, sir. She's very upset about something.'

Dolly gave him a furious look, but it was too late now. Stephen beckoned to her. 'Come here. Now, then, what's wrong?' He smiled kindly.

His gentle tone was the last straw. Dolly's face crumpled and she burst into tears.

Stephen was taken aback, and put the cup of broth down quickly. 'Whatever is it?' he asked, lying back on the pillows, for any effort taxed his strength. 'Tell me, Dolly. Maybe I can help. Are you in my sister's black books, is that it?'

'Oh, no, Master Stephen, it isn't that. I just feel so unhappy for her.'

Stephen looked at her in astonishment. 'Unhappy for her? Whatever for? At this very moment she's dancing the night away with Lord Kane—'

'No, she isn't, Master Stephen, she didn't go to Manchester House this evening.'

'Didn't go? But—'

'Oh, Master Stephen,' the maid wailed, 'it's all so unfair, and I don't know what to do!'

Stephen stared at her in dismay. 'Oh, Lord, please don't cry like that.'

'I'm sorry, sir,' Dolly sobbed, searching for a handkerchief.

Frederick produced one, and ushered her to a fireside chair.

'Sit down, girlie, and tell us what's up,' he said gently. He'd always had a soft spot for Dolly, and was quite upset to see her in such a sorry way.

'I . . . I can't tell you,' Dolly sniffed, wiping her eyes as fresh tears streamed down her cheeks.

Stephen hauled himself up in the bed again, fixing her with a stern look. 'Tell us all about it, Dolly. That is an order.'

She blinked miserably at him and then nodded a little. 'I know I should not tell you, Master Stephen, but I think you should know. It concerns Miss Emma and Lord Avenley.'

Stephen's face changed. 'Avenley?'

'Yes, sir.' Haltingly the maid told him everything she knew, and with each word his eyes became more and more incredulous and angry.

When she finished, he was silent for a moment. 'Are you quite sure about all this?' he demanded then.

'Yes, sir, for I could hear everything through the door.'

Stephen flung the bedclothes aside and got up, hesitating for a moment as everything in the room began to spin. As he became steady again, he nodded at the valet. 'My clothes, if you please.'

Frederick was dismayed. 'But, sir—'

'My clothes!' Stephen snapped.

'You aren't well, sir, you must not leave your bed.'

'Allow me to be the best judge, Frederick,' came the short reply. Then Stephen looked at Dolly. 'You may leave the matter to me, Dolly.'

'But, Master Stephen—' she began.

His eyes flashed. 'Lord Avenley cannot be allowed to get away with such monstrous behavior, and I intend to call him out. No one else need know what my intentions are, indeed I forbid either of you to say anything, is that clear?'

The maid nodded unhappily.

'That will be all, Dolly.'

'Sir.' Wishing that she hadn't blurted everything out, Dolly withdrew from the room.

Stephen then returned his attention to the valet. 'Is it equally clear to you, Frederick?'

'Yes, sir.'

'Good. Now, then, my clothes, if you please.'

Without another word, Frederick hurried to the adjoining dressing room, and a short while later Stephen was dressed in a
mulberry coat, a silver silk waistcoat, a frilled white shirt, a
starched muslin neckcloth, and a pair of cream cord breeches.
Then he sat on a chair while the valet eased on his top boots.

Stephen winced as another searing pain lanced through his
burning chest. The room revolved again, and he clutched the arms
of the chair.

Frederick looked up anxiously. 'Are you all right, Master
Stephen?'

'I'll do. Bring my astrakhan greatcoat, and then go for a hackney coach from the rank around the corner in South Audley
Street.'

The valet was appalled. 'A hackney coach, sir? Surely you will
use the town carriage?'

'I can't wait for you to arouse the coachman, then for him to
harness the team and bring the damned drag to the door. Just get
a hackney coach and have done with it.'

'Yes, sir.' With a heavy heart the valet went to bring the greatcoat, together with Stephen's gloves and hat; then he left the room
to go to the hackney-coach rank in nearby South Audley Street.

As he emerged from the bedroom, he found Dolly still waiting
in the passage.

'Frederick?' She looked anxiously at him. 'Should we tell Miss
Emma?'

'Not if you know what's good for you, girlie. You heard what
Master Stephen said. He forbade either of us to say anything. So
leave it at that.'

Tears filled her eyes again. 'I shouldn't have said what I did,
Frederick.'

'Well, you did, and it's done now.' But he smiled kindly. 'If it
wasn't that Master Stephen is unwell, you wouldn't be in such a
flap, would you?'

'I don't know.'

'Just get to your room, girlie.'

She sniffed. 'I'm afraid, Frederick. Master Stephen is so angry,

171

and when he confronts that horrid Lord Avenley—'

'That's up to them,' the valet interrupted quietly. 'Now, then, I've got to get a hackney coach, so I can't hang about here chitchatting with you.' He hurried away.

Dolly hesitated, still worried that Emma should be alerted, but then she remembered Stephen's stern orders and slowly walked away. Gradually her steps quickened, and then she fled past the grand staircase and on to the little stairs that led up to the servants' quarters on the attic floor.

In her darkened room Emma had fallen into a fitful sleep and knew nothing as her brother left the house to enter the hackney coach, which was soon conveying him across London toward Pall Mall and Avenley House.

19

THE HACKNEY COACH was ancient, cold, and damp, and its springs
had long since ceased to be effective. There was straw on the floor,
the drab upholstery was threadbare and lumpy, and the ill-fitting
window glass rattled as the uncomfortable little vehicle jolted over
the cobbled streets, its single horse trotting wearily with its head
held low. The coachman huddled on his box with several shawls
around his shoulders, and his wide-brimmed hat was pulled
forward over his forehead, for the September night was very cold
indeed, and he knew there would be a frost before morning.

Inside, Stephen sat with his eyes closed. His head lolled against
the poor upholstery, and he was barely aware of the noise of the
coach, for all he could hear was the loud pounding of his heart.
His head was spinning sickeningly, and the pain in his chest
seemed to reach into every corner of his body, turning his flesh to
fire. The effort of what he was doing was taxing what little
strength he had, and it was hard to think clearly, but his anger and
sense of outrage spurred him on. He loved his sister with all his
heart, and the thought of Avenley's vile and lascivious blackmail
was more than he could endure. Avenley would pay for his
monstrous behavior.

Piccadilly was still brightly lit, but there wasn't a great deal of
traffic as the hackney coach reached the corner of St James's Street
and then turned south. Suddenly there was more traffic, for the
small hours of the night always saw a congregation of elegant vehicles as gentlemen sallied forth to their clubs. The hackney coach
moved more slowly, sometimes coming to a standstill as it waited
for a carriage to turn around ahead.

Stephen opened his eyes at one of these temporary halts. The pain in his chest was almost overwhelming, and his vision was confused as he gazed out of the dirty window. He could see a brilliantly illuminated doorway and a sumptuous entrance hall beyond. Gentlemen were coming and going through the doorway, and when he glanced to one side, he saw a gaming-room, with green baize tables, intent players, and interested observers standing watching. He thought he had reached Avenley House.

He opened the coach door and stumbled out, leaving the door open behind him as he strove to maintain his balance and his concentration. The pounding of his heart seemed thunderous, as if the pavement itself were pulsing, and the lights of the gaming club began to revolve around him. There was a high-pitched whistle in his ears, everything began to go dim, as if he were sinking into a bed of black velvet, and then he knew no more as he slipped unconscious to the ground.

The hackney coachman did not realize that he had lost his passenger, and as the way ahead became clear again, he drove on, the coach door swinging idly on its hinges as the tired horse came up to its customary slow trot. The coach vanished at the bottom of St James's Street, turning east into Pall Mall and driving on toward Avenley House.

Two young gentlemen emerged from the club at that moment, halting in surprise on seeing Stephen's unconcious body on the pavement. For a moment they were cautious, suspecting a trick by footpads, for they had just won handsomely and carried a considerable amount of money in their purses, but then they saw that Stephen was well dressed, and they hurried toward him, fearing that he was himself the victim of foodpads.

They crouched beside him, turning him gently over, and by pure chance one of them recognized him. 'I say, it's that Rutherford chap, the one whose sister is to marry Kane.'

The other man put his hand to Stephen's face. 'He's burning up with fever. Didn't I hear something about a sailing accident on the Thames?'

'Yes. Dear God, he hasn't been attacked, he's passed out!' cried the first man.

'You're right. Where does he live?'

'Damned if I know, but Kane's residence is in St James's Square, we'll take him there. I'll get some help.' Scrambling to his feet again, the first man hurried back into the club, returning a minute later with two more gentlemen.

Together they lifted Stephen from the pavement and carried him carefully to a nearby carriage, which belonged to one of them. Stephen was eased gently into the carriage and laid upon one of the seats; then the first two gentlemen remained with him as the carriage set off on its brief journey along King Street, which connected St James's Street and St James's Square. Almack's Assembly Rooms, where high society strove to be seen at the Wednesday night subscription balls, lay on the south side of the street. The building was in darkness now, and presented an almost gloomy façade to the thoroughfare as the carriage drove swiftly by.

Stephen knew nothing of what was happening, for he remained unconscious. He was delirious, his lips moving now and then as if he were speaking to someone, but although both the gentlemen leaned forward to try to hear, they couldn't understand anything.

The sound of the carriage changed as it emerged from the confines of King Street into the openness of the square, and the coachman's whip cracked once as he brought the team up to a smarter pace for the final hundred yards to Gerald's residence, which was in complete darkness.

As the vehicle drew to a halt at the curb outside, one of the young gentlemen leapt swiftly out and ran to the door, hammering loudly upon the knocker. The sound reverberated through the house and echoed around the square. The flicker of candlelight appeared in the fanlight above the door as someone came swiftly to see who was knocking so urgently in the middle of the night.

A cautious voice came from within. 'Who's there?'

The young gentleman was irritated. 'If it's of any consequence, my name is Hamilton-Smythe, but what is more to the point is that I have with me Mr Rutherford, the brother of the lady who is to be Lady Kane. He is very ill, and in need of a doctor, so for God's sake open the door and let us in!'

After a moment there came the sound of bolts being pulled back, and then the door opened and a footman in a nightshirt and tasseled night cap peered out. He was shading a lighted candle in his hand, and he was still cautious, although he relaxed a little when he saw that the unexpected night caller had arrived in a particularly elegant town carriage.

Another nightshirted footman appeared, and soon Stephen was being lifted out of the carriage and carried into the house, where he was laid gently on a sofa. A third footman began to hastily light candles.

Gerald appeared suddenly at the head of the staircase. His hair was tousled, and he was pulling on a green silk dressing gown. 'What in God's name is going on?' he demanded.

Mr Hamilton-Smythe went quickly to the foot of the staircase. 'Kane, it's me.'

'Hamilton-Smythe?' Gerald looked blankly at him, for they were only slightly acquainted.

'Forgive the intrusion, Kane, but we found your future brother-in-law lying in the street. He's dashed unwell, running a high fever.' Mr Hamilton-Smythe indicated the unconcious figure on the sofa.

Gerald came quickly down the staircase, and as he approached the sofa, he could see that Stephen was indeed desperately ill. He nodded at the footmen. 'Get him to the Chinese room, and then send someone for Dr Longford. And do it quickly.'

'My lord.' The footmen picked Stephen up carefully and carried him up the staircase. As they did so, a golden-haired figure in a flimsy white nightrobe appeared at the top.

Raine paused, her hand resting on the banister. 'What is it, Gerald?' she asked, her sweet voice carrying clearly down into the hall below.

Gerald turned sharply, as did the two gentlemen who had brought Stephen. Gerald looked coolly at her. 'Go to your room, Raine.'

'But—'

'Go to your room!' he snapped.

The two gentlemen exchanged glances. So that was the way of it, eh? The future Lady Kane was in town, but Kane was still involved with the Countess of Purbeck!

Gerald ran his fingers through his hair and then turned to them. 'Thank you for all you've done. You may leave the matter with me.'

'Think nothing of it, Kane,' murmured Mr Hamilton-Smythe. 'I'm only sorry we, er, disturbed you.'

There was an angry set to Gerald's mouth as he showed them to the door, and as he closed the door behind them he turned to look darkly up at the place where Raine had been standing a few moments before. A nerve flickered at his temple, and he began to walk toward the staircase.

The butler hurried from the direction of the kitchen. He still wore his nightshirt, but had managed to put on his coat and wig. He carried a candle, which fluttered and smoked as he walked. 'I have sent a man for the doctor, my lord.'

'I trust the urgency of the situation was stressed?'

'It was indeed, my lord.'

'Is someone attending to the fire in the Chinese room?'

'A boy is lighting it at this very moment, my lord.'

'Good.' Gerald paused, his hand on the banister. 'Mr Rutherford's family must be informed without delay. Send someone to tell them, and to reassure them that all is being done that should be done.'

'Certainly, my lord.'

Gerald went up the staircase, his thoughts flying momentarily to Emma, but even as memories of her face and voice moved over him, he pushed her away. He did not wish to think of Emma Rutherford, not now, or ever again.

The Chinese room deserved its name, for it was decorated and furnished entirely in the Mandarin style. There was hand-painted silk on the walls, the canopy of the bed resembled a pagoda, and the chandeliers were like Oriental lanterns. The room was predominantly blue and white, but pink flame shadows danced over the furnishings as the boy dispatched by the butler kindled the fire into roaring life. The footmen had laid Stephen gently on the bed and were removing his outdoor garments. Within a moment or so he was dressed in one of Gerald's own nightshirts and was lying comfortably in the soft bed. He seemed close to consciousness, for his lips moved and he turned his head from side to side, but his eyes remained closed, and nothing he said was intelligible.

The boy finished attending to the fire, placed a guard in front of it, and then scurried out. The footmen then withdrew as well, leaving Gerald on his own. He went to the window, holding the curtain aside to gaze out over the square, where the lamplight reflected on the circular lake in the center.

'How is he?' asked a soft voice from the doorway behind him.

He turned to see Raine standing there. She was still dressed in the revealing white robe, and her figure was outlined very clearly by the bright lamps in the passage.

He drew a long breath. 'Please go to your room and stay there, Raine.'

'I am merely showing concern,' she replied, ignoring the instruction by entering the room and going to stand by the bed, looking down at Stephen. 'There is no family likeness at all, is there? No one could possibly guess that he and sweet little Emma are—'

'I don't wish to discuss it with you, Raine.'

Her lovely lilac eyes were luminous as they swung toward him. 'How very touchy you are, to be sure,' she murmured.

'Have a care, Raine, for I am in no mood.'

'My poor darling . . .' she whispered, leaving the bedside to come to him, but as she raised her slender arms to link them around his neck, he caught her wrists and held her away.

'Enough, Raine. This is neither the time nor the place, and I have already told you that I dislike your attempts to manipulate me in this way.'

'Manipulate you? Oh, Gerald, how could you think such a thing?' She pouted, affecting to be hurt.

'I think it because I know you too well. Now, please go to your room, before I have you forcibly removed there.'

'I will wait for you,' she said softly, reaching up briefly to brush her lips over his; then she left him, her robe whispering softly, her perfect body silhouetted against the light from the passage.

Gerald exhaled slowly, closing his eyes for a moment. When he opened them, he looked toward the bed, and with a shock found that Stephen was awake. He went quickly to him.

The sick man's eyes were glazed and feverish, and he was obviously confused. 'Kane? Where. . . ?' Stephen glanced uncertainly around the strange room.

178

'You were found unconscious in the street, and someone brought you here to my house in St James's Square.'

Bewilderment entered Stephen's eyes, and his brows drew together as he tried to remember. The pain in his chest was hot and dry, as if a fire was burning behind his ribs, and all the time he could hear the urgent, swift pounding of his heart. Memories slid in and out of his head, one moment clear, the next jumbled and forgotten. But then he recalled that there had been something important concerning Avenley. He struggled to sit up. 'Avenley, I must see him . . .'

Gerald's mouth hardened at the mention of his foe's name, but he gently restrained Stephen. 'Be still, man, for you're in no condition to go anywhere.'

'I have to see him without delay. It's important—'

'Later.'

'It's Emma, she and Avenley . . .' Stephen's voice faded away, for he was sinking back into the velvety blackness. Everything was fading around him, even though he tried to cling to consciousness. He stared up at Gerald's face, his lips moving, but no words came out. Darkness engulfed him again.

Gerald released the unconcious man and then straightened. Stephen's last words were still audible in the silent room. *It's Emma, she and Avenley. . . .* A bitter smile twisted Gerald's lips. Yes, Emma and Avenley. Emma and Avenley.

20

IT WAS ALMOST dawn as yet another carriage drove swiftly toward Gerald's residence in St James's Square, this time conveying a distraught Emma, who responded immediately to the message about her brother. She had changed out of her green-and-silver evening gown, and wore her peach-and-white-striped muslin gown beneath a green velvet cloak trimmed with white fur, and her hair was combed up into a loose knot beneath the cloak's hood. Her face was pale and tense, and her eyes still showed signs of her recent weeping, but she was otherwise reasonably composed. Thoughts of Lord Avenley were temporarily pushed into the background, for Stephen was of much more immediate importance. She had not yet informed her father, wanting to be absolutely sure about her brother before she said anything.

She was accompanied by a very subdued and contrite Dolly, who had tearfully confessed her role where Stephen's actions were concerned. The maid sniffed from time to time as she sat opposite her silent mistress. Dolly felt wretchedly guilty, for she had always been a loyal and discreet servant, but tonight she had transgressed, and as a result something terrible had happened. What if Master Stephen should die? It would be all her fault. The maid's remorse did not end there, however, for if Master Stephen's ill health had not intervened, and he had reached Lord Avenley, what might then have ensued? A duel? Oh, the thought was too horrid. . . . Dolly's eyes filled with tears again, and she tried to blink them away as she looked out of the carriage window.

They were just entering St James's Square, where the gray light of dawn cast a steely glint on the central lake. The statue of

180

William III looked cold and isolated in the middle of the water, and the horse's rump was a prime perch for two sea gulls, whose pale shapes seemed almost ghostly. There was a frost, and it touched everything with a sheen of silvery white.

Dr Longford's carriage departed as they approached, and Emma caught a glimpse of the physician as the two vehicles passed. She was immediately panic-stricken. Why was he leaving already? Was Stephen...? She didn't dare finish the thought, for it was too awful to contemplate. Her heartbeats quickened, and she could barely wait for the carriage to draw up at the curb.

She climbed swiftly down and hurried to the door, knocking loudly. There were lights inside, and the butler admitted her without delay. 'Miss Rutherford?' he inquired, guessing that it was she, and wondering if his master would really wish her to be admitted while the Countess of Purbeck was also in the house.

'How is my brother?' she asked without preamble.

'Mr Rutherford is comfortable, madam.'

Relief flooded through her, and through Dolly, who entered the house in time to hear his words. The maid's lips quivered, and more hot tears stung her eyes.

Emma looked at the butler. 'What did Dr Longford say, do you know?'

'That Mr Rutherford had suffered a dangerous relapse, but that he is young and healthy enough to overcome the crisis. Strong doses of laudanum and willow bark have been prescribed, and a poultice of warm cooked cabbage leaves is to be applied to his chest, to draw out the inflammation.'

'The doctor was quite certain that he is not in danger?'

'It was his considered opinion, madam, but if Mr Rutherford should refuse to remain in bed, then the doctor could not say what might happen.'

'May I see him?'

'Certainly, madam. If you will come this way, I will show you to the Chinese room, and then I will inform his lordship that you are here.' The butler glanced a little uneasily up the staircase, only too conscious of the embarrassing fact of having both the Countess of Purbeck and the future Lady Kane beneath the roof at the same time. The situation was potentially very awkward indeed. Clearing

181

his throat, he led Emma and Dolly up the staircase to the first floor, past the doors of the drawing room, and then up to the bedrooms on the second floor. It was there that they came face-to-face with Raine, who had observed their arrival from an upper window and was determined to make the most of her opportunity.

She still wore the revealing robe, and there was a malevolent smile on her lips. 'Why, Miss Rutherford, how pleasant it is to meet you again.'

Emma halted, shaken to so suddenly and unexpectedly find herself confronted by her rival. The shock was so great that she couldn't respond. Why was the countess here in this house? Why, if not because. . . ? Her thought was interrupted by Raine herself.

'You must excuse my *déshabillé*, my dear, but I'm afraid you've caught us unawares. We, er, didn't expect you to actually call here at such an hour.'

'We?'

'Don't be naïve, Miss Rutherford. You may be a little rustic, but I am sure that even you must understand my meaning clearly enough.'

Emma stared at her. 'Yes, Countess, I understand your meaning, I understand it very well indeed. And now, if you will excuse me, I wish to see my brother.' She nodded at the butler, who was waiting a little further on, his face a picture of mortification.

Raine stood aside for them to pass, and she watched as they disappeared into the Chinese room. Her eyes glittered triumphantly, and then she turned to go back to her room. She had timed matters very well indeed, and had achieved the maximum effect with the minimum of effort. Emma Rutherford's hopes were dashed, and soon she would be scuttling back to the provincial lair from which she had so fleetingly dared to emerge.

In the Chinese room, Emma tried hard not to show any reaction to the unpleasant encounter in the passage outside. She teased off her gloves and then allowed Dolly to assist her with her cloak.

The maid looked anxiously at her. 'Oh, miss, I don't know what to say—'

'Then say nothing, Dolly,' Emma replied, glancing meaningfully in the direction of the butler, who could hear everything they said.

Dolly fell silent, making much of folding the cloak over the back of a chair that was upholstered in dragon-adorned blue brocade. Then she watched as her anxious mistress went to the bed, where Stephen lay in a deep sleep.

Emma put out a hand to touch his cheek, and her breath caught at how fiery it was. His face was flushed and dry, and he would have been tossing and turning were it not for the influence of the laudanum.

Emma looked sadly down at him. Oh, Stephen, she thought, how impulsive and quick-tempered you are. How on earth did you imagine you would emerge from a confrontation with Lord Avenley? She had no doubt that he had been intent upon challenging his former friend, for in Stephen's eyes a brother would lack all honor if he did not call out the man who had so callously compromised his sister.

The butler hovered. 'I will inform Lord Kane that you are here, madam.'

'Very well,' replied Emma.

He went out, pausing for a moment after closing the door, for he needed to gather himself for the difficult task of telling his master that Miss Rutherford had not only called but also come face-to-face with the countess. He hoped that he himself would not receive any of the blame for this exceedingly inopportune situation, but he could hardly have refused Miss Rutherford when she asked to see her gravely ill brother, and then if a lady like the countess chose not to remain in concealment, but made much of being present in the house, what was a mere butler supposed to do about it?

In the Chinese room, Emma was also wondering how Gerald would react on being informed that she had come to the house. How would he explain away the Countess of Purbeck, if indeed he bothered to explain at all? She, Emma, had been forced into deception against her will, but Gerald was himself guilty not only of deception, but also of a great deal more as well, apparently. Had the countess ever left London in the first place? Or had she been here all along?

Dolly watched her mistress's sad withdrawn face and then lowered her own eyes. Nothing had gone well for poor Miss Emma since they'd left Dorchester, and the maid wished with all her heart that they'd all stayed at Foxley Hall, where there had not been any unhappiness or sly tricks. London was not to be trusted, for here all was treachery.

The butler returned, his expression a little relieved because he had not received a reprimand for the awkward state of affairs. Instead Lord Kane had merely instructed him to inform Miss Rutherford that he would await her in the drawing room. The butler bowed as he entered the Chinese room. 'Miss Rutherford, Lord Kane will receive you in the drawing room as soon as you are ready.'

'Very well. I will go to him now,' she replied, for there was no point in delaying the moment, and besides, Stephen wasn't in any condition to even know that she was there. She nodded at Dolly. 'Bring my cloak and gloves, for I do not think we will stay long,' she said.

'Yes, Miss Emma.'

The butler conducted them back to the floor below, and Emma left Dolly outside as she went into the drawing room.

Gerald was waiting with his back to the fireplace. He still wore his green dressing-gown, with beneath it a frilled white shirt and cream kerseymere breeches. The shirt was undone at the throat, and his dark hair was tousled. His eyes were very cool and gray in the light from the chandeliers as he faced her. The was no smile on his lips, and no welcome in his manner. He didn't say anything.

The doors closed once more as the butler withdrew, and the two looked silently at each other, neither wishing to be the first to speak. Gerald's glance moved fleetingly over her, taking in the dainty peach-and-white-striped muslin gown and the way her hair-pins only just seemed able to contain her heavy curls. He thought how direct and uncomplicated she seemed, and he marveled again that he had been so taken in by her air of innocence. She was not what she appeared to be, any more than faithless Margot had been, and it was as well that he had found out now rather than later.

At last he inclined his head to her and broke the silence. 'Miss Rutherford,' he said coldly.

She took the cue and replied in the same formal vein. 'Lord Kane.'

'I trust that you are now recovered from your indisposition?'

'I am. Thank you.' Her heart was splintering into fragments with each frozen word, but she did not show it. Her voice was steady, and she did not shrink from meeting his eyes.

'I am very sorry that your brother is so ill, but I assure you that he will receive every attention while he remains under this roof, as I am told by the physician he must.'

'You are most kind, my lord.'

'You are, of course, most welcome to call upon him each day, and to sit with him if you wish.'

'Thank you.' Suddenly his chill manner touched a nerve in her. 'I am sure that any calls I may make will be made most proper by the Countess of Purbeck's presence,' she added, for the first time not quite able to hide the tremor in her voice.

An angry light passed through his eyes. 'Do not presume to act the betrayed soul, Miss Rutherford, for it is a role to which you are singularly ill-suited.'

She stared at him. 'What do you mean by that?'

'Oh, come now, I think you know full well.'

'All I know full well is that you have been found out, sirrah!' she cried. 'Your lies have been monstrous, and I deeply regret that I was so easily gulled into believing you to be both honorable and sincere.'

He looked incredulously at her. '*My* lies? You really do have face, madam! I marvel that you can so blatantly ape the innocent, when all the time your perfidy has been staggering.'

Her eyes flashed. 'Your mistress is here in this house, and you accuse me of perfidy?' she breathed. 'What price your claim to never seducing other men's wives and to regretting a so-called single night of folly last spring? How dare you point a finger at me, when your conscience is anything but clear!' She was shaking with anger and distress. This wasn't happening, it simply wasn't happening. . . .

'Oh, you missed your vocation, madam, for in truth you should be treading the boards with the likes of Mrs Siddons,' he replied icily. 'I really believed your playacting last night, when you pretended to be on the verge of a faint, but it was all a stratagem so that you could slip away to Avenley!'

185

Her breath caught guiltily, and dismay rushed weakeningly through her.

His lips twisted bitterly. 'Your culpability is written very large and clear, madam, but you could not have denied it anyway, for you were seen, both by Castlereagh and by Jerry Warburton. I will not inquire what your purpose was in going there, but I can imagine it well enough.'

'You cannot imagine it at all, sir, and so I will tell you.'

'No, Miss Rutherford,' he said, holding up a hand to stem her explanation. 'I don't want to know what you have to say, for it is evident to me that we are most definitely not suited.'

'You will not hear me out? You don't want to know why my brother left the house tonight, or why—?'

'No, madam, I do not,' he interrupted, his tone as frosty as his eyes. 'I think we should just leave it that you have been caught in your untruths.'

She felt as if she was in a nightmare, but she knew that it was all only too real and that she wouldn't awaken, because she was awake already. She made herself meet his gaze. 'If I have been caught in untruths, sirrah, then so have you. You told me that the countess meant nothing to you, and that she had gone to the country to be with her husband, and yet here she is with you.'

'I don't think that the countess's whereabouts are anything to do with you, madam, and as to my so-called untruths, let me reiterate that I have always told you the facts as they truly are. From the moment you chose to indulge in whatever it is you are indulging in with Avenley, you left me no choice but to end all thought of our betrothal. Accordingly, I am now informing you that negotiations for our match are at an end, and I request only that you return the Keepsake, which is, as you know, a family heirloom.'

She felt numb. Her world was in tatters around her, he was refusing to even listen to her, and at the same time he was behaving as if justice was on his side for having the countess in his house. She, Emma Rutherford, was innocent, but she was being blamed. As for returning the Keepsake. . . . Her head was spinning with confusion, and although she tried to speak, the words simply would not come.

He spoke again. 'Have I made my position clear to you, Miss Rutherford?'

'Very clear indeed, Lord Kane.'

'I trust then that you will return the Keepsake at the earliest possible moment.'

She stared at him. What could she say? She didn't have the Keepsake, Lord Avenley did, but she was certain that Gerald would not listen if she tried to tell him. Suddenly she couldn't even bring herself to try to explain; all she wanted was to escape from his presence, to hide away somewhere. Somehow she contrived to look into his eyes again. 'I accept that there will not now be a contract between us, Lord Kane, and I will return the Keepsake as soon as I can.' But how? How was she going to retrieve it, if not by surrendering to Lord Avenley's shameful terms?

She turned and went to the door. Tears stung her eyes, but she was determined that he would not see them. As she emerged, Dolly looked at her in dismay. 'Oh, Miss Emma—'

'Let us leave as quickly as possible,' Emma replied quietly, hurrying to the staircase.

The maid hastened after her, speaking in a whisper. 'Did you tell him about Lord Avenley, miss?'

'He didn't want to hear anything I might have to say.'

'But what will you do?'

'I don't know.' Emma's voice caught on a sob, and she halted for a moment, her hand on the banister. 'The match is over, Dolly, and he wants me to return the Keepsake as soon as possible.'

The maid stared at her. 'Return it? But—'

'I know, Dolly. I know.'

'You cannot mean to do as Lord Avenley wants?'

'Dolly, I feel so trapped by everything that I begin to see no other way out.'

The maid put an anxious hand on her arm. 'Please don't, Miss Emma. You must tell Mr Rutherford all that has happened. Please say you will tell him, miss.'

'It will break his heart if I tell him, Dolly.'

'It will break his heart if you don't, miss,' the maid replied wisely. 'Besides, you will have to tell him if the match is over, and you will have to give him an explanation. Better the truth than lies he may detect.'

For a long moment Emma was silent, but then she nodded slowly. 'You're right, Dolly. I have to tell my father.'

Dolly's eyes were bright with tears as she helped Emma with her cloak, and then they proceeded down to the entrance hall, where Gerald's butler was waiting to open the door for them.

They emerged into the bitterly cold early-morning air, where the brightness of the rising sun was luminous through the haze of frost. Emma did not glance back as the carriage pulled away.

From an upstairs window Raine watched the carriage depart. A faint smile played upon her lovely lips, and there was triumph in her lilac eyes. She had vanquished her provincial foe, and that was all that mattered.

21

MR RUTHERFORD HAD still not returned when Emma reached the house in Grosvenor Square, and so Saunders was requested to send a footman to him without further delay, to inform him what had happened to Stephen. Emma now fully accepted that her father should be told absolutely everything, and so, with the prospect of a very painful and difficult interview ahead, she waited in the library. Dolly tried to persuade her to take some breakfast, but she had no appetite at all, and could only be prevailed upon to drink a cup of strong black coffee.

A fresh fire had been kindled in the hearth, and the smell of the coffee mingled pleasantly with the leather of the armchairs and the bindings on the books lining the shelves. Outside, the sun had risen now, and the rays shone brightly in through the French windows. The garden was crisp and cold, with splashes of bright color from the Michaelmas daisies and those of the roses that still remained after the recent frost. Autumn tints glowed in the trees, and webs glistened like diamond-threaded lace among the leaves and branches. The sky was an incredible blue, and the air was so clear that it seemed she could see forever beyond the nearby rooftops. How beautiful it all looked, and how at odds with the misery and sense of injustice that enveloped her.

The clock on the mantelpiece ticked slowly, and the fire shifted in the hearth. She could hear the servants going about their morning tasks, and, more distantly, she could hear the street calls in the square. She heard the front door open as her father came in response to her message, and steeled herself for the next few minutes. The last thing she wished to do was acquaint him with what he was about to hear, but she no longer had any choice. Dolly was right, it was unthinkable that she could actually submit to Lord Avenley's despicable terms, and so her poor father had to learn what had been taking place.

She rose to her feet, pressing her trembling palms to the soft folds of her muslin gown, and she raised her chin as bravely as she could as the door of the library opened to admit her anxious father.

He hadn't paused for Saunders to remove his warm cloak or his hat and gloves, and his eyes were full of concern as he hastened toward her. 'What is all this, my dear? Stephen has suffered a setback?'

'Yes, I fear he has, Father.'

'I must go up to him without further delay—'

'He isn't here, Father, he's at Lord Kane's house in St James's Square,' she interrupted quietly.

He stared at her, totally nonplussed. 'He's where? Whatever is he doing there? He was expressly forbidden to leave his bed.'

'Please sit down, Father, for there is something I have to tell you.'

He searched her pale, drawn face. 'What is it, Emma? What's wrong?' he asked, obeying her by going to sit in one of the armchairs. The firelight danced in his eyes as he looked anxiously up at her.

A lump rose in her throat, and she hesitated for a moment. 'I don't want to tell you any of this, but I am afraid that I must,' she said unhappily, and then she began to relate everything that had happened, from Stephen's gambling debts and her troubles with the Countess of Purbeck, to Gerald's infidelities and Lord Avenley's shameful plotting and blackmail. She ended with Gerald's decision to withdraw from the match.

As her voice died away on the last word, there was silence in the room. The fire crackled, sending a shower of sparks fleeing up the chimney, and the clock began to chime the hour, the sweet bell-like notes ringing gently over the room.

Emma could no longer hold back her tears, and hid her face in her hands, her shoulders shaking as she wept. Her father rose quickly to his feet, putting his arms sorrowfully around her.

'Oh, my dear, my dear . . .'

'What am I to do, Father? How can I possibly get the Keepsake back in order to return it to Lord Kane? And then there are the IOUs as well. If I don't do as Lord Avenley says—'

'You will never bow to his loathsome demands! Never!' breathed her father, his eyes furious and outraged as he thought of that lord's base conduct.

'But he has the Keepsake and Stephen's notes!'

'I will meet your brother's debts, so rest assured upon that point. As to the Keepsake, well, I'm afraid that Lord Kane will have to be informed that Lord Avenley has stolen it.'

She drew sharply away. 'If we do that, then Lord Avenley will deny all knowledge of it, and he will say that I have been pursuing him.'

'Lord Kane will surely never believe such a malicious fabrication.'

In spite of her tears, Emma gave a wry and bitter smile. 'Oh, he will believe it, Father, you may take my word for that. Lord Kane is disposed to think only ill of me, even though he is the one stained with guilt.'

Mr Rutherford shook his head helplessly. 'I would have staked my life that Kane was an honorable man, I would even have gone so far as to say that he was as warmly disposed toward you as you were toward him. And now you say that the countess is at his house at this very moment?'

'Yes.'

Mr Rutherford's eyes filled with sadness at the emptiness in his daughter's voice. 'I'm so very sorry, my dear.'

More tears welled from her eyes, drawn forth by his kindness and understanding. He pulled her close again, resting his cheek against her dark, shining hair. 'We will sort it out somehow, my dear,' he murmured.

'But how? How can we possibly prove that Lord Avenley has the Keepsake? He has all the trumps, Father, just as he said he did.'

'We'll think of something,' he whispered, but his eyes were anxious.

Her voice was choked. 'Whichever way I turn, whatever I do, I am faced with scandal and ruin. I will have no reputation left after this, no reputation at all.'

At that moment, unknown to Emma, Dolly was on her way back to Gerald's house in St James's Square. The maid had decided that she must do all she could to assist her wronged, unhappy mistress, and so she meant to somehow speak to Gerald, to tell him exactly what had transpired at Avenley House. She did not know how she would achieve this, for it was unlikely that he would agree to receive her, but at the very least she meant to try.

On the pretext of having to return to St James's Square because Emma had left her reticule behind, Dolly had persuaded Saunders to allow her to use the carriage, and she alighted the moment it drew up at the curb outside Gerald's residence. As she went to the door, she did not notice a second carriage that was being brought around from the mews at the rear of the square. This second carriage was drawn by a fresh team, and was obviously prepared for a long journey into the country. It too meant to draw up at Gerald's door.

Anticipating the arrival of this second vehicle, Gerald's butler opened the door of the house immediately he heard a carriage draw up outside. He was startled to discover that the vehicle he had heard was not the one he expected, and he was even more startled to find himself face to face with Miss Rutherford's maid.

Glancing past her in case Emma herself was also there, he then gave Dolly a rather disapproving look. 'Front doors aren't for the likes of you, my girl,' he said loftily, jerking his thumb to indicate that she should go around to the back of the house.

Dolly held her ground, for she had seen beyond him into the entrance hall, where the Countess of Purbeck was at that very moment taking her leave of Lord Kane. The countess's own maid stood nearby, next to her mistress's luggage, and her eyes were downcast as she toyed with the strings of her little brown cloak. The countess was very beautiful indeed in a peacock silk gown and matching pelisse, and she wore a wide-brimmed black corded silk hat that was adorned with artificial flowers. The brim hid her face, and she was too far away for Dolly to hear what she was saying.

Gerald glanced toward the door, his eyes changing as he recognized Dolly, but he said nothing, for he was listening to Raine.

The butler was irritated that Dolly had not immediately obeyed his instructions. 'To the back door with you, girl,' he ordered, jerking his thumb again.

'I must speak with Lord Kane,' she replied, standing up to him.

The second carriage was drawing up just behind hers, and the butler was momentarily distracted. Dolly seized the moment, ducking beneath his arm and hurrying into the hall.

'Lord Kane, please let me speak with you. Please, I beg of you,' she cried.

Raine whirled about, and Dolly was startled to see that her face was pale and tearstained. Tears or not, however, Raine's temper or venom had not been diluted. Her lips curled as she recognized Emma's maid, and she turned back to Gerald.

'Have her ejected immediately, for it is hardly the thing for a mere servant to demand things of you!'

'Your carriage is here, Raine,' he replied, ignoring her advice.

'Gerald—'

'I have said all there is to say,' he interrupted. 'Please leave now, without further embarrassment.'

Her lips moved, and her magnificent lilac eyes beseeched him to relent, but he remained adamant. 'Goodbye, Raine,' he said gently but firmly.

Without another word she turned and walked out of the house, followed by her maid, and then by some footmen with her luggage.

Gerald then turned to Dolly. 'I cannot imagine that I wish to hear anything your mistress wishes to convey to me.'

'Miss Emma doesn't know that I am here, my lord.'

'I find that hard to believe,' he replied dryly.

'It's true, my lord. I have come here because I think you should know exactly why Miss Emma went to Avenley House, and what happened when she was there.'

'I am not interested in what happened when she was there, because she is no longer of interest to me.'

'If you are not interested in Miss Emma, then I think you will be interested in the Keepsake, my lord,' said Dolly quickly, seeing that he was about to instruct the butler to show her out.

He hesitated, his eyes becoming more sharp. 'The Keepsake?

What of it?'

'It has been stolen from Miss Emma, my lord.'

Dolly felt rather than saw the butler's shocked reaction. Gerald remained very still, but then he nodded. 'Very well, you have my undivided attention.'

Dolly looked earnestly at him. 'I . . . I think we should be more private, my lord.'

'As you wish. Will the drawing room suffice?' He indicated the staircase. 'Please come this way.'

She followed him up to the next floor, and then he stood aside for her to enter the drawing room first. It was sunlit now, the bright morning light reflected in mirror-clad walls and gleaming on gilded wood and plasterwork.

Gerald took up a position by the fireplace, resting an arm along the mantelpiece as he faced her. 'Very well, we are alone, er, Dolly, is it not?'

'Yes, my lord.'

'I am all ears to hear this tale of the Keepsake being stolen, Dolly,' he murmured, his tone indicating that he did not believe she would be telling the truth.

'It isn't a tale, my lord, it is what has indeed happened. Someone came to Miss Emma's room and took the Keepsake from its case.'

'Someone?' He raised an eyebrow. 'Come now, Dolly, why don't you simply admit that you've been dispatched here with this cock-and-bull story so that your mistress can attempt to save the match?'

Dolly stared at him in dismay. 'That isn't true, my lord! Miss Emma doesn't know I'm here, and everything I've said is the truth. It was Lord Avenley who had the Keepsake taken, and he has it now at Avenley House.'

Gerald's eyes grew colder. 'Dolly, if this is indeed a stratagem on Miss Rutherford's part—'

'It isn't, my lord! I swear it!' cried the maid. 'Miss Emma is entirely innocent, she has done nothing wrong at all—'

'Except lie to me in order to go to Avenley House,' he interrupted quietly.

'She had to do it, my lord, for if she had not done that, then Lord Avenley threatened to ruin her and Master Stephen. He sent an anonymous note to her just as she was preparing to accompany you and Lady Castlereagh to Manchester House, and in the note he warned her that if she wished to recover the Keepsake and Master Stephen's IOUs, and if she also wished to save the match with you, then she was to go immediately to Avenley House. Until then she hadn't even realized that the Keepsake was gone, and when she saw that it was, she was afraid to do anything but obey him.'

Gerald straightened slowly, his eyes steel-bright. 'If this is your notion of—'

'It is the truth, my lord!' cried Dolly.

He studied her for a long moment. 'Why did Avenley do it? Did he give a reason?'

Dolly hesitated. 'Yes, my lord, but I'd rather not—'

'Tell me everything, or nothing at all,' he interrupted sharply.

'He gave two reasons, my lord. First of all, it was on account of your previous wife.'

'Margot?'

'Yes, my lord. He said that she had really been his and that you had stolen her from him.'

Gerald turned away, gazing down into the heart of the fire. 'So, the old hatred is as strong as ever, is it?' he murmured. Then he glanced at her again. 'You said there were two reasons?'

'Yes, my lord. The second is because he desires Miss Emma.'

Gerald met her eyes. 'Go on,' he said softly.

'He said that originally his only purpose was to be avenged for the first Lady Kane, and that was why he decided to deliberately lure Master Stephen into debt, so that he could ruin him and make things very difficult for Miss Emma and her family. Then he saw Miss Emma, and found her so attractive that he decided to make her do as he wished.' Dolly had to lower her eyes as she spoke, for she found it almost impossible to say such things, especially to a gentleman of his rank.

'Go on, Dolly,' prompted Gerald. 'I want to hear it all.'

'Lord Avenley theatened Miss Emma that if she did not do as he wished, then he would not only call Master Stephen's debts in all at once but also deny all knowledge of the Keepsake. He also said that he would tell you she was infatuated with him, a fact that would be apparently proved because Mr Warburton recognized me at Avenley House.'

A nerve flickered at Gerald's temple. 'And he said all this in front of you?'

'Oh, no, my lord. I was outside, but I looked through the keyhole, and I saw and heard everything.'

'What did Miss Rutherford say to Avenley's demands?'

'That she would rather die than give in to him,' replied the maid, raising her chin proudly. 'She told him she despised him, and that she would tell you what he had done. That was when he made the threats I've just told you about. She left then, and she was almost crying. We went back to Grosvenor Square, and when she reached her room she broke down. She sobbed into her pillow, Lord Kane, and it wasn't her fault that any of it had happened. She is innocent in all this, but she has suffered dreadfully. I managed to persuade her that she had to tell you, and she at last agreed that she would. I left her then, but I was so upset that I was crying as well, and that was when Master Stephen's valet saw me, and so did Master Stephen. They made me tell them why I was crying, and I couldn't help telling them absolutely everything. That was why Master Stephen left the house tonight, he was on his way to confront Lord Avenley, but something happened to him, and he was brought here to you after being found in the street.'

Gerald closed his eyes for a moment. He could hear Emma's accusing voice. *You will not hear me out? You don't want to know why my brother left the house tonight, or why. . . ?* No, he had refused to listen to her, because his own damned pride had apparently been wounded by what he believed her to have done. May God forgive him. May Emma herself forgive him. . . .

Dolly looked at him. 'She meant to tell you everything when she came here to see Master Stephen, but she found the countess here, and then you were so cold.'

'You have no need to lecture me, Dolly, for I am more than aware of being at grave fault in this.'

'What will you do, my lord?'

'Do? I will call Avenley out for what he has done, even though I will find it damnably difficult to prove anything against him. He isn't a fool, and has planned this so that he can hide his own part of it. The anonymous note will not point to him, of that I am sure.'

'No, my lord.'

'And if he has Stephen's IOUs, there is no proof that he intends to call them in at once. Nor is there proof that he has the Keepsake or that he has attempted to blackmail Miss Rutherford into submitting to him.'

Dolly's eyes brightened suddenly. 'But, my lord, I know where he hides the Keepsake. I saw him through the keyhole.'

Gerald held her gaze. 'Where?'

'When Miss Emma wasn't looking, he took it from a place at the back of a clock on the mantelpiece in the drawing room at Avenley House. When her attention was distracted again, he put it back there.'

'You're quite sure?'

'Positive, my lord.'

'Then I will confront him armed with that secret knowledge. I trust that he denies all connection with the Keepsake, for then I will be able to issue a challenge that is demonstrably justified. I will take a witness with me,' he added, thinking of Lord Castlereagh.

Dolly's eyes stung with tears again. 'Oh, my lord—'

'Please go back to Miss Rutherford and tell her that I beg her forgiveness, Dolly. Tell her that I am very conscious of having failed her, but that I will endeavor to put things right.'

'Yes, my lord. But, my lord. . . ?'

'What is it?'

'I do not know that it will be enough that you believe her now, for the countess was—'

'The countess has now departed,' he interrupted.

'Yes, my lord.'

'I will explain to Miss Rutherford when I see her.'

'You may not be admitted, my lord.'

Gerald was startled. 'Not admitted?'

'When I left, Miss Rutherford was preparing to tell Mr Rutherford everything, including about the countess.'

'I see. Well, that is a bridge I will cross when I come to it. You go home now, Dolly, and tell Miss Rutherford what I've told you.'

'Yes, my lord.' Dolly turned to go to the door; then she paused, looking back at him. 'Maybe I should not tell you this, Lord Kane, for I have already been very indiscreet today, but I think it is something you should know. Miss Rutherford loves you very much. At least, she did until last night. Now I don't know what she feels, except that she is bitterly hurt.'

'As well she might be,' he murmured. Oh, Emma. . . . He looked at the maid again. 'Just go to her and tell her that Avenley will not escape retribution and that she will never have to yield to his demands.'

The maid bobbed a curtsy and went out.

As the door closed behind her, Gerald suddenly seized a silver-gilt candelabrum from the mantelpiece and hurled it furiously across the room. 'May God forgive you, Avenley,' he breathed, 'and may he damn you to hell and back for what you've done!'

22

DOLLY RETURNED TO Grosvenor Square, and after telling Mr Rutherford where she had been, and what she had done, she went up to tell Emma. She found her mistress seated quietly by the fire in her bedroom in a simple leaf-green woolen gown. Her hair was not pinned up, but tied back with a matching green satin ribbon. The gown had a pretty frilled neckline, long tight sleeves, and a gilt belt that fastened immediately beneath her breasts. There was a fringed white shawl around her shoulders, and the book she had bought at Hatchard's lay unopened on her lap.

She looked up swiftly as the maid entered. 'Where have you been, Dolly?'

Dolly lowered her eyes uncomfortably. 'To see Lord Kane, Miss Emma.'

'You've what?' Emma gasped, rising to her feet so abruptly that the book tumbled to the floor. 'I gave you no permission to do that!'

'No, Miss Emma, but I was determined that he should know the truth.'

Emma pressed her hands agitatedly to her cheeks. 'He must think that I sent you!'

'He did at first, Miss Emma,' the maid admitted, 'but in the end he believed me. He told me to tell you that he will see to it that Lord Avenley does not do any more harm, and that he wishes you to forgive him for having spoken to you as he did. He says he knows he has been gravely at fault.'

Emma turned away. Forgive him? How could she forgive him for the Countess of Purbeck? She looked quickly at the maid. 'He said he means to see to it that Lord Avenley does not do any more harm?'

'Yes, Miss Emma. Lord Kane is going to call Lord Avenley out.'

Emma's heart almost stopped within her. Another duel? Oh, please, no.

'He said he will call on you to speak with you, Miss Emma.'

'How can I receive him when the countess is there?'

'The countess has gone, Miss Emma. She was in tears, and I think that Lord Kane had told her to leave.'

'But she was there in the first place,' Emma pointed out quietly.

Dolly lowered her eyes. 'Yes, Miss Emma,' she conceded.

'He may now believe in my innocence, but I cannot believe in his, not when his guilt is so very obvious. If he calls here I will not receive him. I intend to tell my father that I have no wish to see or speak to Lord Kane again and that I would like to go home to Foxley Hall as quickly as possible.'

'But, Miss . . .'

'My mind is made up,' Emma interrupted firmly.

'What will you do if he and Lord Avenley fight a duel?' the maid asked hesitantly.

'Lord Kane will be fighting for the Keepsake, not for me.'

'Please, Miss Emma . . .'

'That will be all.'

'But . . .'

'That will be all, Dolly. You may go.' Emma's tone was emphatic and brooked no further argument.

Without another word, the maid left the room.

Alone, Emma hid her face in her hands.

The carriage drove swiftly out of St James's Square toward Pall Mall and Avenley House. It conveyed Gerald and Lord Castlereagh, the latter having been requested to witness everything that transpired at the intended confrontation with Emma's tormentor.

Lord Castlereagh looked thoughtfully at his friend. 'On whose account are you doing this, Gerald? Your own, because of the Keepsake? Miss Rutherford's, because Avenley has wronged her? Or does it reach back to Margot?'

'Certainly not Margot. On that you have my word. As to your other two reasons, well, there you touch upon more important points.'

'So, Miss Rutherford means something to you, if not everything. I am not referring to the Keepsake, but rather to a certain countess.'

'Raine is of no consequence.'

'No? I wonder if Miss Rutherford sees as you do,' Lord Castlereagh murmured dryly. 'I happened to be looking out of my window this morning, and I saw La Purbeck departing, bag and baggage, having obviously been with you overnight. And I happen to know not only that Miss Rutherford came to see her sick brother at about dawn but also that her maid arrived just as the countess was leaving, from all of which I deduce that Miss Rutherford must be aware of the Paragon of Purbeck's sojourn beneath your hospitable roof.'

'Your deductions are correct, Robert, but your suppositions are not. I promise you that the countess does not occupy a place in my heart, and that I most certainly did not invite her to enter my house.'

'Nor did you turn her away,' Lord Castlereagh pointed out succinctly.

'You have a talent for stating the obvious. Robert, I have no desire to talk about the Countess of Purbeck, for she has not played any part in Avenley's plot, and all I wish to do now is nail his hide to the wall.' Gerald leaned forward to open the carriage door, and then alighted to the pavement.

Lord Castlereagh sighed and tapped on his hat before stepping down as well.

The noise of Pall Mall was all around, a cacophony of voices, footsteps, hoofs, wheels, and street calls, to say nothing of the sudden clamor of church bells. A flock of sea gulls was startled into flight, rising from a nearby roof.

Gerald looked at the porch of Avenley House and the glittering entrance hall, where the chandeliers were still lit. 'Let's get to it, then,' he murmured, stepping purposefully inside.

A liveried footman appeared immediately they entered. He came from the gaming club, where chairs had been upturned on green baize tables and maids were brushing the costly carpets.

The footman bowed, hastily doing up his braided coat as he did so. 'Good morning, my lords. I fear that the club is not open this early in the day, but will be—'

'Is Lord Avenley at home?' Gerald interrupted.

'His lordship is resting, my lord, and left strict instructions that he was not to be disturbed.'

'A plague on his instructions,' Gerald muttered, pushing past him toward the staircase.

'My lord!' began the startled footman, making to pursue him, but Lord Castlereagh tapped his shoulder.

'If you know what's good for you, fellow, you'll toddle off elsewhere,' he murmured.

The footman stared at him, but then discretion got the better part of valor, and with a quick bow he withdrew into the gaming club.

'How very wise,' Lord Castlereagh said softly, following Gerald up the staircase.

At the top, Gerald thrust open the drawing room doors and strode in. A maid was kneeling by the fireplace, attending to the fire, and she gave a squeak of alarm, scrambling to her feet. Gerald glanced swiftly around, but there was no sign of Lord Avenley. He nodded at the maid. 'Please inform Lord Avenley that he has visitors.'

With a rather inelegant curtsy she scurried past them both, and Lord Castlereagh closed the doors behind her. Then he looked toward the mantelpiece. 'The clock awaits, my friend,' he said to Gerald.

Gerald went to it, turning it carefully on the mantelpiece and then opening the back. There, lying on the bottom beneath the mechanism, was the Keepsake. A smile played on his lips, and he turned to look at Lord Castlereagh.

'It's here, just as Emma's maid said it would be.'

'So it's "Emma", is it? How very forward,' Lord Castlereagh murmured.

Gerald didn't respond, but closed the back of the clock and replaced it in its original position.

Angry footsteps sounded at the door, and Gerald moved swiftly away from the fireplace, standing instead near a small table upon which there stood a decanter of cognac and a number of glasses. He picked up the decanter and began to pour two measures just as the doors burst open and Lord Avenley came furiously in.

It was obvious that he had indeed been resting, for he was still tying the belt of his purple paisley dressing-gown, which he had pulled hastily on over his shirt and breeches. His hair was untidy, his eyepatch had been put on in a hurry, and he became very wary and suspicious as he saw who his visitors were. 'What is the meaning of this?' he demanded.

Lord Castlereagh sketched a cool bow. 'Upon my soul, Avenley, you look all of a fluster,' he observed.

Lord Avenley ignored him, giving Gerald his full attention. 'To what do I owe the unexpected honor of this call, my lord?' he asked.

Gerald replaced the decanter on the table and then picked up one of the glasses, glancing around the room as he did so. His gaze fell upon the miniature of Margot. He went toward it, studying it carefully. 'Not a good likeness,' he murmured.

'Why are you here?' Lord Avenley demanded again.

Gerald continued to study the little portrait. 'Margot's eyes were not as large as that, and the artist has prudently omitted her rather unbecoming freckles.'

Lord Avenley's eye was very hard and bright. 'I will not ask you again, my lord. Why are you here?'

Gerald turned to survey him. 'I think you know the answer to that, Avenley. I am given to understand that you have been pestering Miss Rutherford in a very disagreeable and ungentlemanly fashion, and I have come to find out what you have to say for yourself.'

Lord Avenley's gaze slid guardedly toward Lord Castlereagh, and then back to Gerald again. 'You should not believe everything you're told, Kane, for I have not been the one doing the pestering. The lady is very importunate, you know.'

'Indeed?'

'Dammit, Kane, you and I may not have been boon companions over the years, indeed I would go so far as to say that we cordially despise each other, but even so I would not wish such an abandoned creature on you. She is quite without shame, you know.'

'I'm touched that you should show such concern for me,' Gerald replied.

'I am not entirely without redeeming features,' Lord Avenley murmured, going to the table and picking up the other glass of cognac. He appeared to be recovering apace from the shock of the visit, but both Gerald and Lord Castlereagh noticed how he downed the glass in one swallow.

'I'm rather afraid that you have no redeeming features at all, Avenley,' Gerald said quietly.

'I don't much care for your tone, Kane.'

'And I don't much care for the fact that you have purloined the Keepsake.'

Lord Avenley's lips parted, and his eye shone cleverly. 'What are you talking about, Kane? I don't know anything about your Keepsake.'

'How strange,' Gerald said softly, moving to the mantelpiece and turning the clock.

Lord Avenley drew warily back as the Keepsake was removed from its hiding place. 'I know nothing of this, Kane—'

'Don't add insult to injury, Avenley,' Lord Castlereagh interrupted. 'The Keepsake is where you put it, and it is here in this house because you had it stolen. You are a lamentable excuse for a gentleman, sirrah, indeed I think you are simply lamentable.'

Lord Avenley whipped around to face him. 'You have my word that I know nothing of this! I put it to you that in her desire to be avenged because I spurned her advances, Miss Rutherford hid it there herself in order to incriminate me.'

'Miss Rutherford has no idea where the Keepsake is, Avenley, save that you have it here.'

'Then how. . . ? The maid!' Sudden realization brought the words instantly to Lord Avenley's lips.

Gerald gave a cold smile. 'Yes, indeed. The maid. Keyholes are so very informative, are they not?' His smile faded. 'I will have satisfaction for this, Avenley.'

Lord Avenley remained absolutely still, a thousand and one expressions passing through the brightness of his eye.

'I'm calling you out, Avenley,' repeated Gerald. 'That is, if you are man enough to face me equally.'

The taunt found its target, and the mask slipped from Lord
Avenley's face, leaving his loathing there in all its naked ugliness.
'You'll have your satisfaction, Kane!'

'And don't make the mistake of thinking that this has anything
to do with Margot, for she could not matter less to me.'

'Damn you, Kane! Margot was mine!'

'And I surrendered her more than gladly, you may count upon
that!'

'You kept her close, Kane, you refused her her freedom, and
when she ran away from you she was killed in that carriage overturn.'

Gerald shook his head. 'You were but the last of many lovers she
had, Avenley, although I did not realize it at first. When I found
out, however, you may be sure that I gave her her *congé*. When she
saw that I meant to divorce her, she suddenly discovered the error
of her ways. She begged me to forgive her, and she swore she'd be
faithful to me. But I no longer wanted such a wife, and I told her
that you were welcome to her. In the end she accepted that I
would not change my mind, and that was when she left to go to
you.'

'You're lying!' breathed Lord Avenley, his face still ugly with
hatred.

'I fear not, Avenley.'

'If what you claim is the truth, why have you never said
anything? Why have you allowed society to believe that you were
heartbroken over losing her?'

'Because she wasn't worth it, and because I chose not to air my
dirty washing in public, Avenley. She had gone, never to return,
and I saw no point in blackening her name after the event. If you
recall, her father fell dangerously ill after her death, and for his
sake as well I left matters as they were. By the time he died, it was
all so much in the past that it no longer mattered to me. You
should have left well alone, Avenley, for now you not only have to
swallow a rather bitter pill but also to face me with pistols before
this day is out.'

Lord Castlereagh looked at him in surprise. 'Before this day is
out? Would it not be prudent to allow the usual negotiations to

take place between seconds, and so on?'

Gerald shook his head, his gaze not moving from Lord Avenley. 'I see no reason to wait, do you, Avenley?'

A nerve twitched at the corner of Lord Avenley's mouth. 'No reason at all, Kane. I am at your disposal.'

'Then, shall we say at three this afternoon? On Putney Heath, where my friend here bettered the foreign secretary?'

'As you wish.'

Gerald put the Keepsake in his pocket and then gave Lord Avenley an icy smile. 'You're going to pay a very heavy price for daring to hurt Miss Rutherford, and by the time I've finished with you, you're going to wish you'd never even heard her name.'

'You seem to be under the illusion that you're going to emerge the victor, Kane,' replied the other.

'Oh, I am, Avenley. I am,' Gerald said. 'This is one occasion upon which you would be very unwise to wager, unless it be upon your defeat. Until three o'clock.' With a cold nod of his head he walked past Lord Avenley and out of the room.

Lord Castlereagh lingered for a moment. 'How unfortunate that you've upset him so deeply, Avenley, for he is really rather dangerous when provoked. I once saw him shoot an apple from a post at a really unconscionably long distance. Correct me if I am wrong, but are you not somewhat larger than an apple? *À bientôt*, my friend.' Bowing, he followed Gerald, leaving Lord Avenley standing alone in the drawing room.

23

AFTER RETURNING LORD Castlereagh to his house at number eighteen St James's Square, Gerald drove swiftly to Grosvenor Square to make the promised call upon Emma. Saunders greeted him at the door with the polite but firm reply that Miss Rutherford was not at home.

Gerald held the butler's uneasy gaze. 'Am I to understand that Miss Rutherford is really not at home, or am I being refused entry?'

Saunders shifted his feet uncomfortably. 'My lord, I—'

He said no more, for at that moment the library door opened in the house behind him, and Mr Rutherford emerged unwarily, not having realized that Gerald was at the door. In a trice, just as Lord Avenley had trapped Emma before him, Gerald addressed her father.

'May I have a word with you, sir?' he asked.

Mr Rutherford halted in dismay, for after all that Emma had said, he had instructed Saunders not on any account to admit Gerald.

Gerald stepped past Saunders and walked purposefully toward the library. 'I must speak with you, sir.'

Saunders was in a quandary, for the thought of maybe having to lay hand upon a peer of the realm in order to forcibly expel him from the premises filled the butler with dread. He lingered by the door, praying that Mr Rutherford would consent to Lord Kane's request.

Emma's father faced Gerald a little frostily. 'My lord, I do not think that you and I have anything to say to each other. Your conduct has been abominable, and since it has also pleased you to end the negotiations for the match, I—'

'I have been gravely in error, sir, and I freely admit it. It is most certainly not my wish to end the match, and it is about this that I need to speak with you. My purpose in coming here was to see Emma, but she will not see me.'

'Can you blame her, sir? And as to your free and ill-placed familiarity in using her first name, I think that more formality is called for now, do you not agree?'

Gerald exhaled slowly, nodding his concurrence. 'I more than understand, sir, but all I ask of you now is that you hear what I have to say.'

'In mitigation?'

'Yes.'

Mr Rutherford pursed his lips. 'My lord, I fail to see what can be said in mitigation where the Countess of Purbeck is concerned.'

'The countess was not at St James's Square at my invitation, sir.'

'But nevertheless she remained beneath your roof for at least one night,' Emma's father replied coolly. 'My lord, do you deny that the lady has been more to you than she should have been, seeing that she is another man's wife?'

Gerald shook his head reluctantly. 'I can hardly deny something which is common knowledge in society, sir, but I repeat to you, as I have already said to Miss Rutherford, that the countess was a very fleeting and much-regretted mistake on my part. The inter-lude was over and done with well before I had even heard of your family, and there has certainly not been any repeat of the error.'

'Nevertheless, the lady stayed with you last night.'

'She came to me in distress, Mr Rutherford, and she has now left my residence to go to her sister in Northumberland.'

'Distress?'

'Her husband has indicated that he intends to divorce her, not because of her infidelities, but because she had persistently and willfully lied to him about the character of his son. The son was believed to have died in Greece, but has recently returned, and the countess's malice toward him has been revealed. As a consequence, she was turned out of Purbeck Park, and so she—'

'And so she came to you,' Mr Rutherford interrupted quietly.

'My lord, I find it a little odd that she should turn to you, if indeed your, er, dealings with her were so very transitory.'

Gerald drew a long breath. 'I concede that it must look questionable to you, sir, but I swear that what I have told you is the truth. What I haven't told you is that although I very swiftly ended the liaison with her, she did not wish the matter to come to a close. She has persistently endeavored to regain my affections, and I have resisted her importuning, both because I deeply regret breaking my own rule about becoming involved with other men's wives and because I no longer feel anything for her. If this makes me appear shabby, then there is little I can do about it, but I am telling you because I wish to convince you that what seems to have been going on has in fact not been going on at all. I gave the countess shelter last night, and I did so in the firm knowledge that she would use the opportunity to her advantage if she could. She failed, and this morning she departed for her sister's home in the north. Whatever the countess has said or done where Miss Rutherford is concerned, has been done out of jealousy and spite, you have my word upon that. Since knowing your daughter, sir, I have not given the countess any reason at all to hope that I would return to her.'

Mr Rutherford studied him. 'And you swear that at no time at all have you succumbed to the countess's unwanted advances?'

For a moment Gerald's thoughts flew back to the evening before, and the way Raine had come to him in the drawing room. He had succumbed then, because he had been in a turmoil over learning that Emma had lied about being ill and had then gone to Avenley House. Guilt washed over him anew as he recalled giving in to Raine's seductive embrace, but his senses had not been long in cooling, and after one single kiss he had held her away.

Mr Rutherford watched him. 'You do not answer, my lord,' he said quietly.

'Whatever may have passed between the countess and me, it was transitory, and meant nothing. She has no place in my life or my heart, and last night I merely gave her shelter.'

'Lord Kane, it seems to be that you cannot categorically deny that something occurred last night, and so I am afraid that you have not offered sufficient evidence in mitigation for your appalling conduct. Stained with guilt yourself, you had the gall to accuse my innocent daughter of your own misdemeanors. I find that monstrously ignoble, sir, and I do not care that you now express a desire to continue with the match, for I have decided that my daughter is too good for you. I am exceedingly sorry that the Keepsake is now in Lord Avenley's possession, and if I can persuade him to return it, then I will do so, for you may be assured that I have no intention of allowing any cloud to hang over my family. The Keepsake was in our possession when it was stolen, and so I regard it as my duty and obligation to do all I can to restore it to you. I intend to call upon Lord Avenley this after-noon.'

'Mr Rutherford, I have already repossessed the Keepsake, and I can tell you that Avenley will very busy this afternoon.'

Emma's father was relieved to hear about the Keepsake, but then looked quickly at him. 'You've challenged him?'

'Yes.'

'Well, I am sure that the theft of a family heirloom is indeed cause enough,' Mr Rutherford replied.

'You may feel justified in applying such a qualification to my reasons, sir, but I assure you you are not. The Keepsake is actually of little consequence to me in all this, but Miss Rutherford is not. It is primarily on account of Avenley's unspeakable treatment of your daughter that I intend to face him this afternoon, and whether you believe it or not, sir, the fact remains that she is my sole concern in this. I accept that my conduct has led to the ending of the match, but I now intend to redress the balance, and I promise you that your daughter's honor will be defended. Good-bye, Mr Rutherford, I only wish that things had not reached this pass.' Inclining his head, Gerald turned and left.

Mr Rutherford gazed after him, and then lowered his eyes as Saunders closed the door. He too wished that things had not reached this pass, for in spite of everything, he could not entirely dislike the man who had broken Emma's heart. There was some-thing about Lord Kane that encouraged belief, and denied mistrust.

Outside, Gerald paused on the pavement. Turning quickly, he glanced up at the drawing room windows, and was just in time to see Emma's pale, tearstained face before she pulled hastily back out of sight. He continued to gaze at the window, but she did not reappear, and after about a minute he climbed back into his waiting carriage to drive back to St James's Square to prepare for the duel.

From the drawing room window, Emma watched him drive away. She felt empty inside, as if her whole being had suddenly lost all substance. She had listened from the landing to everything that Gerald had said to her father, and she had so wanted to believe him that it had been all she could do not to run down to him. But pride, and a need to protect her heart from further pain, had held her back. She didn't trust him anymore, and without trust, what was left?

When it was time to leave for the appointment on Putney Heath, Gerald's carriage drove around St James's Square to Lord Castlereagh's residence on the western side, by the corner of King Street.

It was a four-story building, with a basement that was separated from the pavement by a fine iron railing. Built of brick, with stone facings, it boasted a full-length iron balcony that stretched across all four windows of the first floor, and although not the largest or most beautiful house in the square, it was certainly one of the most elegant.

The carriage halted at the curb, and Gerald alighted. He wore a wine-red coat, gold armazine waistcoat, and gray breeches beneath an astrakhan-collared greatcoat. The greatcoat was double-breasted and fitted to the waist, with a long skirt that reached almost to the ankles of his highly polished Hessian boots. There was a high-crowned hat on his dark hair, and at his throat he wore a full starched neckcloth which sported a fine ruby pin. He carried a gold-handled cane in his gloved hand, and he swung it idly to and fro as he approached the house.

Lord Castlereagh's butler admitted him immediately, and he stepped into the blue-and-cream entrance hall, where Lord Castlereagh and his wife were just descending the curving black-marble staircase. Lord Castlereagh wore a dove-gray coat and gray breeches with a sky-blue brocade waistcoat and a golden pin in his neckcloth. His black greatcoat, hat, gloves, and cane lay waiting on a console table.

Lady Castlereagh was dressed in a pink velvet gown, with a matching bandeau around her forehead, and her eyes were large and anxious as she hurried across the black-and-red-tiled floor to greet Gerald.

'Please do not proceed with this madness!' she cried, taking his hand urgently. 'Lord Avenley may not be a finer shot than you, Gerald, but he is capable of any ignominy to win the day.'

'I'm his match, Emily,' he replied, fondly kissing her forehead.

'Please withdraw, Gerald, I beg of you.'

'This is as much a matter of honor for me as Robert's confrontation with Canning was for him. I must defend Miss Rutherford's reputation, Emily.'

Lady Castlereagh studied him earnestly. 'You love her?'

He gave a wry smile. 'As I've never loved before in my life. For her I would face a thousand of Avenley's kind.'

'Then why on earth did you allow that she-cat countess to stay with you last night?'

'Not for the gratification of my lust, of that you may be sure. No, the truth of it is that her long campaign of lies against her much-loathed stepson has come to light now that said stepson has returned to the paternal fold. The long-suffering Earl of Purbeck has had his blinkers removed at last, and in the time-honored fashion has given his wife her marching orders, and she came to me to try one last time to win me over, but she is now *en route* to her sister in Northumberland. Emily, I have been a fool to end all fools, both in my dealings with Raine and in my accusations toward Emma. I should have known that Emma would never have betrayed me with Avenley, and I should never have allowed Raine across the threshold, let alone to remain overnight.'

Lady Castlereagh took his hand, resting it sympathetically against her cheek. 'Oh, Gerald, whatever am I going to do with you? But it is never too late to right wrongs, and if you love Miss Rutherford, then you have to go to her and tell her so.'

He gave a dry laugh. 'I did go to her, but I was told she was not at home, even though she most definitely was. I have blotted my copybook, Emily, indeed I have spoiled it beyond redemption, and that is a sad fact that I have no choice but to accept.'

'But, Gerald—'

He put his finger to her lips. 'There is no point in saying anything more, Emily, for the matter is sealed.' Then he looked at Lord Castlereagh. 'Are you ready?'

'As ready as I ever will be.'

'Then let us proceed with the business in hand.'

Lord Castlereagh waited only until the butler had assisted him with his coat, and then he accompanied Gerald out to the waiting carriage.

Lady Castlereagh watched it drive away, and then she turned with sudden decision to the butler. 'Andrews, have the town carriage made ready as quickly as possible. I wish to go to Grosvenor Square.'

'My lady.' He bowed and hurried away.

Lady Castlereagh gathered her skirts to run back up the staircase, and she called her maid as she did so. 'Kitty? Kitty, I need you immediately!'

Ten minutes later, her face flushed from having dressed in such a hurry, she emerged from the house to climb swiftly into the carriage. The coachman's whip cracked loudly, and the team strained forward, coming quickly up to speed for the urgent drive across London to the Rutherford residence.

There was much shouting and waving of fists from other road users as the coachman flung his team along St James's Street and then across Piccadilly to the narrow, choked confines of New Bond Street. He ignored the curses and accusations, for when her ladyship instructed him to drive with every haste, he was not one to shirk the challenge. The carriage jolted and bumped on the uneven cobbles, and swung wildly around the corner into Grosvenor Street. Lady Castlereagh held on tightly to the handgrip, oblivious of the breakneck pace. All she could think of was the duel, and convincing Emma that Gerald loved her. Maybe there was nothing to be gained, maybe the foolish chit didn't return his love, but while there was a chance, then it had to be seized, before it was too late.

The team was sweating as they were reined in at the door of Lady Bagworth's house, and the carriage had barely halted when Lady Castlereagh flung the door open to clamber down. She wore a fur-edged green wool cloak over the pink velvet gown, and the matching bandeau had been replaced by a wide-brimmed silk hat from which curled a luxuriant white ostrich plume that fluttered and streamed in the cool September air as she hurried to the door of the house.

Saunders almost ran to answer her urgent knocking, and he stood aside in surprise as she rushed inside. 'My lady. . . ?'

'I wish to see Miss Rutherford without delay!'

'I . . . I will inform her that you have called.' But as he turned to go to the staircase, Emma herself appeared at the top in her leaf-green gown.

Dolly had applied a little rouge to her cheeks, and had tied her hair back with a green ribbon, but she still looked tense and drawn, and there was a sadness in her green eyes as she came slowly down the staircase.

'You wish to see me, Lady Castlereagh?'

'It seems you are at home after all, Miss Rutherford,' Lady Castlereagh replied a little tersely.

Emma reached the bottom of the staircase and paused with one hand on the lowermost newel post. 'From which I take it that you are here on Lord Kane's account?'

'I am, but not, I hasten to add, with his knowledge. Will you answer an important question, Miss Rutherford?'

'If I can.'

'Do you feel any affection for Lord Kane?'

'I . . . I hardly think that that is any concern of yours, Lady Castlereagh.'

'On the contrary, Miss Rutherford, it is every concern of mine. Well? Do you feel any affection for him?'

Emma didn't reply, and had to look away.

Lady Castlereagh advanced a little. 'If you still harbor doubts because of that wretched Purbeck woman, let me assure you that her stay was only fleeting and that Lord Kane regrets his decision to allow her to remain overnight. He did so because he is a gentleman, Miss Rutherford, and a gentleman does not turn a lady out into the streets at night.'

'I know that that is what Lord Kane says, my lady.'

'I believe him, Miss Rutherford, and I rather think that you

214

should as well.'

There was a discreet cough, and they both turned toward Saunders, who was standing nearby. He looked apologetically at Emma. 'Begging your pardon, madam, but there does appear to be confirmation of what Lady Castlereagh says. Master Stephen's valet has just returned to collect some of his master's things, and—'

'I had no idea Frederick had gone to see him,' Emma interrupted.

'Oh, yes, madam. I took the liberty of dispatching him this morning. I trust that that was in order?'

'Yes, of course. Do go on.'

'Yes, madam. Frederick informed me that the talk among Lord Kane's servants is that the Countess of Purbeck only stayed there with his lordship's extreme reluctance, and that he gave in only when she resorted to tears. He sent her away first thing this morning.'

Saunders cleared his throat, looking very uncomfortable. 'Begging your pardon for any offense my next words may cause, madam, but it seems of considerable importance that you should know that the countess slept in a guest chamber, and his lordship in his own room.'

Lady Castlereagh raised a wry eyebrow. 'What would we do without servants' gossip?' she murmured. Then she turned to Emma again. 'Does all this make any difference, Miss Rutherford?'

Emma's lips had parted, and her heart had begun to pound in her breast. She looked anxiously at the butler. 'Are you quite sure about all this, Saunders?'

'Absolutely certain, madam. I can send for Frederick, if you wish—?'

'That won't be necessary.' Emma was suddenly full of emotion, and her eyes shone with tears.

Lady Castlereagh's face softened, and she went to her. 'You love him, don't you?' she asked gently.

'Yes,' Emma whispered.

'As he loves you, my dear. He told me so himself just before he and Robert set off for Putney Heath.'

'He loves me?' Emma whispered.

'My dear, of course he does. He isn't fighting this duel because of the Keepsake, or your brother's gaming misfortunes, or even that unlamented *chienne* Margot, he's fighting it for you.' Lady Castlereagh smiled a little. 'We can follow them to Putney if you wish. They left some time ago, and it's all of eight miles there, but if we make as much speed as my team can manage—'

Emma didn't wait for her to finish, but was already fleeing back up the staircase to put on her cloak.

24

SHORTLY AFTERWARD, ONCE more to the considerable annoyance of other traffic, the Castlereagh carriage was again to be seen flying along the streets toward Putney Heath. The team's hoofs struck sparks from the cobbles as the coachman urged them down Park Lane, reining them in impatiently at the toll gate by St George's Hospital, before bringing them up to speed again to travel west toward Knightsbridge, along the very road Emma and her father had traveled on their way to London barely a week before.

After all the sunshine of recent days, there was now a change in the weather. A breeze had sprung up to rustle through the trees, and clouds burgeoned overhead, bringing the promise of rain. Dry leaves scuttered over the road, and the autumn tints lost their glow on the trees as the wind stirred across the countryside.

The carriage drove over the bridge that spanned the narrow Westbourne stream, which in January had overflowed its banks to inundate the surrounding fields, turning them into a lake. London's tentacles were beginning to reach out from its present confines, inundating the countryside in the same way, and already there were villas linking the hamlet of Knightsbridge with the capital. As the carriage turned south toward the Thames, it passed along another villa-lined thoroughfare, called Sloane Street.

Soon they reached the large riverside village of Chelsea, where a thirty-year-old wooden toll bridge crossed the Thames. Trees overhung the water, and rolling countryside stretched away to the west. Sailing barges slid on the river, sometimes so close to the banks that they brushed through the rushes that grew so thickly on either side. The carriage's wheels rattled dully on the toll bridge as the coachman urged his willing team toward the southern bank and the hamlet of Battersea.

The minutes ticked by slowly, and Emma gazed anxiously out of the carriage window. By her little fob watch she knew that there was still half an hour to go to the appointed time of the duel, and it seemed that there was still an unconscionable way to go before they reached the heath. Please let them be in time. Please. If she could persuade Gerald not to proceed with the duel, then she would, for nothing was worth risking his life for. All that mattered now was the future, and the happiness that might yet be enjoyed.

At last the carriage turned west again, making the slow climb over several hills, including Lavender Hill, and then passing through the village of Wandsworth. Putney itself lay ahead now, and beyond it the heights of the famous heath, where highwaymen lurked, and duels without number had been fought.

The horses were tired now, and they moved much more slowly as they strained to draw the heavy carriage up Putney Hill toward the open four-hundred-acre expanse of heathland. The skies were now very lowering, with clouds beginning to scud across the heavens. From time to time a spot of rain was dashed against the carriage window, and torn leaves fluttered by.

The whip cracked again as the coachman urged the flagging horses past a wayside inn and then down a narrow tree-lined lane that led onto the heath. There were elegant villas dotted around, among them Bowling Green House, where the late prime minister, William Pitt, had died only three years before. It had been William Pitt who had set the precedent for government ministers to fight duels, for he had faced the Irishman George Tierney here on Putney Heath, and honor had been deemed to be satisfied after the exchange of shots.

The with blew freely in so high and exposed a place, blustering around the carriage as it jolted along a way that was now rough and rutted. There was a crossroad ahead, and a gibbet to remind all wrongdoers of the fate that awaited them if caught. Both Emma and Lady Castlereagh averted their eyes from the grisly sight as the carriage turned sharply to the left, bumping along a little-used track that led toward the designated spot for the duel.

Heather grew on the hummocky ground, and silver birch trees

bent in the wind. The air smelled sweet, as it always does up on a heath, and a small flock of sheep fled into the trees of a small copse.

Lady Castlereagh leaned forward to look out. 'We're almost there,' she said.

Emma glanced again at the fob watch and saw that it was three o'clock. Were they too late?

The carriage halted suddenly, and she flung the door open to climb down, pausing only to shake, out the heavy folds of the rose velvet cloak she had hastily donned over her leaf-green gown. The wind snatched at the cloak's fur-trimmed hood, whisking it back so that her dark hair fluttered in confusion, almost tearing loose from its green satin ribbon as she cast anxiously around for a glimpse of the duel.

The ground sloped away to the right, and there, in a tree-fringed dell, she saw Gerald and Lord Avenley selecting their weapons from the case held out for them by Lord Avenley's second, a rather foppish gentleman by the name of Francis Teggerton.

She called out anxiously, but the wind tossed her voice away into the wild air, and no one in the dell heard her.

Lady Castlereagh had alighted from the carriage behind her. 'You must go to them, my dear,' she said.

Emma needed no second bidding, but gathered her skirts to run down the slope toward the dell, where Gerald and Lord Avenley were now standing back to back, about to take the obligatory twelve paces.

Lord Castlereagh was endeavoring to reason one last time with Francis Teggerton, who could only shrug, for Lord Avenley had hitherto refused to listen to any advice. With a sigh, Lord Castlereagh withdrew to stand with the surgeon who waited in readiness, and Francis Teggerton prepared to conduct the duel.

'Twelve paces, if you please, gentlemen,' he said.

They obeyed, walking slowly away from each other, their pistols safely lowered. Both men had discarded their coats ands waistcoats, and their shirts were very white in the dull afternoon light. The wind ruffled Gerald's hair and fluttered the costly lawn of his shirt against his lean body as he halted at the end of the twelve paces.

Francis Teggerton looked at them both. 'Turn and cock your pistols,' he commanded.

Both duelists obeyed, and the clicking sounds were audible as the wind dropped away for a moment. Lord Castlereagh suddenly saw Emma running down toward them, and he stepped anxiously forward, afraid that she would distract Gerald, who had his back toward her. Gesturing urgently for her to halt and remain quiet, Lord Castlereagh at the last moment managed to catch her attention, and to his relief, her steps faltered and she stopped, her hair blowing around her face as she stared wretchedly at the scene in the dell.

Francis Teggerton spoke again. 'Take your aim, gentlemen.'

Slowly both men raised their pistols, leveling them at each other, but as Teggerton's lips parted for the order to fire, Lord Avenley anticipated him, squeezing the trigger before a word had been uttered.

Emma stifled a scream, pressing her hands to her lips as she looked anxiously at Gerald. The smoke from the pistol was snatched away as the wind rose again, but Gerald remained standing, and she almost cried out with relief as she realized that the bullet had not found a target.

Teggerton was thunderstruck, and Lord Castlereagh whirled about to furiously face Lord Avenley. 'That was the act of a cur and a coward, sir!'

Lord Avenley's face had grown pale. 'It was an accident!'

But his own second looked uncomfortable, for no one, not even his friend, believed it to have been an accident.

Lord Castlereagh was contemptuous. 'You deliberately loosed that shot, Avenley, as everyone here witnessed. Now it pleases me greatly to have to advise you that you must stand where you are while Kane takes aim at leisure.'

Lord Avenley's tongue passed dryly over his lips, and his face was ashen. He trembled visibly, and there was terror in his single eye as he watched his opponent take grim pleasure in very slowly leveling his pistol at his heart.

Francis Teggerton prepared to issue the final command, but before he could do so, Lord Avenley sank cravenly to his knees, begging for mercy. 'Spare me, Kane, I beg of you! I will do anything you ask, if you will just spare me!'

It was too much for Teggerton to stomach, and he turned in disgust to speak to Gerald. 'Take aim as you wish, Kane, and I trust you put an end to him,' he said; then he turned and walked away toward his carriage, which was drawn up together with those of Gerald and the surgeon just beyond the trees edging the dell.

Lord Avenley was filled with abject terror. Gone was the arrogant, ruthless, contemptuous lord who had tampered so callously and viciously with the lives of others, and in his place was a quivering poltroon.

Gerald savored his moment of vindication, making as if he had every intention of squeezing the trigger of his pistol, but at the last moment he lowered his weapon. 'I won't bother to waste a good bullet,' he said.

Lord Avenley was so relieved that he hid his face in his hands, his shoulders trembling as he wept.

Gerald, who still did not realize Emma was close by, walked across to his wretched foe, reaching down to seize him by the hair and force him to look up into his face. 'You make me sick, Avenley, and ashamed to be an English lord!'

Lord Avenley could only stare up at him, his lips shaking.

Gerald's mouth curled back with disgust. 'I marvel that Margot was ever interested in you, but one thing is certain, you and she richly deserved each other, for you are both equally worthless. Now, then, I want your full and unqualified admission that Miss Rutherford is innocent of everything of which you've accused her.'

'She is innocent, I swear it!' cried Lord Avenley.

'That won't do, my friend, for I want those present to be quite clear that you are absolving the woman I love from all guilt or complicity in your plotting.'

Emma had taken hesitant steps toward them, and now was close enough to hear what he said. Tears filled her eyes, and she longed to run to Gerald, but he hadn't finished with Lord Avenley yet.

'Proclaim her innocence, my friend, or I may yet put an end to you,' he breathed, his fingers still gripping Lord Avenley's hair.

'I swear she is virtuous and free of all complicity!' Lord Avenley cried. 'I acted out of malice, and I sought to ruin her because of Margot. I swear it upon my honor, Kane!'

221

'Honor? You have no honor!' Gerald replied, his voice filled with loathing; then he tossed the other man aside so that he fell to the grass.

Lord Avenley looked fearfully up at him, still not sure if he would be finally spared. 'I will not transgress again, Kane. I promise you!'

'I know you will not, my friend, for I expect you to see the merit of leaving the country for a while. A little self-imposed exile will prove the making of you, don't you agree?'

'If that is what you wish.'

'It is what I'm telling you you'll do,' Gerald snapped. 'I am also telling you to return Stephen Rutherford's IOUs immediately, and to see to it that you undo any other mischief you may have put in motion. You had better leave with a clean slate, Avenley, or I promise you I'll come after you and finish what I started today.'

'I will do as you say, Kane.'

Gerald glanced toward Francis Teggerton's carriage, which was beginning to drive slowly away; then he looked at Lord Avenley again. 'I suggest you hurry after him, my friend, unless you wish to walk all the way home.'

Lord Avenley did not wait to be prompted again, but scrambled ignominiously to his feet and ran stumbling away after the departing carriage. He did not pause to retrieve his clothes, but ran in his shirt and breeches.

The surgeon stepped foward to shake Gerald by the hand. 'That was splendidly done, my lord. The act of a true gentleman.'

'The last thing I feel right now is gentlemanly, for it was all I could do not to tear his venomous throat out,' Gerald replied, tossing his pistol aside.

As the surgeon walked away to his own carriage, Lord Castlereagh grinned at Gerald. 'A convincing victory, I think.'

'A hollow one, Robert, for I have still lost the one thing that matters in all this.'

'Have you?' Lord Castlereagh pointed behind him, to where Emma stood.

Gerald whirled about, his lips parting in surprise. 'Emma?'

She ran to him, flinging her arms around him and holding him close. He closed his eyes, his lips moving against her hair as he embraced her. 'Oh, Emma, my darling . . .' he whispered.

She raised her lips to meet his, and he kissed her long and sweet, tasting her tears. He could feel her body quivering against his as he twined his fingers richly in the warm hair at the nape of her neck.

Then he looked into her eyes. 'I love you, Emma, and I think I have done so from the first day I saw you in the library at Foxley Hall.'

'I've loved you since then as well,' she whispered in reply, 'but I was so afraid that Margot still meant everything to you.'

'She meant nothing, and if I wore my wedding ring, it was to remind me never again to rush into a marriage because I fancied myself in love. I do not fancy myself in love with you, my dearest Emma, I adore you with all my heart, and when I thought I'd lost you forever—'

'You will never lose me.'

'If you still doubt me because of Raine—'

'I don't care about her, I only care about you,' she replied, smiling up into his eyes.

He drew back for a moment, pausing to take something from the pocket of his breeches. It was the Keepsake, its diamonds flashing brilliantly even though the skies were lowering. 'This belongs to you, Emma,' he said, pinning it carefully to the shoulder of her cloak. 'I gave it to you because I loved you, even though I did not tell you that was why. I asked for it back because I was a fool, but now I give it to you again, because I've regained my senses, never to lose them or you again.'

Her eyes shone with tears, and his name was a whisper on her lips as he pulled her close to kiss her again. They were oblivious of everything except each other, and they did not see Lord Castlereagh smiling to himself as he turned to go to his wife, who had observed everything from the slope above, and whose glad smile at the outcome of everything was visible even at that distance.